# PACIFIC RIM™
# U P R I S I N G

ASCENSION

FROM DIRECTOR
**STEVEN S. DEKNIGHT**

NOVEL BY
**GREG KEYES**

**TITAN** BOOKS

Pacific Rim Uprising: Ascension
Print edition ISBN: 9781785657665
E-book edition ISBN: 9781785657672

Published by Titan Books
A division of Titan Publishing Group Ltd
144 Southwark Street, London SE1 0UP

First edition: March 2018
1 3 5 7 9 10 8 6 4 2

A CIP catalogue record for this title is available from the British Library.

Printed and bound by CPI Group (UK) Ltd, Croydon, CR0 4YY

Did you enjoy this book? We love to hear from our readers.
Please email us at readerfeedback@titanemail.com
or write to us at Reader Feedback at the above address.

To receive advance information, news, competitions, and exclusive offers
online, please sign up for the Titan newsletter on our website:
**www.titanbooks.com**

# PACIFIC RIM™
## UPRISING
### ASCENSION

Also available from Titan Books:

## PACIFIC RIM UPRISING:
### THE OFFICIAL MOVIE NOVELIZATION

FOR TERRI SHAW

# 1

FOR OU-YANG JINHAI, SHATTERDOMES WERE OLD news. He had spent most of the first seven years of his life in family housing in the Hong Kong Shatterdome, and he had visited several others. In Hong Kong he had been one of only a handful of kids living in the dome, and generally kids were meant to stay out of the way, and usually they did.

But sometimes, when nothing much was going on, he and his little group of friends would sneak to see the Jaegers, the giant mechs that fought the nightmares from the deep, the Kaiju. They stared up in wonder at Cherno Alpha, Crimson Typhoon – and his favorite, of course, Shaolin Rogue. They made Jaeger and Kaiju costumes of cardboard boxes and fought their own battles; they played in dead storage and explored Mechspace, where transports and Jumphawks were stored and repaired, and spare Jaeger parts were kept ready.

And then everything changed. The Kaiju – which had been attacking the human race since before he was born

– were defeated. He remembered the night it happened, the muted celebrations among the J-Techs and mechanics, their joy subdued by profound loss.

After that, his parents moved away from the Shatterdome, to one of the nicer inland suburbs, and the smell of ozone and machine oil became a distant memory. Ten years passed. He grew up. The world changed.

But it was all coming back now, as he and the others looked up and down the Jaeger bays, the immense man-shaped machines that stood in them, the thirty-story tall ocean doors through which they could be taxied to deploy.

Of course, Jinhai had never been in this, the Moyulan Shatterdome. It was only recently built, and a bigger, shinier, more modern place than what he remembered from Hong Kong, which – by the time he came around – was dingy, rundown and more than a bit rusty. Still, on many levels it felt more like home than the sprawling, quiet, nearly empty house in the suburbs.

What was clear to him from the beginning was that none of these other cadets had ever seen the inside of a dome. Doubtless they had seen images and videos, but until you stood at the foot of a two-hundred-fifty-foot plus Jaeger – and realized you were in a space that housed six of them – you couldn't truly get a grip on the scale. He remembered the first time his mother had shown him Shaolin Rogue. It had made him feel little, of course, but it also – for the first time – made him realize that his mother wasn't that big, either. Or Dad. Or even Marshal Pentecost. No one looked big next to a Jaeger. The difference in degree between a child and an adult seemed trivial in comparison.

He watched the others gape up at the mighty frame of Titan Redeemer with amusement and a certain amount of disdain.

*Get over it*, he thought. *I have.*

They were all – him included – cadets. They were all within a year or so of his age – seventeen – and all of them hoped to one day climb into one of those metal behemoths and go off to save the world.

Most of them, anyway. He was over that, too. He was here for his own reasons.

Only one of the other cadets wasn't all open-mouthed and wide-eyed, and that was Viktoriya Malikova, a Russian girl who didn't outwardly express much of anything except perhaps annoyance. He liked that about her, right away.

Most of the cadets had arrived the day before, but Viktoriya had arrived a little later, just in time for the orientation. They had begun in a conference room, where they turned in all of their personal electronics and were given PPDC-approved devices. Then they had been orally refreshed on all of the stuff they and their parents had signed concerning the rules and expectations of the Pan Pacific Defense Corps Jaeger Training Academy. Now that that was out of the way, two Rangers named Lambert and Burke were giving them a tour.

It wasn't as if nothing had changed since he was seven – technology had come a long way since the Jaeger program had begun, back in the mid-teens. The Mark-6 series impressed even him, although he wasn't going to admit that out loud. Or ooh and ahh like a groupie. But they were cool.

"Don't get used to this," Lambert told them. "You'll go through a lot before you ever pilot one of these. Some of you never will. After today, we start with the basics – Kwoon combat drills, basic Pons training to evaluate your Drift compatibility – then eventually you will fight simulated battles in the Mock-Pods. If all of that goes well, you'll get a turn in Chronos Berserker, here."

The Jaeger bay was a huge, circular space; Jaegers stood in niches along the walls. Chronos Berserker was an older Mark-5 that had never met a Kaiju, although it had done its part in law-enforcement and rebuilding efforts.

"As you can see, Chronos doesn't have a head," Burke said. "It's there, up above."

He pointed to the dark recesses of the dome's high ceiling, where a mess of gantries, walkways, scaffolds, head clamps and the like obscured the shadow that was Chronos Berserker's control pod.

"The head – in this case, a Conn-Pod – is being prepared for a test run by two of our graduating cadets," Lambert went on, "soon-to-be Rangers Braga and Vu. You'll meet them tomorrow. Meantime, we're going to take the lift up to CB's Conn-Pod, which I'm sure all of you know is where the pilots control her from. You'll go in twos. Everything important is offline, but don't mess with anything. It isn't a toy, and this isn't kindergarten. The reason we're doing this at all is because I want you to be able to visualize what it will be like to be inside one of these magnificent things and know you're ready and equipped to battle *anything*. This training will be hard, and at times you'll want to quit, I promise. When you feel like giving up, I hope this experience will give you something to motivate you."

They took the lift to the very top of the dome, where a head clamp was positioned to drop the Conn-Pod to Chronos Berserker and thus complete her. There they waited their turns to go inside.

He noticed Viktoriya step away from the others and look out over the rest of the place. After a moment, he followed her.

"These guys are easily impressed, aren't they?" he said, sotto voce.

"It is impressive," she replied, although her diffident tone seemed to belie her words. "Many of them never dreamed that they would be here. Some of them, probably, should not be."

The way she said it, the little flicker of a glance from the corner of her eye, suddenly made him feel defensive.

"You don't know me," he said.

"I know you arrived in Fuding in a PPDC executive jet," she said, "while I arrived in third class on the train from Vladivostok."

"Look," he said. "I didn't mean to rile you up. I was just making conversation."

"I didn't come here to make conversation," she said. "I came here to train, and learn. To become a pilot." She lifted her chin toward the Conn-Pod.

"It's your turn."

Lambert gave the two cadets a final inspection before escorting them to the Jaeger bay. Braga, as usual, was trying to suppress a big grin. There was still a lot of kid in him, but in the best way. His sense of wonder didn't interfere with either his focus or his drive; in fact, it propelled both. His thick, wavy black hair was a little disheveled, and bordering on being too long for regs. Typical, but he never let it go over the line.

Next to Braga's six-foot frame, Vu looked diminutive. She was just under five feet and weighed less than a hundred pounds, but he had never seen anyone perform better in the Kwoon. She was all business, Vu, and very contained.

"I shouldn't say this," Lambert told them, "but I'm proud of you guys. You've both worked hard, and you deserve to be Rangers. I know this feels like it will be a big deal, but the fact is, it's not all that different from being in the Mock-Pod."

"With all respect, Ranger," Braga said, "actually being in a Jaeger – that's got to be different."

"It's a little different," he admitted. "But it's the Drift

that's important, and you guys have demonstrated your ability many times. Just stay cool, and don't get excited, and everything is going to be fine, right?"

"Right, Ranger," they said in unison.

"Great. Let's take a swing through the cadets so they can see what they're working toward."

"I've met most of them already, Ranger," Braga said. "Seems like a good bunch."

"Don't get too attached to them," Lambert warned. "Just think about the attrition rate in your cadre."

"Nearly sixty percent," Vu said.

"Closer to seventy, in our class," a new voice said.

"Ranger Burke," Vu said.

Burke was a little shorter than Lambert, but they weighed about the same due to the other Ranger's impressively muscled upper body.

"Well, there he is," Lambert said. "Where've you been, buddy?"

"Oh, out and about," he said. "I guess I'm not too late, though."

Lambert tried to hide his irritation. He liked Burke, and they were excellent Drift partners, but lately he'd been a little squirrely. Not unreliable, exactly, but it felt like things were edging in that direction.

"We were just headed out to see the new recruits," Lambert said. "Why don't you come with us?"

"These kids look really young this year," Lambert whispered to Burke where the two Rangers stood in a corner, largely ignored. The cadets were focused on Braga, who was giving an encouraging little speech about dreams and persistence.

"I was just a street kid in Rio," he was saying. "And Vu here, she's the daughter of a fisherman and a seamstress.

The PPDC doesn't care where you come from – rich or poor, high or low. It's who you *are* that matters…"

"That's because you're old," Burke said.

"Last time I checked, twenty-seven wasn't considered 'old'," Lambert replied.

"It's relative, isn't it?" Burke said. "When you were in your twenties, you still sort of felt like you were one of them, right? Like there isn't a huge difference between seventeen and twenty-one, or twenty-one and twenty-five. It's the difference in, well, everything else. Listen to Braga. Can you imagine being that fresh, that idealistic, ever again? I mean, think about how we were at that age. We had dreams."

"I've still got dreams," Lambert protested.

"Not like they do, you don't. They seem young because you really aren't one of them anymore. We're almost a different species from those guys."

Never shy about the hyperbole, Burke. But he had a point. When Lambert looked at cadets, he had to recognize that his feelings weren't friendly, or even brotherly, but much closer to what he thought a father might feel.

*Oh, God, I am getting old*, he thought.

They finished up with the cadets and headed on to the main event.

Even after more than a decade, the Jaeger bay still gave Lambert goosebumps; it was just the sheer size of it, the magnitude of the accomplishment. Humanity had stared into the face of extinction and then built *this*.

Currently, five Jaegers stood against the walls, including his own ride, Gipsy Avenger. An homage to the Mark-3 that Mako Mori and Raleigh Becket had piloted into the Breach, his Gipsy was a Mark-6, a true thing of beauty. A very deadly beauty.

One of the Jaegers stood ready for deployment. It was the older model he'd mentioned to the cadets, the

Australian-built Mark-5 known as Chronos Berserker. The Conn-Pod was still up in the "rafters" so Braga and Vu could board her.

Braga looked up. "Heard you let the kids climb around in there yesterday," he said.

"Yes," Lambert replied. "Don't worry, we gave her a full diagnostic run as soon as they were done. Not that there was anything for them to really mess up."

"No, it's not that," Braga said. "I just – I remember when you took my bunch up there. It really inspired me, sir. I'd like to thank you again."

"Thank me when you pin on your Ranger patch," he said.

He shook hands with Braga and Vu, and watched as they rode the lift to their Conn-Pod.

Then he went into LOCCENT Control to help monitor what amounted to the final exam of two very promising cadets.

He nodded at Xiang, the new LOCCENT controller.

"How are they doing?" he asked.

"Getting situated like old pros," she replied. "Braga is in a bit of a rush, Vu is taking her time."

That was good. He couldn't help but think that they had it a little easier than when he had started, and they still used the old-style "Pinocchio" rigs, where a pilot's arms and legs directly manipulated machinery that then translated their motion to the Jaeger. Chronos Berserker had been upgraded to the newer system, in which pilots were actually suspended over pads via magnetic levitation. It gave them – and thus the Jaeger – a much greater and more fine-grained range of motion.

"Okay," Xiang said. "Ready for the drop."

"Ready," Braga said.

The head descended briskly from its gantry, guided between Chronos Berserker's shoulders, where it latched into place.

"Oh yeah," Braga whooped with glee. "That is *way* better than a Mock-Pod. Let's do that again!"

"Okay," Xiang said. "Settle down, Braga. Ready to engage pilot-to-pilot protocol."

"We are ready, Control," Braga confirmed.

"Hemispheres calibrating," Xiang said. "Left, yes, right, yes. Initializing neural handshake."

She pushed back a strand of onyx-black hair that had escaped her queue. Lambert didn't know her all that well. They had been through three LOCCENT controllers since Moyulan was founded – Xiang had only been in Moyulan for a few weeks. She had trained under the famous Tendo Choi, which meant she was probably okay – but you never really knew how someone was going to perform until they came under pressure, and things had been quiet lately.

"Neural handshake engaged," she said. "They're drifting."

The earliest Jaeger prototypes were built to be controlled by one person. That hadn't gone well. The neural load was just too much for a single pilot to bear. Nor could two people, working independently, control half of the machine and achieve anything approaching the coordination necessary to actually battle a Kaiju.

But two people, bearing the neural load together – their minds "bridged" by the Pons technology – could.

So, Jaegers were designed to have two – in some cases, three – pilots.

This meant that Jaeger pilots were different from other people who controlled machines; like, for instance, the pilot of a plane. In addition to all of the intellectual and physical qualifications, there was one more necessary ability that stood out above all the others – Drift compatibility. Some people had it, some people did not, and few were compatible with everyone. Drift partners were often siblings, or lovers, people who had already shared a lot of mental territory.

Others just got lucky in training, and came across someone they really clicked with.

It had happened to Lambert, twice.

Braga had been compatible with several other cadets, but Vu was only able to successfully Drift with Braga. But as a team they were *so* good together, there hadn't been any question that they would be partners.

Right now, Lambert knew, they were experiencing one another's fears, dark secrets, traumas; settling into each other's heads, and into the artificial nerves of the machine that surrounded them, trying to find silence, to ignore the memories, let them go, not latch on to any of them.

And now they were ready.

"Chronos Berserker, move your right arm," Xiang said.

After the briefest of pauses, the right arm shot up. Scattered applause could be heard from the engineers and J-Techs on the floor.

"Good. Now, left arm."

Up went the left.

"Now your right leg. Just one step."

Nothing happened.

"Chronos Berserker, right leg, please."

Again, no response.

"Braga? Vu?"

"*Meu Deus!*" Braga suddenly screamed. Then Vu started yelling, too.

"*Dab tsi, dab tsi?*"

Then the two cadets abruptly went silent.

"What's happening?" Lambert snapped.

"I don't know," Xiang said. "We just lost the feed from Chronos."

"Lost the feed? Everything? How——"

All heads turned as Chronos Berserker suddenly lurched forward, threw an air punch, then another.

What were they doing? Braga liked to kid, sure, but he wasn't so dumb to not know he was already crossing the line on this. And Vu, she would never tolerate this sort of horseplay.

Chronos turned, ran four steps, and crashed into the wall.

"What the hell?" Lambert yelped. They weren't messing around. Something was wrong. Really wrong.

"Shut it down!" he told Xiang.

"I can't," she said. "The fail-safe system has been overridden."

"By who? By what?"

"Ranger, I do not know. Oh, crap."

Lambert saw it, too. Chronos Berserker carried two hammerhead missiles, one in each arm. The port in the right arm had just raised out of its frame.

"No, no—"

"All personnel, evacuate to safety," Xiang snapped.

Everyone knew it was too late for that, and were jumping for the nearest cover. He didn't see the point of even that. Hammerheads contained the most powerful non-atomic warheads available. One of them could do a very decent job of hollowing the Shatterdome out.

With a flash and the roar like a jet taking off, the missile leapt from Chronos Berserker's arm.

It slammed into the bay wall, about halfway up, narrowly missing Gipsy Danger. He watched the wreckage expand and fall, stunned, only then remembering that while the missiles could be fired for training purposes, their payloads had been removed.

Which for everyone in the building was a very, very good thing.

What was going on? Something in the Drift, obviously. They thought they were fighting something. What? Why?

Chronos threw another punch; this one hit Valor

Omega, visibly damaging the other Jaeger's shoulder.

There had to be something...

"Wait," Lambert said. "You said all of the fail-safes. What about the Pons Intercessor?"

Xiang's eyes widened, and she shook her head.

"That's a separate system," she said. Her hands flew over the controls. "It's still intact."

The intercessor was designed to allow an outsider to drift with those in the Conn-Pod. It was a safety precaution – useful, for instance, if one of the pilots passed out for some reason. A third party could enter the Drift to help stabilize the situation.

But maybe he could use it to shut things down.

"Put me in," he said.

# 2

HE ENTERED NOT A DRIFT, BUT A MAELSTROM. Braga and Vu were both utterly panicked, nourishing each other's terror in a feedback loop that was already so strong, Lambert had trouble not caving in to fear himself.

Of course, now that he was in, he saw they had a reason to be afraid. His field of vision was all Kaiju, a monster so gargantuan and so close he could only make out parts; he got a sense of Gila monster and ground sloth as three huge claws ripped through the right side of the Conn-Pod.

He knew it wasn't real, couldn't be real.

But it seemed real. And Braga and Vu were utterly convinced. He couldn't see them, of course, because he wasn't really in the Conn-Pod – but he could feel them, the bright mental stuttering of total panic.

But even though they were terrified, they were fighting, or trying to.

The Kaiju swiped at them again with those black claws; Chronos countered with a double high block, then brought both fists back down on the monster's head. It staggered a bit, but shook it off, and then its muzzle filled the screen as its jagged teeth closed on the Conn-Pod and started worrying it like a dog with a bone. Chronos responded with an uppercut and began warming up the other missile, stepping back to give her room to fire.

Lambert tried to force his thoughts into the whirlpool theirs had formed, but it was hard to make headway; if there was a downside to their compatibility, it was that they were so strongly connected he couldn't get through to them; the strength of their bond was shutting him out. He couldn't reach both of them at once.

He had to pick one.

Of the two, it felt like Vu still had the most control, so in a split-second decision, he went for her.

*It's not real. This is just a training sim. Snap out of it, Vu. Let's shut this down.*

She wanted to believe him. But it was just so real, and the Kaiju was coming back…

*Think. Before you started to drift you were in the bays; Chronos never went outside…*

He felt suddenly dizzy as the Kaiju lifted Chronos Berserker into the air. He saw the sea below, sheeted in ice, land in the near distance, mountains covered in snow.

*Ice, Vu, see? Snow! We're at the Moyulan Shatterdome. China. Late summer. No ice for a thousand miles…*

They slammed into the water. Braga screamed and thrashed wildly as the Kaiju drew them into the depths. Water started pouring through a tear in the Conn-Pod, and it was cold, shockingly cold.

*Vu!*

*Noicenoicenoicenoice,* Vu repeated. *NO. ICE.*

"Yes, Ranger!" Vu shouted, aloud.

He felt her go, suddenly, explosively. She must have ripped off her headgear. Braga's mental scream rose, peaked in utter anguish and despair as the Conn-Pod seemed to flood with icy water.

Lambert broke contact. Braga couldn't drift by himself. With Vu gone, the neural handshake would not hold, the illusion would end, and everything would stop.

Out in the bay, Chronos Berserker hit the wall again, took three steps back, and then became very still.

The feed from inside the Jaeger was still cut off; all Lambert could do was watch helplessly as the emergency crew descended from the ceiling and opened the Conn-Pod. When they finally got in there with the medical team, there was a long moment of silence.

"Vu is unconscious," the medic reported, finally.

"And Braga?" Lambert asked.

"I'm sorry, Ranger – he's gone."


Dr. Ysabel Morales had always intimidated Hermann Gottlieb. It was nothing she meant to do, and came from no deficit in her character. His feelings were entirely derived from comparing himself to her. Her early work in the PPDC – her equations that outlined the first intimations of what scientists would call the Anteverse – were sheer genius, the kind of forward leap in mathematical thinking that only came along once in a century or so. In the old days, when they had been colleagues in the research division of the PPDC, she always seemed to reach the answers before he did. Along with that she had been social, and funny, able to easily converse about anything from Victorian literature to the contents of a Sazerac cocktail or the string theory with equal enthusiasm and aplomb. She had exuded confidence and self-reliance without seeming conceited or stand-offish. In short, she made him and most of the other scientists look rather... inferior. Even so, he had always liked her.

Now she was in his lab. It was the first time he had seen

her in almost a decade, and he was starting to fear she was going to cry.

She didn't, but she must have read something in his expression.

"I know," she said. "This is much harder than I thought. It's the first time I've been back in a PPDC facility since… well, since not long after Sean died."

"Ah, yes," he said. "I had forgotten. Not – not that he died, you understand. It was tragic. I didn't know him all that well, but I know that you did…" he trailed off, realizing that things were going wrong, as they often did when he spoke. Of course she had known him better. They had been engaged.

"It's okay," she said. "I'm just not as at peace with it as I thought I was."

"I never understood—" he began, but then realized that once again he was about to intrude on her grief, and didn't finish the sentence.

But she knew where he'd been going.

"Why I blamed myself?" she said. "Because it was my fault, Hermann. I was responsible for the containment system."

"But we knew so little back then," he said. "And it was important work. Transforming our mathematical theories – *your* mathematical theories, really, since you first saw the implications in the data and wrote it into equations – into practice – we were able to build generations of better technology. Ultimately, those experiments were also the start of what let us close the Breach."

She shrugged. "He was going to be my husband," she said. "He died – in – in agony. Knowing it was me that failed him. I could see it in his eyes."

"Nonsense. I can't believe he would have blamed you. No one else did."

She tilted her head down, and now he understood she

*was* weeping. He stood frozen, unsure what to do. But after a moment, he gave her an awkward side-hug and patted her shoulder, hoping she did not misinterpret his intentions.

Perhaps a change of subject.

"It's going to be fine," he said. "Listen, why don't you tell me what brings you here. You're still employed by Geognosis?"

"Yes," she said, wiping her eyes. "You're right. I should focus on doing something. That's how I got through it. I'll get through it this time."

She smiled thinly. "After I left the PPDC I went back to university, but it didn't – well, after a few years it didn't fulfill me the way I hoped. So, yes, I found a job in the private sector, with Geognosis. They've just taken a contract with PPDC to design the plasma cells for a new generation of energy refineries. I'll be heading up our team, here, in the dome. I've been provided facilities in Mechspace."

"I can think of no one better suited for the job," he said. It was an understatement; the job actually seemed well beneath her, or at least beneath the woman he had known. But the person before him seemed considerably more fragile than the one he remembered.

"And if you need anything at all, please – do not hesitate to come to me."

"That's very kind of you," she said.

There followed an uncomfortable silence, in which he began to wonder if there was something she was expecting him to say, or do. He did empathize with her, but of course there was a lot to do. It was good to see her, but at work there was – work. Should he invite her over? He would have to check with his wife first, of course, but he might at least suggest a more social, after-hours setting if she needed more emotional support.

He hadn't quite formulated how to say that when her eyebrows lifted.

"I'm sorry, Hermann," she said. "I quite forgot. I brought something to show you."

She reached into her bag, removed a small memory stick, and handed it toward him.

"What's this?" he asked.

"I'm not sure," she told him. "The last project I was on involved building better predictive models for locating geological assets – oil, natural gas, rare earths and the like. We used a wide range of data sets, and some things jumped out at me. Inside the tectonic data there are some very subtle rhythms which increase and decrease in frequency and amplitude over a six-month span, but they generally trend up. Which I might not have noticed if there wasn't a similar upward trend in neutrino emissions from the Earth's upper mantle. It's not exactly an Anteverse signature, but it – well, it reminded me of one. I didn't have time to give this the attention I think it might need, and frankly, this field has left me way behind. I haven't read a paper on the subject since – since I left here. You're the expert on this, Hermann. It might be nothing. It probably is nothing. But I wanted to afford you the opportunity to give it a look."

He took the stick and synchronized it into his workstation; the data began appearing instantly. He hunched over it.

"Yes, I see," he murmured. "Very interesting. This is like nothing I've ever seen before. I will certainly have a look at this."

He stared back at the data uneasily. Lately he had had his own worries about such things. He hated the very idea of intuition, but occasionally it was hard to deny its value.

The building suddenly shuddered, violently, and again.

Alarms were going off. He checked the status matrix.

"Something is going on in Jaeger bays," he said. "Ysabel, I'm afraid you must excuse me."

"Of course, Hermann," she said. "Do what you need to, I'll talk to you later…"

He hardly heard her as he hurried toward the door.

# 3

**"SECRETARY GENERAL MORI?"**

Mako didn't turn right away, because she was transfixed by the sunset and because "Secretary General" still didn't sound like it went with her name. It felt too big for her, like a coat made for someone else. At the same time, it felt small, considering that when she was a Ranger she stood two hundred and sixty feet high. That had seemed just right.

And like so many things, that had been taken from her.

And there was the sunset seen from fifty thousand feet – beautiful, almost too big to grasp, layer upon layer of clouds soaked in light, each higher heaven a little brighter. But the sea below, that was already dark. Tonight and yesterday seen all at once.

"What is it, Airman?" He was a young man, his uniform so crisp it seemed like he'd ironed it after he put it on.

"You've got an urgent message from the Moyulan Shatterdome. They've been trying to get through to you."

"Thank you," she said.

Once the airman was gone, she sighed and checked her redline comm. She had only meant to turn it off long enough for a moment with the sunset, but since they were chasing the sun, that moment had stretched on and on. What was wrong with her? She felt a little out of it. Not fatigued, exactly, but more attenuated. She knew her work was important, she just wasn't sure she was important to the work. But someone did, obviously, or they wouldn't be calling her.

LOCCENT.

She returned the call and asked the controller for Marshal Quan. There was a bit of shuffling, then Quan's voice was in her ear.

"Secretary General," he said. "I hope you are well."

She almost smiled, knowing that translated to "where the hell have you been?"

"I'm well," she replied. "What is it?"

"We've had a problem here," he said. "In the Jaeger bay."

She listened with growing horror as he gave the details. It took her back to a place and a moment she did not care to remember: her own Drift gone bad. This time it was worse: one person was dead and another would never pilot again. But it could have been far worse still.

"Was anyone else injured?" she asked. "Are the cadets all okay?"

"They are, Secretary General. No other injuries, in fact."

That was good. *Okay, take a breath.*

"Let me talk to Ranger Lambert," she said. "He's there, isn't he?"

"He's practically standing on top of me. Here you go."

"Lambert here."

"I just want to get this clear in my head," Mako said. "You cut into their Drift, and they thought they were fighting a category V Kaiju?"

"Yes, Secretary General."

"We've only ever seen one category V."

She should know. She had sudden remembrance of Slattern, appearing from the watery void, a monster so large that it seemed to have no end to it...

"That's true, Secretary General," Lambert said. "And this wasn't it. This was a new Kaiju. An imaginary one, I guess."

She let that sink in. When she had first drifted with Raleigh, he had experienced again his fight with the Kaiju Knifehead, and the loss of his brother. His violent memory had triggered her, and she had slipped into a memory she thought was real: the recollection of the Kaiju attack on Tokyo that had killed her parents. It had very nearly been a disaster – she had begun the process of firing Gipsy's plasma cannon inside the Hong Kong Shatterdome.

But the two trainees – Braga and Vu – neither of them had ever fought a Kaiju, not unless they had done it when they were nine, so what memories could they use to conjure up such a situation?

"Were either of them in Kaiju attacks?" she asked.

"No," Lambert replied. "Braga was from outside of Rio and Vu from Houston, and neither traveled to any city that was attacked."

"So, this didn't come out of their heads."

"No. It was like Mock-Pod simulation but more... real."

"Then this was not an accident of some sort."

"I don't see how it could be," Lambert said. "This was sabotage – and murder."

"I assume you've locked the place down?"

"Of course. Marshal Quan gave the order immediately."

"I'll be there in five hours," Mako said. "I'll put the other Shatterdomes on high alert. If someone is attacking us, this may just be the first strike. We should be prepared for follow-ups."

She kept the phone on this time, but turned her attention back to the sunset. The sun was winning their race; only a sliver of it remained. All but the highest clouds were dark now.

She thought about enemies. When she was little, they had seemed simple, almost grotesquely so – a giant monster had destroyed her city and killed her parents. She had grown up believing that one day she would climb into a Jaeger and kill those enemies. And she had, and so doing she had found something infinitely precious.

Raleigh.

People who hadn't drifted didn't understand. They thought when they said "love" they were somehow talking about the same thing she and Raleigh had experienced. Attraction, connection, trust – these were words that could not quite carry freight for what two people felt when they had a link of some kind to begin with, and then literally joined their minds together. The things most hidden often appeared first, things that in a normal relationship might take years to come to light – or might never surface at all. Honesty had almost no meaning when you drifted.

She and Raleigh – and her adoptive father Stacker Pentecost, and others – they had beaten the enemy, killed the Kaiju, and destroyed the portal by which those monsters entered the world. And everything was fine. The world was saved.

In ten years, nothing had come out of the Breach.

But they had taken Raleigh anyway, hadn't they?

Both of them had been poisoned by the radiation from the Anteverse; she remembered days in bed, blood transfusions, highly experimental treatments for both of them. Still they had been together in a sense, going through the same thing, victims of the same affliction. She drew strength from him and he from her.

But then she started to get better.

Raleigh did not.

The scientists called it the throat, a sort of interdimensional tube through which the Kaiju emerged into their world. She and Raleigh had gone down the throat, and Raleigh had ejected her before rigging the atomic core of their Jaeger – Gipsy Danger – to melt down.

Once she was out, he descended further. As she rode, unconscious, in her escape pod, he and Gipsy drifted out the other end of the throat, into the Anteverse itself. Raleigh used Gipsy's nuclear vortex turbine to propel the Jaeger back into the throat, and then ejected himself, seconds ahead of the detonation. He'd spent a handful of heartbeats in the Anteverse, but those were seconds longer than she had been there. He tried to describe to her the things that he saw there, but they didn't make that much sense, even to him.

Poisoned by the radiation of another world, he fought, as he always fought.

She was holding his hand when he died. She heard his last words. He had been asleep, but when he opened his eyes, the old brightness was still there. *He* was still there.

"Mako," he whispered, squeezing her hand. "All you have to do is fall. Anyone can fall."

And then he wasn't there. Not in a rush, not in battle, but in a quiet moment that did not seem nearly big enough for the weight of his person. Raleigh had been cheated. *She* had been cheated – of Raleigh, of her adoptive father, of her life as a pilot.

And even if she could still pilot a Jaeger, even if she could climb into one and make it go, who would she fight? Where was her revenge for Raleigh?

# 4

2035
MOYULAN SHATTERDOME
CHINA

THE APPROACH TO THE MOYULAN AIRFIELD WAS
steep; the PPDC's newest Shatterdome was built into a
mountainous speck of rock in Qingchuan Bay, off the rocky
east coast of China's Fujian province. The view from the
approach of mountains and countless fractal inlets of the
sea was quite beautiful. Far from any really large population
centers like Hong Kong, it had never been attacked by Kaiju;
the shoreline was pristine and the small city of Fuding a little
inland. Once resort towns and spas had dotted this coast,
but that was long ago. Even without a direct Kaiju threat,
beachfront property was no longer seen as... premium.

Moyulan also filled an important gap, putting the
island of Taiwan and the mainland cities of Shanghai and
Hangzhou within easy deployment range and reinforcing
the Japanese capacity to protect the region.

Quan and Lambert met her at the airfield. Marshal
Quan was in his early forties; his compact, fit frame carried

a great deal of authority, as well as a certain amount of style. Lambert was more than a decade younger and had what Mako couldn't help but think of as an all-American sort of look, with his chestnut hair and steel-blue eyes and a bearing that bordered on – but was not quite – arrogant. She knew him well; he was a true believer in the PPDC and its mission, and had little patience with those whom he perceived as not having the same level of commitment. He and her adoptive brother Jake had once been close friends and Drift partners, but they were now estranged. She hadn't seen her brother in many years, either, but that was more... complicated.

The two men first escorted her, at her insistence, to the Jaeger bays to review the damage.

It wasn't as bad as she had feared. The Jaegers had suffered only minor dings, and that included Chronos Berserker. The damage to the interior of the dome was a little more extensive. Even without warheads, the missiles had made quite a mess of some of the gantry and loading equipment, and it would take some time before all their standing Jaegers could be deployed at once. Still, most of the harm was cosmetic.

Except, of course, for the death of one of their most promising cadets.

Before they left, she let her gaze linger on one of the Jaegers, Gipsy Avenger. It was all Mark-6, gleaming and beautiful, but it reminded her – as it was meant to – of the old, refurbished Mark-3, Gipsy Danger. Raleigh's Jaeger. The first and last she had ever piloted.

"She is a beauty, isn't she?" Lambert said.

"Yes," she said. "She is. And she has an excellent pedigree."

"I hope one day to live up to that," Lambert said. "It's an honor to be given the chance."

"You're a good pilot, Ranger," she said. "Probably

the best we have. I'm sure when the time comes, you will acquit yourself quite well."

Lambert looked uncomfortable; she felt the awkwardness, too, and lowered her voice.

"It is good to see you, Nathan," she said. "Now is not the time, but later, when you have a moment, I should like to catch up."

"I would like that too," he said.

But she wasn't sure he meant it.


In Quan's office, Dr. Gottlieb joined them. The room was neat, professional, balanced; an excellent reflection of the Marshal himself. She waved off an offer of tea.

"What do we know?" she asked.

Dr. Gottlieb cleared his throat. "I've put several of our best people on the problem," he said. "I've been correlating their reports. What I'm telling you now is what we know for certain."

"I understand," Mako said. "Go on."

"What the pilots of Chronos Berserker experienced was essentially a Mock-Pod training program with some modifications. The Kaiju was entirely made up, and was essentially unbeatable in any scenario involving any Jaeger we have. The program also targeted all of the safeguards put in place to prevent something like this."

"Could it have been inserted remotely?"

"No," Gottlieb said. "I don't think so, and no one I've talked to does, either. After all, we can't have someone remotely reprogramming our Jaegers while they're in the middle of a fight. Like those people in Serbia tried to do a few years ago. No, the most plausible explanation is that someone manually inserted the code."

"And we have this," Quan said. He lifted a plastic

evidence bag. Inside was a small pen drive.

"That's one of our own drives," Mako said.

"Yes. More specifically, it's the kind we issue to the cadets on their first day, when they turn in all of their personal electronics."

Mako frowned. "You think either Braga or Vu did this to themselves?"

"No," Quan said. "All of the new recruits were in Berserker's Conn-Pod yesterday. This drive was issued the same day, to one of the cadets."

"The recruits?" Mako said, surprised. "You think one of them did this?"

"The evidence points that way," Gottlieb replied.

"No," Lambert said, shaking his head. "No. I take the new recruits up there every year. Then the J-Techs do their final check – after they leave. There's no way – if one of those kids left so much as a piece of gum stuck under the Drift harness, it would have been noticed. There's no way they would miss a pen drive lying around."

"Obviously they did," Gottlieb replied.

"Uh-uh. It had to have happened later, at night or early that morning."

"The security data disagrees," Quan said. "Once the Conn-Pod was sealed that night, it wasn't opened again until just before Braga and Vu stepped in."

"Then maybe it was one of the J-Techs that did the final inspection," Lambert said.

"Or maybe all of the cadets are not what they seem," Gottlieb said. "When two or more solutions are suggested to a problem, it is usually the most simplistic which is correct."

"I'm familiar with Occam's razor, Doctor," Lambert said.

"The pen drive was issued to Ou-Yang Jinhai," Gottlieb said.

"It could have been stolen from him. When would he have had time to transfer a program from one of his personal devices to a drive he was issued yesterday?"

"In any number of ways, while he was turning his things in, Ranger. Jaegers are resistant to wireless reprogramming. But pen drives are not. And I believe he had outside help."

"Your theory is getting more complicated, Doctor," Lambert said. "I think your Occam's razor is getting dull."

Mako had been listening without comment, but now the conversation seemed to be becoming unproductive.

"So either one of the cadets did it," she said, nodding at Gottlieb, "or someone wants us to think a cadet did it." This time her gaze shifted to Lambert.

"Are any of the cadets capable of creating a program like this?"

"Unlikely," Gottlieb admitted. "That's what I was getting at a moment ago. It would have been possible for one of them to access a Mock-Pod scenario and modify it, and at least one of the cadets – Ou-Yang Jinhai, as it turns out – has a record of successfully subverting security procedures."

"Ou-Yang," she murmured. "That's the son of Suyin and Ming-hau. Is he really a suspect? Even if the pen drive was his, as the Ranger noted, it could have been stolen by any one of the other cadets or someone else in the Shatterdome."

"He's shown a certain disregard for authority in the past, I'm sure you recall."

"Yes," she said. "I reviewed his entrance materials. I didn't want him. I was overruled. But I wouldn't have thought he would do something like this."

"If he did," Gottlieb said, "he didn't do it alone. He might have inserted the program, but the features of it that over-wrote our fail-safes were – in my opinion – far too complex for any of our cadets to have accomplished.

Whoever created it had inside information about our systems that no new recruit could have obtained. In addition, certain segments of the code resemble some we've intercepted from the Akumagami Front. The likelihood is that whoever planted it in the Jaeger was merely a delivery boy – or girl."

"You're saying one of our cadets is a Kaiju worshipper?"

Probably from the moment Trespasser – the first Kaiju – appeared, there were people who believed it had been sent by God or the gods to punish humanity for its sins. Over time those people had found each other and organized religions around those beliefs, building temples inside the skulls of dead Kaiju, creating hymns, devotions, and ceremonies. When the Kaiju stopped coming, the cults remained. Most of them, though – however deluded and objectionable Mako found them – were not dangerous. They prayed and chanted and took drugs made from Kaiju body parts. A few committed suicide through means of an elaborate tea ceremony, where the tea was made of dehydrated Kaiju fluids.

The Akumagami Front was different – they were violent extremists, dedicated to destroying the PPDC and somehow bringing the Kaiju back into the world. They had made dozens of attempts to destroy or sabotage Jaegers – although none of them had succeeded remotely as well as what had just happened in Moyulan.

"It's not impossible," Quan said. "Our checks are good, but some of these kids come from questionable backgrounds."

"Some of our best Rangers come from 'questionable' backgrounds too," Lambert said.

"What I mean," Quan said, "is that they often come from places where records are incomplete, due to the widespread chaos in the aftermath of Kaiju attacks. To a certain extent, we have to take their word about their history."

"What about their psych evaluations?" Gottlieb said.

Quan shrugged. "Irregular psych profiles are almost a trademark of good Rangers. It's not like we're looking for the best-adjusted individuals on the planet. Anyway, their psych evaluations are necessarily incomplete until they finish their training here."

For a moment, the conversation paused, as if everyone was trying to think of something to say and coming up empty.

"I'll look into this," Mako said.

"Secretary General," Quan objected, "I'm sure you have far more important matters to occupy you. I assure you, we can mount an internal investigation, and we will discover the truth."

"The cadet program as it stands is the legacy of Stacker Pentecost," Mako said. "And for the last decade it has been a particular project of mine. If there is a problem with one of our cadets – or with the way the program is formulated and administered – it is certainly my concern. Marshal Quan, if you can make an office available to me and provide me with dossiers on the cadets, I will begin immediately."

# 5

WHEN THE FIRST BITTER FLAKES OF SNOW BEGAN to fall, Viktoriya's toes were already numb, despite her boots and three layers of socks. The day had fooled her; it had begun in sunshine, cool but not cold, a warm day for April – spring days could be like that. But now the sky was like the old chalkboard in her schoolhouse. The wind was from the sea, smelling of salt but thick with wet and chill. She knew she must be close. She even thought she could hear seagulls. Yet the stands of Jezo spruce and Sakhalin fir here were young and thick, and even from the hilltop, she could see nothing. But she was sure that if she went just a little farther, she would. It would be there, like she had seen in pictures, white-capped waves coming into the shore, an immense blue plane of water.

But as the snow fell harder, and the brown needles of the forest floor began to vanish beneath an ashen pall, she found she couldn't walk any further, not without a rest. She was only seven, after all, and not used to walking so far. It was getting dark, too, and she was starting to feel sleepy. Her jacket and pants were stiff, rubbing her uncomfortably with each step. And it seemed to be snowing harder every moment.

She sat down on a fallen log and huddled into herself. She would rest, she told herself, just for a moment, and then continue on to the coast.

Or maybe she should go back. But Babulya would be so angry, and anyway, the sea couldn't be far. Another few minutes, over the next hilltop, and it would be there. And then maybe she could see him, *them*...

It grew darker, and her limbs became heavier, and she was so sleepy she could barely keep her head up. But she knew she had to go on. She had a reason.

Taking a deep breath that seemed to bite deep into her lungs, she used the trunk of a fir tree to push herself up. She took a step, but now her pants felt completely frozen, and she cried out in pain as her already chafed skin felt like a knife had cut into it. Her eyes stung, so she closed them, gritted her teeth, and with all of the determination in her small body, took another step. Then she felt all dizzy and swirly, and she seemed to fall onto a bed, a soft, cozy bed warmed by the little cube heater back home.

The next thing she knew, someone was trying to shake her awake. She wanted to be left alone, and tried to say so, but whoever it was wouldn't stop. She felt herself pulled up, and she finally opened her eyes to find a bright light shining in them.

"Viktoriya," a rough voice grated. "Come along."

She couldn't see his face – everything was darkness and the one bright light. But it sounded like her grandfather.

Later, she realized he must have carried her. She didn't recognize where they were; a little wooden room, a small fire flickering in a little metal stove connected to the low roof by an aluminum pipe. She was on the floor, wrapped in several blankets.

"Dedulya?" she murmured.

He looked old in the firelight, with his scruff of black-and-white beard. The hood of his coat covered his balding head.

"Where were you going, Vnuchka?" he asked.

She didn't want to tell him, so she said nothing. After a moment, he sighed and pushed another few sticks into the fire. Sparks twirled up the flue.

"Where are we?" she asked.

"I was on a logging crew here, years ago," he said. "We cut most everything, and now it's growing back – that's why the trees are all so small. But we built some shacks and such so we didn't have to trek all the way back to town every night. A few of the shacks are still here. We were lucky this one still had a sound roof on it. I suppose we might have made it back home. Probably not – with my bad back. You're lucky I even found you. In another few minutes, your tracks would have been completely covered. Even so, if you hadn't yelled…" he shook his head.

"Babulya will be mad," she said.

"Oh, yes," he replied. He looked at her. "Was it because of the boy? The one you hit with the rock?"

"Maksim is bigger than me," she said.

The faintest grin turned his lips up.

"That's smart," he said, so quietly she almost didn't hear it.

Maksim had made fun of her, and she'd hit him. But he was nine, and big for his age, and it hadn't hurt him at all. He'd pushed her down and started to walk away. But her hand found a rock, and she'd called his name. When he turned around, she smacked him right in the forehead with it. She'd been surprised by all the blood, and how loudly he screamed, but soon all she could think was how much trouble she would be in.

"So you decided to hide in the woods?"

She looked at him to see if he was kidding. He still didn't understand.

"No," she said. "I was trying to get to the sea."

"Why?"

"I never saw it. It's just over there, and Babulya won't let me see it."

He sighed. "The sea is dangerous, Vikushka. Especially on days like this. Your grandmother only tries to protect you. But why now, why—" he stopped, and his green eyes shone clearly before he turned away.

"Ah," he said. "The Jaeger. Is that it?"

"Yes," she admitted. "Cherno Alpha is there. I saw it on the monitor at school. Dedulya, Cherno Alpha is fighting a Kaiju, out in the water. I want to see."

He shook his head. "The sea is a big place," he said. "The Kaiju is south of here, and on the east coast. We're on the west side of Sakhalin, so you could never see it from where you were heading. And for this you almost died." He coughed, a heavy cough deep in his chest.

"Your grandmother..." he began, but he didn't finish. He just looked away.

"This boy. Why did you hit him?"

"He said I was a liar. He said I was an orphan."

"What did you tell him, that he said you were a liar?"

"I told him that Sasha Kaidanovsky is my mother and Aleksis Kaidanovsky is my father, and they ride in the chest of Cherno Alpha, and one day, when all of the Kaiju are dead, they will come back here and get me."

Her grandfather again fell silent, and seemed to sink into himself. When he did speak again, it was very quietly, as if he was afraid the snow outside might hear him.

"What has your grandmother said about this?" he said. "She told you they were your parents?"

She dropped her head.

"Yes. But she also said I am never to say that. Never to speak their names or tell anyone."

"That is so," he said. "Your grandmother is very wise. You must obey her in this."

"Why? Why should I let Maksim call me an orphan?"

"It does you no harm, what he says," the old man told her.

"Because I know the truth?" she asked.

He was quiet for a moment. Then he put his hand on her shoulder.

"Does it make you feel strong, knowing who your parents are? Does it inspire you to become great, like them?"

"Yes," she said.

"Very well," he sighed. "That's good then. But you must not run off like this again," he said. "You must promise me."

"I promise you, Dedulya," she said. "But can you tell me – is the battle over? Has Cherno Alpha won once again?"

Her grandfather laughed. "How should I know? I've been out here, looking for you."


They finished the night in the hut, and the next morning her grandfather walked her to their little cottage in the low hills outside of town. Then he went to catch his ride to work, cutting trees in the north.

"You're a thief," her grandmother scolded her. "Your grandfather needs his rest – he works so hard. And you stole that rest from him."

"I'm sorry," she said.

"And what of me? If you had frozen to death, what could I say? Your parents left you here with me, to care for you, see you grow strong – what would they say if all I could deliver to them was a little ice princess, a frozen block of meat?"

"I only wanted to see the sea," she said.

"The sea is death. It is cold, and miserable, and it is a murderer and a stealer of souls. That is why we live here, away from it."

"You once lived near the sea, Grandfather said."

"Yes, once. Before, but not now. Not ever again, do you understand?"

She didn't answer. Grandmother sat on the little bed, next to her. She had big gray eyes and a wide nose and ears that stood away from her head. Her hair was blonde, like Viktoriya's, although shot with duller strands. She'd told Viktoriya several times that came from her great-grandmother, who had been one of the old people of Sakhalin, an Ainu. Most of them had been deported when Russia took the island from Japan, but a few had stayed. Grandmother's people went deep into the island – Grandfather's parents had come from Perm, to work in the oil business.

"Why isn't Grandfather's name Kaidanovsky?" she asked.

"What?"

"Maksim said Sasha and Aleksis weren't my parents because Grandfather's name isn't Kaidanovsky."

"Your other grandparents are the Kaidanovskys," she replied.

"Where are they?"

"Moscow, I guess."

"But then shouldn't my last name be Kaidanovsky?"

"We've been taking care of you for so long," she said,

"it's easier for you to use our name. The government asks fewer questions."

"But my magazine said Sasha's name was Vasilev before they got married…"

"What magazine?" her grandmother demanded. "Let me see it."

She hesitated, but Babulya gave her the look, and she dug the old magazine from beneath her mattress. Grandmother took it and thumbed through the fading Cyrillic lettering until she came to their pictures. Sasha was tall and strong, but Aleksis was nearly a giant. Both had shocks of blonde hair, but Sasha had dark eyebrows, like Vik's grandmother, and she suddenly felt bad for asking.

For doubting.

"You know," her grandmother said, "back in the old days there were demons everywhere, just roaming the earth. They loved to destroy, but they loved to attack children the best. I don't know why. It's how demons are. So, back then they didn't name children right away, because once you have a name, a demon can find you, and attack you. In those days, even when you had a name, you kept it hidden, and went by a nickname instead. Over the years, we let that slide, along with a lot of other things. We forgot, because we thought the demons were gone, first driven away by heroes with swords of steel and later by electric lights and algebra and all of that. But you know what, Vikushka? They came back, didn't they? And they still hear our names when they are spoken. If the Kaiju knew your real name, they would come for you. Your parents are strong, your parents kill them. But if the Kaiju knew you were their daughter, your mother and father could not protect you – they could not guard Russia at the same time. So, I have hidden your name, child, to hide you. We have hidden it, you understand? So we go by my maiden name, Malikova."

"But what if they learn my first name?"

"That's a very good point," her grandmother said. "Viktoriya is a long, beautiful name. It might be noticed. Perhaps from now on we should call you something else. Tori, maybe."

"I think I like Vik better," she said. "It's shorter. Less noticeable."

"Vik," her grandmother said. "Very well. You will be Vik Malikova, understand?"

"Okay," she said. "But – is that why they never come to see me? Because they're afraid the Kaiju will know where I am?"

Her grandmother just smiled, and kissed her on the head. Then her face became stern.

"Don't think I've forgotten what you did. You hurt a boy, you ran away. You could have gotten yourself killed and your grandfather as well. Three days with no vidiot, do you understand?"

Vidiot was what Babulya called anything you watched for fun. She thought all of it made you stupid.

"But I want to see about the fight."

"Cherno Alpha won, of course, and that is all you need to know."

But that didn't satisfy her. She knew how to find out; on the way home from school she stopped by the bar, where all the old men too injured to work hung around, drinking away their stipends. Three of them were sitting outside, and they told her about it, two of them slurring their words a bit.

The Kaiju's name was Vodyanoi, named for a water monster that figured in dark, ancient stories of the Russian people. Like all Kaiju, he was terrifically huge. They all looked different, like normal things mashed together with really not normal things. Vodyanoi looked sort of like a big, fat, puffed-up toad, and he was really nasty. Two Jaegers went after him – Cherno Alpha and Eden Assassin. The monster spit some kind of acid on Eden Assassin and it ate right through its metal skin, killing both pilots.

"Cherno Alpha didn't like that," an old man named Vladimir said. "She pulled an iceberg right out of the water. And she beat it to death. With an iceberg. A *grobanyy* iceberg. Right before it got to the capital."

He lifted his glass. "Screw them and their wall. The Russian machine, the Soviet Slammer, she's our savior! To Cherno Alpha, and all the other Jaegers and their pilots!"

They gave her a little of what they were drinking so she could toast with them. It made her mouth and nose burn, and she couldn't swallow it. She wondered if the stuff Vodyanoi spit on Eden Assassin was anything like it.

She went home; Grandmother wasn't back from work yet, so before doing her chores, Viktoriya went to her room. On her wall hung a once-glossy poster of Cherno Alpha with her huge, barrel-shaped head and massive chest. She imagined her parents in there, making the gigantic Jaeger move, fight, kill.

Next to it, on the wall, she had written a list of names. Reckoner, Raythe, Tengu, Denjin, Atticon. The Kaiju Cherno Alpha had battled with and not only survived, but triumphed over.

To this list she now added Vodyanoi.

Then she went to wash the dishes.

That night, she had to go to bed early, part of her punishment. Her grandparents had the news on, and she wasn't allowed to watch. So she lay in bed and thought.

She'd seen Maksim that day, with a big bandage on his head. He hadn't said a thing to her. But she'd heard he was telling people she'd cheated, using a rock.

But now she thought about Cherno Alpha, beating a

Kaiju to death with an iceberg. That wasn't cheating. That was winning.

Even her grandfather had said it was smart. Maksim was too big for a girl her size to beat. But not if that girl had a rock.

What she hadn't told her grandfather was what she'd been pretending when she hit Maksim. She had been pretending she was a Jaeger; armored, powerful, controlled by pilots hidden away and protected by her chest. And Maksim, he was a Kaiju – mean, big, not too smart, breaking things and hurting people just because he could. Because it was his nature. And when she had hit him, she hadn't felt sorry, or ashamed, or shocked. Because she was a Jaeger. Armored, doing what she was supposed to do. It wasn't her hand that picked up the rock; it was the Jaeger's.

She thought of Cherno Alpha, striding through the frozen sea, unbothered by the cold or the snow, of the man and woman who rode within her. Were they thinking of her, too? Of the day when the fighting was finally over, and they could climb out of their steel giant and be her parents again?

She thought they were. She hoped they were.

Thinking that, she went to sleep.

# 6

MOTHER'S HYSTERICAL LAUGHTER FROM THE *next room so cold and what is that smell Russell's little casket so tiny sting of the slap on her cheek taste of blood smaller kids scattering from his path smell of vodka on her breath brother's playing but say she's too young first taste of vodka in his mouth burns sees her curled in the cell what is she doing here the callouses on his fingers the stillness of his presence the strength the fire the anger burning inside her soothing touch he smells of machinery, the power, Reckoner so* grobanyy *big, all legs, battering, beating shock after shock, riding the bright line between fury and control...*

Present. Sasha and Aleksis were in the Drift.

"Initiating neural handshake," LOCCENT control informed them.

And now they were Cherno Alpha.

And Cherno Alpha was a monster. Two hundred and

eighty feet tall, two thousand four hundred and twelve tons of high-tech metal armor and technological guts, and between them Sasha and Aleksis controlled every inch of her through their fused minds and the Pinocchio rig they were fitted into. If Sasha raised her right arm and made a fist, Cherno Alpha lifted the many tons of her massive right limb. When they walked, Cherno walked, and when they ran she ran. She was a Mark-1, a first-generation Jaeger, but while there were newer, shinier models out there, Cherno was theirs. The monster *they* lived inside.

It took a monster to fight a monster, and a monster was headed their way.

Five years before, the first of the Kaiju had burst from the depths of the Marianas Trench, where one continental plate was pushing beneath another, where nearly unimaginable vertical pressure and literally earth-wrenching tectonic forces met. The place of its emergence was later called the Breach, but it wouldn't be recognized and named until later. All scientists had at the time was a lot of strange data that didn't seem to add up to anything until a *thing* arose from the depths. They called it Trespasser, eventually, but at first it was just a three-hundred-foot-tall nightmare that came out of the Pacific and began to destroy the works of man. It surfaced near San Francisco, and over the course of six days left three cities in smoking ruin. The United States and United Kingdom threw everything they had at it, including, finally, a nuclear weapon.

The nuke worked. But the cure was as bad as the disease.

Which would have been one thing, if Trespasser were both the first and the last of its kind.

It was not. Another came, and another, and humanity began to wake up. After destroying, marginalizing, or mastering every predator – every dominant form of life on the planet, for that matter – something had come along to shake *Homo sapiens* out of their self-congratulatory comfort zone.

They were now ants beneath the feet of giants.

But they were clever ants, and they were determined ants, and with the same minds and same hands which had constructed their nests of wood, steel, and plastic, they built their own giants.

And these they called Jaegers.

Jaegers carried as much potential energy as a nuclear weapon – the early ones, Cherno included, were nuclear-powered – but they kept it contained, kept it local, prevented the kind of collateral damage a bomb would cause.

The war effort was international. Cherno Alpha was Russian built; others came from United States, from Japan, from China, Panama, Mexico – but all were housed in the Hong Kong Shatterdome. All along the Pacific Rim, other Shatterdomes were being built. Soon – perhaps by the end of the year – Cherno Alpha would rest on Russian soil, in Vladivostok, where she could better serve the motherland. Other facilities were being constructed in Sydney, Anchorage, Tokyo, Lima, and so forth, forming an arc of protection for the world.

But for now, all deployments started from Hong Kong.

But since this Kaiju was headed toward Russia, it was Cherno Alpha's honor and duty to dispatch it.

The helicopters had lifted it out of the Shatterdome when the Kaiju – Raythe – was nothing more than a tectonic and sonar signature moving through deep water. No one knew what made a Kaiju go this way or that, but this one stayed in deep water, skirting far west of the major Japanese islands, on a straight line toward Kamchatka, so they had flown out to meet it, suspended beneath the rotating wings of eight V-50 Jumphawks. Now they stood in the shallow, icy water about ten miles off the Kamchatka Peninsula, waiting.

"This time will be different," Aleksis said. He spoke out loud; their minds were merged, they felt everything and knew everything the other felt, but the best way to relay something focused and specific was still spoken language.

Even without the Drift, Sasha wouldn't have had to ask him what he meant. Their first fight had been almost two years ago, and it hadn't gone so well. The Kaiju named Reckoner had broken through the Miracle Mile and reached the Hong Kong waterfront. Cherno Alpha had been able to punch it back for a time, but they had suffered crippling damage in the hours-long fight. In the end, it had been China's Horizon Brave that finished the beast by hurling it into an electrical plant. The Blackout Knockout, the press had dubbed it.

That had been sitting in Aleksis for two years now: two years of private recriminations, hard training, waiting for his chance to redeem Cherno — and himself. What he wanted — what Sasha felt — was to beat the Kaiju to death with his bare fists.

With Cherno Alpha's fists, motivated by the most powerful energy cell of any Jaeger, that was possible. But it would do no good to get cocky.

"We fight defensively," Sasha said. "We do not let it out of the water. Not one toxic foot on Russian soil."

A third voice suddenly inserted itself into their conversation: Konstantin Scriabin, in LOCCENT control.

"I'm glad you guys are so gung ho," he said. "But there's been a little snag."

"Explain," Sasha said.

"Target has changed trajectory. It's turned west, toward Hokkaido."

"What then?" Sasha asked. "We're miles from there."

"You're still a lot closer than anyone else, by a power of ten," Scriabin said. "The best we can do is get you down there as quickly as possible."

"It faked us out," Aleksis said. "We should have known better. Why Kamchatka? There's nothing there. Reindeer and snow. Sapporo makes a better target. It has cities. And beer."

"Who knows why the Kaiju attack where they do?" Sasha said. "They're mindless beasts."

"This mindless beast faked us out," Aleksis said. "Bring the Jumphawks back. Get us down there!"

"On their way, Cherno, but they have to refuel at Okha. They've already flown a long way today. Maybe you two should break Drift, take a rest."

There were limits to how long anyone could Drift – some pilots could only make it a few hours before the connection began to fall apart.

But Aleksis was growing frustrated. He wanted a straight-up fight, a cage match, and instead they were now playing cat-and-mouse. Worse, the telemetry suggested that once again, a Kaiju was going to make landfall, this time before they even had a chance to stop it. It wasn't Cherno's miscalculation, but there was no point in blaming LOCCENT control, either. Raythe had deviated from pattern. No one was to blame but the Kaiju.

But it was maddening, nonetheless. Cherno Alpha's dream of succeeding where before she had failed – of killing the Kaiju before it could do any harm – was already impossible. They could never reach Japan in time.

"Negative," Sasha told Scriabin. "We must be ready as soon as we arrive. We will maintain Drift. It's not a problem."

# 7

"THIS ISN'T GOOD," SURESH SAID. "WE HAVEN'T been here a week. It sucks."

Suresh usually looked worried, or at least he had in the handful of days Jinhai had known him. But now his thick eyebrows were threatening to become permanently fused together.

But Jinhai agreed with him. It was difficult enough being in a new place with strange people, but for disaster to strike before they had even gotten to know each other – that really didn't make things any easier.

Added to that, he couldn't find the pen drive he'd been issued. It was a small thing compared to the rest of it, but he would have to ask for another, which would make him seem like a flake who couldn't keep up with his things.

"I liked Braga," Meilin said. The other Chinese cadet, she was tall, long-limbed, striking, although he thought her bangs made her look too severe. "He was very funny. And enthusiastic."

"He was an idiot," Viktoriya grunted. She may have meant to say it under her breath, but everyone heard her except maybe Tahima, who was either asleep or pretending to be asleep on his bunk.

"Why would you say such a terrible thing, Viktoriya?" Meilin asked.

Viktoriya frowned. "Don't call me that, please," she said. "I prefer 'Vik'."

Meilin seemed to shrink a bit from the conflict, but Renata, now paying full attention, stepped in to take her place. Renata – a Chilean – was outspoken and a bit of a smartass. He liked her. Of course, he'd liked Viktoriya too, at first glance.

"Okay, 'Vik'," Renata said. "Why would you call Braga an idiot? I think we'd all like to know."

Vik rolled off her bunk and squared off against Renata. The Russian stood a few inches taller than the Chilean.

"Braga thought the world was soft," she said. "Like a big pillow for him to play on. He did not respect it for what it was. And so it killed him."

For once, Renata did not have an immediate comeback.

"That's my favorite bedtime story ever," Suresh said. "Can you tell another, please?"

"That's pretty harsh," Jinhai said. "You barely knew the guy."

"There are some things you know right away, Ou-Yang."

*Oh, crap*, Jinhai thought.

"What's your deal?" Renata said. "Now you're after Jinhai?"

"Ou-Yang," Vik said, repeating his family name. "Why not tell them how you got here?"

"Same as you guys," he said. "I worked to get in here. My parents had nothing—"

He stopped when he realized that everyone was staring at him.

"Hang on," Suresh said. "I just assumed the name was a coincidence – I mean how many Ou-Yangs must there be in China?"

"Your parents were *those* Ou-Yangs?" Renata said.

"Yeah," he sighed. "Those Ou-Yangs."

The thing was, he wasn't sure the Russian girl wasn't right. Even if his parents hadn't pulled any strings, he might have still gotten preferential treatment.

He could tell they were all now thinking the same thing.

At least now he knew why Vik didn't like him.

"Soooo," Suresh said, after a moment. "Anyway. What do you think happened? Anyone?"

Jinhai shrugged, glad to have the conversation take a different turn.

"I mean, we all heard the racket, right? It sounded like a war going on."

"Obviously the Jaeger malfunctioned," Renata said. "But I've never heard of anyone getting killed in the bay like that. Something must have gone really wrong."

"You figured that out all on your own?" Vik asked. "Something went wrong."

Ilya, the other Russian cadet, said something to her in their native language. She shot back at him in the same. He nodded and shut up, looking abashed.

"Well, Vik," Renata said. "If you must know, I think it was sabotage. That's why they aren't telling us anything. There was a bomb, or something. Is that specific enough for you?"

To Jinhai's surprise, Vik nodded agreement. "I think so too," she said. "It doesn't feel like an accident to me."

Renata seemed to be starting a reply, when she suddenly jumped to her feet.

"Ranger on deck," she said.

Jinhai bounced out of bed and came to attention. Ranger Lambert was paused at the door, giving them a second to compose themselves. He looked them over, a solemn expression on his face.

"I know all you have heard about Braga and Vu," he said. "We'll have a memorial for Braga tomorrow at nine hundred hours. I expect you to all be there and looking sharp. Most of you didn't know Braga very well, but you can take it from me that he was one of the finest cadets I have ever seen. He was a good man, and he will be missed."

Did his gaze linger on Vik when he said that? Were they eavesdropping on the cadet barracks?

Very probably. Jinhai decided he'd better try to watch what he said, from here on out.

"As for Vu," Lambert went on, "the doctors think she's going to be okay. She's being taken off site, where she can get better care. I will keep you informed of her condition."

"Ranger, sir," Renata said. "Can you tell us what happened?"

Lambert shook his head. "The matter is officially under investigation, and until there is a determination, I'm not at liberty to share anything about it with you. Nor should you concern yourselves with it. You're here to train, and as of now that training will continue. When we're done, you'll either still be here and be a Ranger, or you'll be back wherever you call home."

*Or,* Jinhai thought, *we might be leaving in body bags, like Braga.*

Later, he found Ilya and asked him what he and Viktoriya had said to one another. Ilya just shook his head.

"Take my advice, friend," he said. "Don't mess with Russian girls."

The Ranger hadn't been kidding. He took them to the Kwoon, ran them through an hour of brisk exercise, and then started matching them up. Naturally, Jinhai's first match was Vik, because the universe hated him.

They hadn't been in the Kwoon before, but he'd heard a lot about it. It was like a gym or dojo where cadets and Rangers honed their fighting skills; after all, a Jaeger was no better at fighting than its pilots were. If the pilot couldn't throw a proper punch or execute a shoulder-throw, neither could the Jaeger.

"I'm just going to assess you today," Lambert said. "I've seen your test results, of course, but I want to observe you myself. We're going to start without weapons, but you can use any style or combination of styles that suits you. I want to see good, practical form, and I want to see control. I do not want any smashed noses, lost teeth, or broken bones. Do you understand?"

"Yes, Ranger," they said, together.

"Good. Renata and Ilya, you two are first. I—" Lambert snapped suddenly to attention. "Secretary General. Good morning."

"Good morning, Ranger. Good morning, cadets."

No one said anything. Everyone just stared.

Because it was Mako Mori, one of the pilots who had closed the Breach. The only survivor of the fighting team that had been humanity's last stand against the Kaiju, when two Jaegers had taken on three Kaiju at once, two Category IVs and a Category V. Even Jinhai, whose parents were heroes of the Kaiju Wars, was a bit starstruck in her presence.

"To what do we owe the honor?" Lambert asked.

"I'm just here to observe," Mori said. "Please. Carry on as if I weren't here."

Yeah. Like that was possible.

Renata and Ilya went at it – at first tentatively, but after Ilya scored the first touch, Renata really opened up. He could guess she had studied some Shotokan and boxing; she liked to use her hands, and her footwork was really good. Ilya tended to kick, which with Renata was a problem; twice she did the same thing to him, stepping into his high kick, catching it with crossed arms, and then delivering a back-fist to his face – almost, but not quite hitting him.

Then Suresh and Tahima fought. Suresh fared surprisingly well, but Tahima – despite being the biggest of them – was also really fast.

Then it was Jinhai's turn.

Vik came at him hard. He wasn't sure he should have expected anything else. He blocked a flurry of blows from her hands, but in so doing, he neglected her feet. She clipped his front foot, putting him off-balance long enough for her to pop him lightly in the throat. Lambert called the point for her and put them back to guard.

This time he broke her timing by pretending to move into her attack and then quickly stepping back. He threw out a back-fist, she faded to the side then punched low, toward his gut. He caught her arm and threw her, following her as she tumbled to the floor. She almost – but not quite – blocked his punch to her head.

Point for him. He was starting to enjoy himself.

This time when they were told to fight, Vik didn't do anything at first. She just stood there, not even in a good guard position.

"Come on," she said. "You want the point. Come and get it."

It threw him off a little. He had trained in fencing and several hand-to-hand fighting styles, but all of his coaches had disapproved of trash talk. In fencing, it was expressly forbidden and could result in being expelled from the match.

Bouncing on the balls of his feet, he closed the distance.

She was still just standing there.

He threw a punch. It was meant to be a feint, but she caught it, twisted his arm, and hit him on the side of the head with her open palm so hard he saw spots.

*I should have seen that coming*, he realized.

"Stop," Mako Mori said. She said it quietly, but everyone heard her.

*Yeah*, Jinhai thought, shaking his head. *Good idea.*

Mako walked out onto the floor of the Kwoon. She looked at Jinhai for a moment.

"You may sit down," she said.

He nodded, bowed, and sat.

Now she faced Vik.

"Malikova, yes?"

"Yes, Secretary General."

Mori held out her palm.

"Hit me," she said. "Full speed, but only so much as to touch me. I should feel wind only."

Vik stared at her for a moment, took a stance, and struck.

It was fast, and it landed as instructed, with no real contact.

"Very good," Mori said. "Now hit my hand again, so I feel it. Strike through, toward my heart."

Vik hesitated. For the first time since he'd met her, she seemed uncertain. "Secretary..."

"Do it."

Vik lowered herself into stance, then punched Mori in the hand. It landed with a painful-sounding thud.

Mori didn't blink.

"You know the difference, then," Mori said.

Vik nodded, red-faced.

"When you are asked for control," Mori said, "you will show control. Do you understand?"

"Yes, Secretary General."

"I would guess you've heard this before," Mori said, more lightly. A few of the other cadets chuckled, and even Vik cracked a little smile.

"Yes, ma'am," she admitted.

"Have a seat."

Mako then addressed all of them.

"Training in the Kwoon has two goals. The first is to ensure that you have the skills necessary to win a fight. But as important is a way of learning compatibility – who you might be able to Drift with – whether you can Drift at all. You will learn fighting techniques, and you will practice them. But when you spar one another you must think of the other cadet not as an opponent, but as a partner."

Jinhai, to his surprise, understood exactly what she meant. Some of the others looked puzzled, and Vik looked like she had swallowed something sour.

They spent the remainder of the day in the Kwoon, over seven hours. By the time they were done, he could barely walk back to the barracks.

# 8

THE SECRETARY GENERAL STAYED AFTER THE
cadets left, so Lambert figured she expected him to
stick around, as well. He had been dreading this; the
conversation he feared was inevitable, but which he had
no interest in having.

"They seem a solid bunch," Mako said, once the cadets
were out of earshot.

"Some of them have promise," he agreed. "I don't
expect all of them to make it."

"We didn't expect you to make it, you know," she said.
"You were such a loner, so convinced you could take on the
Kaiju all by yourself. There was just that one little thing…"

"Yes, Secretary General."

"I understand the importance of rank, Nate," she said.
"But we're alone now, and my title is intolerably clunky. I
would be happier if you would use my name. We were on
a first-name basis, yes?"

"That was a long time ago," he said.

"To you maybe," she said. "To me, that time seems very
near."

"Okay," he said. "Mako."

"Thank you," she said. "How many Drift partners did you fail to bond with?"

"Six," he said. "It was six."

"We should have washed you out at five. But my father – my adoptive father – believed in you. So did I. So did Jake."

"I remember," Lambert said. "I felt like I belonged. Like all of you – the PPDC – were my family. And then as soon I was starting to get comfortable with that, Jake…"

He realized he was getting angry, and tried to dial it back.

"I don't know where Jake is," Mako said. "I have tried to find him. His name surfaces now and then…"

"Yes," Lambert said. "In criminal circles. How—" he stopped, bowed his head. "I'm sorry," he said. "I know you think of him as a brother."

"As do you, Nate," Mako said.

"No," he said. "Not anymore. And I'm sorry if you can't find him, but – honestly – it might be for the best."

She pursed her lips, and for a moment didn't reply.

"I feel that way myself, sometimes," she said. "But he is still my brother."

By the end of evening mess, most of the cadets had garnered at least some little bit of information on what had happened to Braga and Vu. Rumors were racing around the Shatterdome, and they would have had to stuff their ears with something to keep from overhearing them.

That night they did a round robin, sharing what each had heard. The only total agreement was that something had gone wrong in Chronos Berserker – that Braga and Vu believed they were in a real fight. Suresh had eavesdropped on two low-level J-Techs speculating that Vu was somehow connected to a separatist organization of some sort. Vik said she had heard Kaiju worshippers were involved.

"Didn't those Kaiju nuts try to kill your parents, or something?" Ilya asked Jinhai.

He shook his head. "Not my parents. The couple that piloted Shaolin Rogue before my folks took over were murdered in their apartment," he said. "Everyone kind of thought Kaiju worshippers were involved, but as far as I know, nobody ever proved anything. My parents got plenty of death threats from them, though. I think a lot of the pilots did."

"Nasty business, Kaiju worship," Tahima opined.

"Nasty doesn't begin to cover it," Vik said. She said it like she knew something about it.

"Yeah," he said. "Agreed."


After Braga's memorial the next day was more Kwoon action, but they didn't fight each other, instead working with instructors, and today it was knife-fighting, close-quarters stuff, really savage.

Not too surprisingly, Vik was really good at it, close to being as skilled as the instructor. Jinhai watched her with grudging admiration. It wasn't fencing, which was the only martial art he had ever found to be beautiful, maybe because it had so much in common with dance. But there was a fierce loveliness about the way she did it, and he began to enjoy seeing what move would come next.

And if he thought he'd been sore the day before...

So it was a nice break the next day, when they started covering Kaiju – their nature, anatomy, natural weapons, and so on. The things they would have to know to fight them.

Of course, it was Vik who pointed out the obvious that afternoon, at mess. Jinhai was trying to figure out exactly what the stuff on his noodles was when she sat across from him.

She looked at her noodles.

"What a waste of time," she said. She moved the noodles around with her chopsticks. "This is the closest thing to a Kaiju you and I will ever see."

"I hope so," he said.

"Yes?" she said. "Then why the Academy? Did Mommy and Daddy insist?"

"You know," Jinhai said, "if you're trying to be friendly, you're doing it all wrong."

"I'm not trying to be friendly," she said. "I don't like you. I think you're soft, and you've had everything given to you. I don't think you deserve to be here—"

"Listen," Jinhai said. "You don't know me. You don't have a clue about my life."

"—but I think we're compatible."

That stopped him.

"What? You mean like, ah – you don't like me, but you think we should get cozy?"

"Cozy? Idiot. I mean Drift compatible. You didn't feel it when we were fighting? A connection?"

"I felt the connection of your hand with my face," he said.

She shrugged. "Maybe I'm wrong. But we'll see."

The next day, Renata was called from training for an hour, and then later Ilya. By the end of the day, four of the cadets had vanished and returned, and none of them would talk about where they went or what happened.

The next day, it was his turn.

He ended up in a small office with Mako Mori. He was surprised such an important person had such a small accommodation. She hadn't done a lot to pretty the place up, either.

"So, how are your parents?" she asked, when he came in.

"They're, ah, fine, I guess," he said. "I don't really see them that much."

She nodded. She looked at something on a screen he could only see the back of.

And then she began asking questions. They started off simple – where did he go to school, who were his friends when he was little. Tell her about his fencing instructor, what did he remember about first meeting Dustin.

In fact, there were several questions about Dustin, a disproportionate number of them.

There were a lot more questions and by the time the interview was over, he finally realized what this was about.

The sabotage of Chronos Berserker – the death of Braga.

He was a suspect. The other cadets she had called in, they must be suspects too.

Mori dismissed him from the interview, but he hadn't yet reached the door when she asked him to stop.

"One last question," she said. "When you arrived here, you were issued a pen drive. May I see it?"

His heart dug a little deeper into his chest.

"Secretary General, I seem to have misplaced it," he said. "I couldn't find it the first day of instruction."

"I see," she said. "Very well. You may go."

As he left the office, he wondered what she had asked the other cadets. Maybe she had been asking them all about *him*.

# 9

JINHAI WAS ALMOST OUT OF BREATH WHEN HE reached the stairs down to the train. He had never run so fast in his life, and the heavy backpack didn't help. He figured he had just about two minutes, if even that.

He leapt down the first flight of stairs, landing so hard it hurt his knees. Someone shouted after him in indignation, but he ignored them. He continued down, deeper into the earth – and more importantly, into the field of the superconductors that powered the train. Normally that wouldn't shut the transponder under his skin down completely, but the station was known for its poorly insulated power node. His pursuer wouldn't be able to track him as long as he was close to the leaky field.

The train doors were just opening when he arrived. He dashed on, sat long enough to stick the contents of his hand under the seat, then got up as if he was moving to another car. Instead he went to the next door and exited the train.

Then he went to the bathroom and hid in one of the stalls.

Now he would find out how clever he was. He'd made a recording of his transponder's signal and uploaded it into an old phone. On the train, it should now be transmitting a facsimile of his personal code. An expert with the right equipment would be able to tell the difference – or probably even someone sort of competent with so-so gear – but as it was, he might get away with it.

He waited what he thought was long enough and then waited a little longer.

He poked his head out of the bathroom and had a quick look around. The station was almost empty; he didn't see the guy who was chasing him.

A few minutes later the train he wanted arrived, going in pretty much the opposite direction as the first. He found a seat, doffing the backpack and letting it rest on the floor, and took out a water bottle and some power bars and began to recover his strength – where he was going, he would need it. This was just starting.

"Is that a sword in your backpack?"

He turned and saw a man maybe ten years older than him, briefcase in his lap.

"Well, sort of," he said. "It's a fencing épée."

"Like in those movies? Zorro?"

"Kind of like that, yeah."

"It's got one of those little things on the end, so you can practice, right? But if you unscrew it, it's sharp."

He was always surprised by comments like that. How would that work, exactly? If the tip screwed on, that meant the blade was threaded, right? Which meant to stab someone you would have to somehow spin the blade into them. And did anyone think someone would give little kids a sword they could make lethal with a few twists of the wrist?

"No, sir," he replied. "They make them blunt. On the non-electric ones, they do have a little rubber tip, but that's just for extra safety. We're all about safety in fencing. None of our weapons are made sharp."

"Okay," the man said. "Thanks. Sounds like fun."

"Lots of fun," Jinhai confirmed.

And he hadn't lied. Épées *did* come from the factory with blunt points.

But that's where a file came in handy.

He was rested, fed, and ready to run when he got off the train, but there was no one there to greet him. So far, so good – his clever plan apparently hadn't fallen apart on him yet. He remembered the directions he'd been given.

He'd never been to this part of town. It was near the old waterfront, a part of Hong Kong torn up by the Kaiju Otachi and never really rebuilt. Seaside property wasn't what it used to be, at least not on Pacific-facing coasts. People tended to do their new development inland these days; putting money into a mega tower with a bay view didn't seem like such a good investment.

That would change, if enough time passed without another Kaiju attack. People were stupid that way.

But right now, this was a good playground for people who didn't necessarily want their games noticed. Where he was, many of the buildings – parts of them anyway – were still standing, but they were thoroughly abandoned.

A few turned corners and he saw them, waiting for him.

One of them – a girl about his own age – stepped up.

"You showed," she said. "Tan didn't think you had it in you. He said you would bail."

"Tan doesn't know me nearly as well as he thinks he does," Jinhai said.

She regarded him skeptically.

"You can still back out," she said. "With honor. If you put your gear on, you can't."

"Watch me as I put my gear on, then," Jinhai said.

There were maybe fifteen of them, but only the girl was dressed out, so she must be the one he had to fight. It was hard to tell how that was going to be, looking at her. Medium height, broad shoulders, long legs. She just stood there, so he got no sense of how she moved.

He got everything on, finishing with the mask. A shortish guy came over and examined his blade, then wiped it down with a disinfectant towelette.

"It's good," the guy said.

"Okay," the girl said. "Whenever you're ready."

Was he ready? He stared at the girl's blade, at the needle point on it. That could really hurt.

Screw it. He was ready.

He settled into an en guard stance.

"No referee, no quarter," the short guy said. "Understood?"

"Yes, sir," Jinhai said.

"Okay, then. Begin when ready."

Jinhai began bouncing lightly on the balls of his feet, slowly rotating his blade in wide arcs, keeping moving, making it uncertain where the attack would come from.

Twenty seconds into the fight, Jinhai knew he was outmatched. His opponent knew it, too; he could see her mean little grin through her mask. He bounced back, trying to keep away from her until he could figure out what to do; he nearly tripped. This wasn't the smooth aluminum *piste* he was used to fencing on; streets were uneven, here especially, with pits and chunks of concrete to trip him up.

It was only a slight stumble, but it was enough for her. She seemed to fly at him; he tried to parry the point

PACIFIC RIM UPRISING

of her épée, but her blade slipped around his. He only avoided impalement by throwing himself to the side; the unsharpened edge of her blade slid along his arm.

She stepped back and waited for him to recover.

"This isn't sport fencing, Famous," she said. "You should take it back to your *salle*, where it's safe."

"But I feel so safe here," he replied. "Like I've just been tucked into bed."

"Well, come get a night-night kiss," she said.

He decided if he was going to get anywhere, he had to press her, so he went on the attack. She faded, floating on her feet as if her body had no mass. She found his disengage, caught his épée in a bind. He started a receding parry to catch it, but she slipped out of that, and just like that the point of her weapon slid into his shoulder; he felt the impact on his scapula as if she'd hit it with a hammer instead of a few kilograms of sword.

Once his body was sure he had recorded the impact, the pain asserted itself. It went through him almost like electricity, and he dropped down to his knees.

"There we go," she said. "Goodnight, sweet prince."

His eyes were watering, but he forced himself to stand again.

"Just a flesh wound," he said.

It was true, but flesh wounds hurt a hell of a lot more than he had ever imagined they could.

"Stay down, Ou-Yang," one of the bystanders advised.

Whatever thoughts of yielding he might have been entertaining, that was over now. They knew who he was. Now he had more than his own honor to defend.

He got back on guard, trying to focus.

At least she'd hit the shoulder of his off-weapon hand. That arm wasn't much use in fencing to begin with.

She attacked, and he saw an opening on the inside of

her arm and went for it. That was her plan, of course; she beat away his counter-attack and drove her point into his arm with terrible force. He let his blade drop so it pricked into the top of her thigh.

The pain was instantaneous, this time. He dropped his weapon. His opponent let hers fall, too, but that only made matters worse; the needle-sharp tip had gone in one side of the triceps of his upper arm and out the other, and now it was stuck there. He fell to the ground, trying unsuccessfully not to scream.

His only consolation was that he heard his opponent swearing too.

Someone pulled the sword from his arm, which if anything hurt more than it had going in.

"He's going to bleed out," someone said. "I'd say he has five minutes."

"*You've* got five minutes," Jinhai said, but now fear was rising through the pain. Was it true? There was so much blood, a ridiculous amount of blood...

"Shut up," the girl he'd been fighting snapped. "Don't try to scare him. He did okay. He let me hit him so he could scratch my leg. That's cool. Dress him up."

Someone put pressure on the wound, and then started applying a field dressing. He kept his eyes closed; he didn't like the sight of blood.

When he opened them again, he saw the girl sitting cross-legged on the ground. She had removed her mask and fencing pants and was now in shorts, with a bandage on her thigh.

"You know my name," he said. "What's yours?"

"No offense," she said. "But I don't need the heat your parents could bring."

"Okay," he said. "How about if we just get married, then?"

"You'd marry a girl who can beat you?"

"Only kind I would consider," he said.

She looked like she was about to reply. Instead she scrambled to her feet. By the way she and everyone else were reacting, he thought he knew what was going on.

"Dustin," he said. "I was just about to come and find you."

He turned. It was Dustin, all right.

Dustin wasn't a big guy, but he was dangerous-looking. Part of that was his muscular build and sharp blue eyes, but the pistol he held against his chest didn't hurt. It wasn't pointed at anyone, but with a shift of his wrists, it could be.

"This is not cool," the girl said.

"It's okay," Dustin said. His American accent was unmistakable, but his Mandarin was perfectly clear. "He and I are leaving, and he was never here in the first place, right?"

Most of them nodded. The girl looked defiant.

"Yeah," she said. "He was never here. And he'd better not even think about being 'never here' again."

"Agreed," Dustin said. Then to Jinhai, "Come on."

"Ciao, guys," Jinhai said, as he unsteadily stood up. "It was fun."

# 10

MING-HAU LOOKED DOWN AT HIS SLEEPING SON, hoping the sirens didn't wake him. At the moment, with eyes closed and the covers drawn up to his chin, Jinhai looked more like his mother than he ever had – the way his eyes were set in his face, the soft curve of his chin. At other times, he could see himself in the boy. It was incredible how much the child could change from one day to another.

*You can never step in the same river twice*, his own father had been wont to say.

It was true. But one day, there would be no one to step into the river, and for Ming-hau and his wife Suyin, today might be that day. They might never see their son again.

"We told him we would go hiking by the lake tomorrow," he whispered.

"There will be many days to go to the lake," Suyin

replied. "Let Mei take him to the playground. He will be happy enough. When we return, we will make it up to him."

"Yes," he replied, exhaling. *But if we don't return...*

Suyin squeezed his hand. She could read his face so well.

"Life will go on for Jinhai," she said. "There can be no safer place than the Shatterdome. Whatever happens today, our boy will survive. Now come. There is no time to waste."

But as they made their way to the Jaeger bay, Minghau thought of the lake, and the last time they had taken Jinhai there; how happy the boy had been, how content he himself had felt. It had seemed, in a way, that the day would never end, but that he – that all of them – would stay somehow embedded in it forever.

The Kaiju was a category III, code-named Huo Da. It had emerged from the Breach less than an hour before and seemed to be headed for Shanghai, which meant they had to be airlifted from the Hong Kong Shatterdome via V-50 Jumphawks and carried nearly eight hundred miles across China to meet the beast. In the old days, before all but the Hong Kong Shatterdome was closed, Jaegers from the Nagasaki or Tokyo Shatterdomes would have been deployed to intercept a Kaiju on this heading. But those days, at least for now, were done.

Fortunately, Jumphawks were fast, even carrying a Jaeger, but that still meant some down time, even after checking the systems a dozen times.

Shaolin Rogue was a Mark-3 and she had been in operation for seven years, but this was the first time he and Suyin had piloted her into battle. Or piloted any Jaeger into battle, for that matter – and in this, their first fight, they were slated to take point. When the Wei triplets checked into Crimson Typhoon, some problems had been found in the coolant system. Typhoon, with its more experienced crew, would be around an hour behind them.

They watched China go by below them, reminding themselves what they would soon be defending. They tried to name the moonlit rivers, mountains, and towns they flew over from memory. They played word games. And they kept up to date with what was known about their foe, which wasn't much.

"From what we can tell, this one looks lower slung than some of 'em," Tendo Choi, the voice of LOCCENT control informed them. "Stays close to the bottom, basically linear, but we've been surprised like that before. The silhouette resembles a flat, segmented arthropod – sort of like a centipede, or a really long trilobite. It looks to have from six to eight major limbs, all bunched toward the front. Big head. It moves in short, fast spurts, so K-Watch thinks it could be propelling itself with some kind of water jet, like a squid. It has a top speed greater than anything we've seen yet – in the water, at least. It may be more aquatic in nature than some we've seen."

"Like Shaolin Rogue," Suyin said. "We should meet it as far out at sea as possible."

As every Kaiju was different, so was every Jaeger, each with its own strengths and specialized weapons. You never knew what the Kaiju were going to be like, especially now, when they seemed to be adapting to the tactics and technology of their human adversaries. What worked five years ago – or a year ago – might not work now. The engineer in Ming-hau suspected that if this war went on long enough, eventually Jaegers would settle into something like an optimal design; but then again, if the Kaiju evolved to deal with that design and render it obsolete, once again innovation would be important, much as it was in biological evolution.

Shaolin Rogue, more than most Jaegers, had been built to

fight underwater. She had a vastly increased oxygen supply, and in fact could extract oxygen from seawater through electrolysis. She also had back-mounted turbines that could drive her horizontally through the water like a submarine or lift her toward the surface if she was upright but totally submerged. Her Meteor Chain worked almost as well below water as above it, and she had a system of liquid ballast and gas cells that could quickly orient her in the depths. She had proven herself once already fighting a battle almost entirely submerged, against the Kaiju named Tentalus.

But in that battle Rogue had had other pilots.

Finally, they reached land's end, and saw the sun rising from the Yellow Sea, just as they were passing by Shanghai and its enormous port in Hangzhou Bay. He watched the muddy waters of the Qiantang and Yangtze Rivers give way to the clear turquoise of the bays and inlets, the shallow sea, and that in turn darkened to a cobalt blue as they moved farther and farther from land, until the coastline and its millions of inhabitants were only a distant, thin line on the horizon.

"Okay," Tendo said. "We're about ready to set you down. The depth here is about two hundred feet, but it gets twice that if we go much further. Huo Da's path hasn't deviated. It'll be under you in fifteen minutes. We're going to go ahead and initiate pilot-to-pilot protocol, if that's okay with you guys."

"We're ready," Suyin said.

The first time he and Suyin had drifted, they had already been in love, were already married, already had a son.

But it had still changed everything. Suyin called it their "second wedding". Some experienced the meeting of minds almost violently, he had heard, as one or both personalities either pushed back against the other or latched on to bad memories. But with Suyin, it was always gentle – like a voice in another room coming toward you, like waking to her beside him in the morning. And once the neural handshake was engaged, it was difficult to tell his thoughts from hers. But that also didn't matter, or bother him in the least. It was how he wished it was all the time. He was better in every way when they shared their minds. He felt his fear and trepidation flow away. They were Shaolin Rogue, and they would win this battle.

Once they were ready, the Jumphawks lowered them toward the water. They watched flying fish skip away from them, gliding from swell to swell. Farther away, they saw the smooth gray backs of dolphins.

It was good to see, but at the same time, Ming-hau's heart sank. Shallow water marine life had suffered terribly from Kaiju incursions and the toxic blood spills resulting when Jaegers killed them. The Yellow Sea had endured damage from human-caused pollution for years, but had so far been spared the far greater insult of a dead Kaiju.

That was about to change, and he and Suyin would be to blame, in a way. But there was no help for it, unless they could kill the beast without somehow bleeding it out.

He put it out of their minds. They would kill it however they could. Shanghai was counting on them.

When their feet hit the bottom, only their head and the upper reaches of their shoulders remained above the waves.

"Sonar enhancement on," Suyin said. "There it is."

Huo Da was coming, and they were almost directly in its path. In fact, it seemed to be veering a bit toward them, and speeding up.

They dropped into a crouch, submerging the Conn-Pod. Instantly they were in a different world, a wonderland forest of olive-green kelp teeming with flickering silver life. It was beautiful, but also cut their optical visibility to nearly zero. Hopefully that worked both ways, and they could surprise the Kaiju. They could still see it approaching as an image compiled from sonar and LOCCENT telemetry.

Ming-hau heard something, a long, rising note, then a deep, falling one.

"Whale song," Suyin murmured, awestruck. "I never thought I would hear—"

Suddenly the Kaiju blip on the sonar became a full silhouette, complete with scale.

"It's big," Suyin said. "I hadn't imagined—"

"We're bigger," Ming-hau reminded her.

And then, after all the waiting, the kelp forest parted before them, and a thing from nightmares appeared. And it was – as Suyin observed – *big*. Even travelling horizontally, like a worm, it was more than half their height, and what they saw at first were its four huge, hemispherical eyes and a cluster of colossal, armored, multi-jointed forelegs, maybe eight of them, maybe more. Two of the limbs were so long that he thought at first they were horns or very thick antennae, but then he saw they were flexible, already reaching around them like tentacles, probably to pull them toward the smaller, scythe-like legs below its eyes.

Shaolin Rogue pivoted, deflecting one of the reaching arms, so that Huo Da just missed them, then pounded one great fist into the top of the Kaiju's skull. Now they could see, in the aquamarine light, the rest of its body – as Tendo predicted, Huo Da was long, lozenge-shaped, covered in overlapping plates of scale or chitin. They could also now see – to their dismay – its tail, which was whipping toward them through the kelp fronds, much like the tail of a scorpion.

They weren't fast enough to avoid it; a spike forty feet long speared into their midsection and sent tremors all through the Jaeger. It didn't cut through their armor completely, but it did stick there, holding them in place while Huo Da's body flexed around, reaching again with its long, tentacle-like arms.

Rogue grabbed the tail with both hands and ripped it out of their midsection, then turned to face the monster head on.

# 11

MAKO SAVED VIKTORIYA MALIKOVA FOR LAST. THE young woman answered her first few questions matter-of-factly, but became more guarded when the subject turned to her childhood.

"I didn't know my parents," she said, when asked about them. "I was raised by my grandmother and grandfather."

The longest pause came when she was asked what inspired her to try out for the Academy.

"Cherno Alpha," she finally said. "Sasha and Aleksis Kaidanovsky."

"I see," Mako said.

"You... knew them, didn't you, Secretary General."

"I did indeed," she said. "I have never known braver, more capable pilots."

"Yes," Malikova said. "They were my heroes."

When the interview was over, Mako had an uneasy feeling about the girl. Like the psych evaluation, her interview suggested that Malikova had deep – very deep – wounds. And she was hiding something, something big.

In many ways, Viktoriya Malikova reminded Mako of herself.

That might not be good.


As she expected, Mako found Dr. Gottlieb in his lab, busily scrawling on his chalkboards. Some people found it odd that he used such antiquated equipment: even if you felt the need to write things out long hand, there were plenty of touch-screen or holographic displays that would allow for that. Mako thought she understood, though. One thing you learned in the Drift was how much everything was mediated by memory, by personal history. She suspected that if she drifted with Gottlieb there would be a solid foundation of memory connecting his thought process to the tactile sensation of the chalk in his hand, the squeak of it on the board, the smell of the dust – it was the thread on which the beads of his mathematical thinking were connected from childhood until the present day.

Or perhaps he was just peculiar.

He hadn't noticed her yet.

"Dr. Gottlieb."

He continued scrawling as if he hadn't heard her, but then, belatedly, her voice seemed to register. He looked up, surprised.

"Secretary General," he said. He looked a little flustered. "We – don't we have a meeting at eleven hundred?"

"We did," Mako said. "That was half an hour ago."

"Oh dear," he said, casting about. "I'm dreadfully sorry. I fear time quite got away from me."

She regarded the equations on the board.

"Does this have anything to do with Chronos Berserker?"

"No," he said. "This is, well – I'm very concerned. I was going to bring it up at our meeting."

"Very well," she said. "Tell me about it now."

"A colleague of mine brought me a set of data derived from deep scans of the ocean floor," he said. "It's quite puzzling, but there is a definite pattern – and a very worrying one."

"Go on."

"Well, without going into detail, what I see is a pattern similar to what little we know about the months leading up to the opening of the Breach."

"You believe the Breach is going to reopen? But K-Watch monitors it quite closely."

"Yes, the location of the former Breach in the Marianas Trench is under watch, of course. But the fact is that the conditions that formed the Breach could occur at any number of locations around what we know as the 'Ring of Fire'." He waved at a map on the wall, where a red line began east of Australia, bent toward China through the Philippines, up the eastern coast of Asia, around the top of the Pacific from Siberia to Alaska and then down the coastline of the Americas.

"More like a horseshoe than a ring, isn't it?" he mused. "But here's the point. This line represents most of the volcanic and seismic activity on the planet. There is an enormous amount of energy concentrated in these areas, and especially in the deeper parts. The Marianas Trench is the deepest, but I believe it's possible for a breach to open in other locations. The Kuril Trench, for instance, or the Java, or the Aleutian. I mean, if you were the Precursors, would you open a breach in the same spot as the one we collapsed?"

"I suppose not," she said. "Is this real? Do you think this is imminent?"

He took a moment; his eyes became slightly unfocused, and then he closed them before opening them again and going on.

"You have to understand," he said. "I – I was connected to them. When Dr. Geiszler and I drifted with that Kaiju brain. The Precursors – they are implacable in a way no human being could ever be. Their desire for our universe is more... more like an elemental force than a... a motivation. They cannot be dissuaded; they will not be deterred. We frustrated them once, briefly, but what I saw – what I *felt* – is that they believe the time is *now*. Not in another ten million years, not in another million, but *now*. They *will* be back, and when they do return, I fear the rules might be entirely different. Everything we've done might not be enough."

He stopped; he seemed to be trying to get hold of himself.

"But it's not just my – ah, *feelings*," he said. "Based on this data, yes, I think it is a strong possibility that we could face another breach in the next two to four months. But I need more information to be certain."

"Of what sort?"

"If we convince K-Watch to allocate some resources to a few key spots, I should be able to test the validity of this theory," he said.

"That shouldn't be a problem," Mako said. "Not considering what's at stake if you're right. We certainly don't want to be caught flat-footed again."

"Thank you," said Gottlieb. "I hope that I'm wrong, of course. I would rather be wrong. It's just that I'm so rarely incorrect..."

"I'll talk to Command this afternoon. In the meantime, is there anything you can tell me about the sabotage of Chronos Berserker?"

"Not much," he said. "It really isn't my field; I've just been collating the information from Tech and Forensics. But I did scan the pen drive that contained the program with some equipment they don't have. And there is one thing. It's very, very faint, but I found the slightest trace of Kaiju blood on it. Almost undetectable, but it suggests that whoever had this got it from someone proximate to supplies of the stuff."

"The black market," she said.

"Or the Akumagami Front," Gottlieb said. "They use Kaiju blood in some of their rituals. I know it doesn't really tell us anything we didn't already suspect, but it does help confirm those suspicions."

She nodded. "Thank you, Doctor," she said. "I'll let you know what K-Watch says as soon as I hear from them."

She went back to her office and made her call to Command. It took a little wrangling; although it was implicit in everything the PPDC did that one day the Kaiju would be back, nobody really wanted to think about it, and far too many in the upper ranks of Command had become altogether too comfortable with things as they were.

But she had pull, and Gottlieb had credibility, so she got what she wanted. Maybe not as much of it as Gottlieb would prefer, but it was better than nothing.

After that was off her plate, she turned her attention back to the problem of sabotage. She contacted Lambert. He wasn't all that happy with what she had to say, but after she made her argument, he agreed.

Two to four months. If Gottlieb was right, perhaps they needed to accelerate the training program.


Jinhai woke from troubled dreams and reluctantly rolled out of his bunk. He saw Renata and Suresh were already up. Ilya was stirring.

Vik wasn't there at all. Which was suspicious.

In fact, the barracks had become a very uncomfortable place. No one seemed to want to talk to anyone.

"Where's Vik?" he asked.

"She went for a run," Renata said. "I'm about to join her. I think we could all use a run."

Ah. They wanted to talk. Away from possible eavesdroppers.

"I'm in," Jinhai said. "Just give me a few."

The sun was just a promise in the east, and off in the distance he heard the weird bubbling wail of a nightjar, while early-rising fish-eagles cut profiles against the gray sky.

Vik was still warming up, waiting for them, so they all started jogging together, across the multi-acre deployment zone and airfield the Jaeger bays opened on to.

"We have to talk about this," Renata said, a few minutes in.

"What's to talk about?" Suresh said. "They think one of us carried out the sabotage. I think maybe they're right."

"I don't believe it," Meilin said. "I know I didn't do it, and I don't believe any of you did, either."

"It must be an awfully pretty world you live in," Vik said.

This time the Chinese girl didn't shy away from Vik. "Why would one of us do something like that?" she demanded.

"No one is what they seem," Vik said. "Everyone has secrets. Anyone is capable of almost anything, under the right circumstances."

"Sounds like you know all about that," Jinhai said.

"I didn't do it, if that's what you're getting at," Vik said. "But you're right to be suspicious of me. Just like I'm suspicious of you. Must be hard, being the son of heroes, right? So much to live up to. Maybe you decided to make a name for yourself in your own way. Really show them you're your own man."

"Come on, Vik," Tahima said. "Lay off Jinhai."

"No," Jinhai said. "She's right. It could be me. It could be any of us."

"Maybe," Renata said. "Maybe one of us is the bad guy, or maybe somebody found it convenient to frame us. We don't even know why they think one of us is responsible. For all we know, they're questioning everyone in the Shatterdome."

"We were all in the Conn-Pod, two at a time," Meilin pointed out. "We each had the opportunity. Did anyone see the other do anything?"

"Ryoichi held up his arms and said, 'I'm a Jaeger,' in a fake German accent," Suresh said. "I might or might not have farted."

"You did," Ryoichi said.

"This isn't a joking matter," Tahima said. "A guy died."

"What could any of us have done in the Conn-Pod anyway?" Renata asked. "Whatever. I'm with Meilin. I don't know any of you that well, but I don't think any of us worked our asses off just to get here and put a bug in a training Jaeger. If I was here to do sabotage, I would wait until I could do it really big, wouldn't I?"

"You would think," Vik said. "That would make much more sense."

"Guys," Ryoichi said. Everyone turned their heads in surprise. The Japanese cadet was usually quiet.

"It could be one of us," he said, "and we wouldn't even know it. My dad works for Interpol. He said some guys in the underworld figured out how to use Pons technology to, like, make people zombies – no, not zombies, not the right word. Put commands in them they don't know about, and then they forget them."

"Are you serious?" Renata asked.

"Dad doesn't joke about things like that," Ryoichi said. "Or anything, really. But if any of you has any funny thoughts, gaps in your memory when you don't know what happened..." he trailed off.

"...you might be a zombie," Suresh finished.

"More with the jokes," Tahima grumbled.

"You mean like, every night when I'm asleep?" Jinhai scoffed. "Come on."

But as they continued to run, he began to feel the doubt creep in.

*No, shake that off, Jinhai.* It probably wasn't true anyway. Just because Ryoichi said it didn't make it real.

"Anyway," Renata said, breaking the uncomfortable silence. "All we can do is keep our eyes and ears open. But we can't let this tear us apart. You heard Secretary General Mori – to do that we have to work together."

# 12

2024 WAS A BAD YEAR. THE KAIJU HAD BEEN coming since way before Viktoriya was born – since 2013 – but at first they came maybe one, two, three a year. There were three the year she was born, she'd been told. But Vodyanoi was the second Kaiju of 2024, and they just kept coming – Insurrector in Los Angeles, Bonesquid in Papua New Guinea (she liked saying "Papua" – it was a funny name for a place), Biantal in Taipei – by the middle of December, thirteen Kaiju had emerged from the deep water of the Marianas Trench. All had been killed, but six Jaegers were also destroyed.

Thankfully, Cherno Alpha was not among the dead. But there weren't many Jaegers left. Instead, everyone was talking about the Wall.

Like the old men at the bar, most people on Sakhalin didn't think much of the Wall. Japan had been building walls for years, and now they were putting them up in

America and Australia and other places. But no one was going to build one for a little Russian island in the Sea of Okhotsk. If one got built at all, it was most likely going to be along the coast of mainland Russia, which would leave them outside with the Kaiju.

So her grandfather grumbled, anyway, until – five days after the Kaiju called Vermin was slaughtered by Vulcan Specter in Colombia – he died in a logging accident. Her grandmother wouldn't tell her the details, but Viktoriya had been to a few funerals, and usually the dead were laid out at home, so people could come and say goodbye. But that didn't happen with her grandfather. She simply never saw him again. Babulya wouldn't say why, but Vik heard one of the neighbors say Grandfather was too messed-up to lay him out.

She cried for a while, but then she reminded herself that she was a Jaeger, that she had armor, and whatever she felt inside, it was the armor people would see, and they would think she was strong even if she wasn't.

But it was a bad year, and it only got worse. With Grandfather gone, her grandmother could no longer keep up the rent on their little house, and no more than a week after her Dedulya was in the ground, she and Grandmother were on the train to the capital, Yuzhno-Sakhalinsk, where a cousin had promised Babulya work. Viktoriya was excited at first, because YS was a big city, the biggest on the island, and the maps told her it was close to the sea. It was also where the corpse of Vodyanoi lay, right at the edge of town. Her enthusiasm dimmed a little when she realized they were still many kilometers from the water, but there was still a lot to see, and in theory a lot to do, if one had money, and quite a lot of people in the city seemed to have money. There were two Christmases, which seemed fun: one in December – celebrated by expatriates from lots of places and many old Korean families – and the unusual one in January.

They moved into a tiny apartment in a gray five-story building crammed with tiny homes. At first it seemed very interesting and modern to Vik, with its small electric kitchen and beds that folded out, but soon it just seemed little, dingy, and boring.

A lot of the people in their building hailed originally from the country, she found, which made things a little more familiar. Her grandfather had once told her Sakhalin had three things of worth – trees, oil, and cheap labor. But now there were a lot of jobs in or near the city as factories grew. At first, most had manufactured Jaeger parts, but now they mostly produced things that went into the Wall. Grandmother's job was in a chemical plant where they made some sort of stuff used to render concrete super-hard. Grandmother cleaned the bathrooms for the workers and washed the coveralls they stripped out of at the end of the day. She got home late, and didn't have much energy left for housekeeping. School hadn't started yet, so she left Vik with a little money every day along with instructions on what to buy with it and how to make dinner.

The market was only a few blocks away, an easy walk. One afternoon a few days before regular Christmas she made her way there, carrying less money than usual, with directions to buy a cabbage, a can of tomatoes, a little rice, beef powder – and if she had enough, some sour cream.

It was during the day, and the streets weren't too busy. About a block from the store she noticed a guy watching her. She had seen him before. She didn't like the way he looked at her, but she didn't know why, exactly. He had gray stubble, but his hair was black. He wore boots with his pants tucked in, and a fancy shirt with diamond-shaped designs in brown, red, and dark yellow.

"How's your grandmother?" he asked, as she got close. She wanted to keep going, but he asked again.

"Your grandmother? Ilyana?"

He knew Grandmother's name, so he was probably okay.

"She's fine," she said. "She's at work."

"I see you're going to market," he said. "I hope you have enough for some meat."

"I don't think I do," she said. "Anyway, Grandmother told me not to buy any. Too expensive."

"Yeah," he said. "But it would be nice, wouldn't it? If you had a little more money?"

"What do you mean?"

He held out his hand. In it were forty rubles. She stared at it. It was more money than she had ever had in her hand.

"Take it," he said. "Buy something good for your supper. And if you ever want to know where it came from, come back and see me, okay? Ask around for me. My name is Andrei."

That afternoon, when her grandmother bit into the *golubtsy*, her eyebrows went up.

"There's meat in there," she said.

"It was cheap," Vik answered. "They were going to throw it away. It's just a little."

Grandmother's eyes narrowed. "Did you steal it?"

"No, of course not," she said.

She felt guilty for lying. She hadn't stolen it, but it hadn't been cheap, and yet she still had a whole ten rubles in her pocket. She didn't think she should tell Grandmother about Andrei, even if he did know her name.

"It's good," Grandmother said. She looked pleased, and Vik's misgivings evaporated. She hadn't hurt anyone, and she had made Babulya happy.

She didn't see Andrei the next day, but there was a crowd of people gathered in front of the market, which had a video screen in one of its windows. She tried to push through to the front to see what they were watching, and soon found it was video from K-Eye. Another Kaiju, the fourteenth of the year. Its name was Mutavore, and it had plowed through the coastal wall around Sydney, Australia in less than an hour. She watched, entranced, as the monster was finally put down by one of the few remaining Jaegers, Striker Eureka. The crowd cheered.

"I knew the *grobanyy* wall was pointless," she heard one man opine. "I say they build more Jaegers. That's how we kill those things."

"It doesn't matter what we do," someone else said. "There were fourteen of those things this year. Next year it might be twenty. Or sixty. We're doomed, pure and simple. There's no way around it. Walls, Jaegers – nothing is gonna stop them."

"Cherno Alpha will stop them!" somebody yelled. It took her a second to realize it had been her.

"That's the spirit!" a woman told her. "Don't listen to this nonsense about doom. As long as Cherno Alpha is out there, we'll be safe here."

"Yeah?" a man said. "Tell that to Tomari."

Vik felt a weird chill when she heard the word. It was a word her grandmother had forbidden her and her grandfather to speak. She knew what it was, of course. It was a town, a place that no longer existed. It had been destroyed by a Kaiju named Raythe, before Cherno Alpha caught up with it.

But it seemed unfair to blame Cherno Alpha for the loss of one town, not when so many had been saved.

She saw Andrei again the next day, pretty much in the same place he'd been before. She didn't think he had noticed her, so she ducked behind a building, wondering if she should go a different, longer way.

But she decided that would be cowardly. She was a

Jaeger, after all. She didn't feel things like fear.

To her surprise, he didn't say anything to her when she went by – he just nodded his head at her and smiled.

She went into the store, just behind a woman with two children – an older boy, and a girl about her age. They were all dressed well. The girl, she noticed, had very nice shoes – not drab little flats with plastic soles, but shiny red shoes with little heels. She tried to ignore the kids, but they were loud, and kept asking their mother for things. If Vik had ever acted like that with Grandmother, she would have regretted it, but to her surprise, the mother actually bought both of them pastries at the bakery counter.

She found what she was looking for: a potato, two carrots and two turnips.

But she had to pass the pastry counter on the way to check out. She had stopped there before, on her first day in the store. She had stared at the beautiful treats, salivated, and written the whole business off as pointless because they were so expensive.

But with the extra rubles in her pocket, everything suddenly looked different. With what she had she could get three pastillas – or four mochis, a cupcake, or a piece of almond and pistachio paklava.

The lady behind the counter asked her if she wanted anything and somehow, moments later, she walked out the shop with the paklava wrapped in brown paper.

It was so good she almost cried.

She was still licking her sticky fingers when she saw Andrei again. Once again he smiled and nodded.

But this time, she stopped.

"So how do I get it?" she asked. "The money?"

He smiled. "I knew you were a smart girl," he said. "Go on home, now, and make dinner for your grandmother. You aren't in school, are you?"

"It's out for the winter," she said. "And Grandmother hasn't registered me yet. They said I might have to wait months for a spot."

"Good. So come back in the morning, after your grandmother goes to work, okay? Meet me right here, and we'll see."

She waited a moment, hoping he might give her more money, but he laughed and shook his head.

"No," he said. "From now on, you earn it."

That night, she dreamed that her grandmother caught her under the covers, eating paklava. She tried to hide it, but Babulya shook her finger at her.

"Tomari!" she said, accusingly. "Tomari!"

A shadow fell on them, and she heard people screaming. In the darkness, she thought she saw a woman's face, but she didn't know who it was.

She woke up, gasping, but it didn't take long to calm down. And the next morning she went to meet Andrei.

He led her down the street to where an old van was parked. It was so beaten up and worn-out-looking she wondered if it even ran. He banged on the door, and after a minute, a girl stuck her head out. She was older, maybe eleven or twelve. Her black hair was something of a mess. She looked sleepy. Some movement and chattering in the van told Vik there were at least three or four others in there.

"Yeah?" the girl said.

"This is – what's your name?"

"Vik," she said. She thought it was funny he knew Grandmother's name but not hers.

"Vik?" he grunted. "Okay, Vik. This is Eun. Eun, take Vik to the dig."

"Yeah. Got it, boss," Eun said. "You wait there," she told Vik.

Eun emerged a few moments later, wrapped in a

tattered coat. She led her through the streets of the town, to the east, where Vik never ventured, to where the houses grew fewer, and the trees were stunted or did not grow at all. Her sense of dread grew stronger with each step, and she became increasingly certain where they were going.

She was starting to wonder if it was over the hill ahead, but then she realized it *was* the hill.

She stopped then. Eun went a few more steps before she realized she was no longer following.

"What's the matter?" she asked. "You know it's dead, right?"

"It's a Kaiju," Vik said. "Why are we going to the Kaiju?"

Eun rolled her eyes. "You know what's in a Kaiju?" she said. "You know what they're made of?"

"What?" Vik asked.

"Money," Eun said. "Rubles. Everything we pull out of there, someone will pay for it. It's like going into a mine, but the whole thing is made of diamonds. And you, you're little. You can crawl up into the bones and guts, places where the grown-ups can't."

"I'm not crawling around inside of a Kaiju," Vik said.

"It's not that bad, you'll see. We wear special clothes, so we don't get sick. Andrei and the overseers, they take care of us."

"I'm not going inside a dead Kaiju," Vik insisted.

"Fine," Eun said. "I don't care one way or the other. But you can walk back by yourself. I've got a quota to make, and you're wasting my day."

# 1 3

ONCE AGAIN, RAYTHE PROVED FRUSTRATING, breaking the usual Kaiju pattern – instead of attacking the populous cities of Hokkaido, it again deviated northward, to the sparsely settled island of Sakhalin. Once home mostly to the aboriginal Ainu and Nivkh people, in the twentieth century it had gone back and forth between Russia and Japan until after the Second World War, when it became and remained Soviet territory until the collapse of the USSR; then it became simply Russian. Raythe missed or ignored the capital city on the far southern tip of the island and rampaged across a thinly populated area, obliterating a small town before the Jumphawks even managed to get Cherno in the air again.

Raythe took back to the water and churned up the Strait of Tartary, the narrow gap between Sakhalin and the mainland, breaking the sea ice that had formed in the narrowest spots, but doing little or no harm to the villages and towns along the coast. Once again, it was heading almost single-mindedly north.

"It's looking for something," Aleksis said. "What is it looking for? Like I said before, there's nothing up here."

A moment later, an update from LOCCENT control came in.

"Subject has just entered the Sea of Okhotsk, and is now bearing to the northeast."

"Toward Kamchatka?" Aleksis said. "That's where we were. What is it with this runaround?"

"Maybe it's blind," Sasha said. "Or it's following some other sense than sight. Maybe it smells something. The way it's going, it reminds me of a hunting dog my cousin had."

"Listen," Scriabin said. "We think it's heading for the Okhotsk oil fields."

Sakhalin didn't have a lot, as far as modern industrialized economies were concerned. At one time it had been an important center for the whaling industry, but by and large most inhabitants of the island had gotten by fishing and cutting timber. Geologists knew about the offshore oil pretty early on, but it wasn't until the first decades of the twenty-first century that they'd had the technology to drill in the deep, freezing waters. Now there were seven large platforms around the north end of Sakhalin. Aleksis had even been to one of them a year ago, as part of a PPDC publicity campaign.

"Give us a map," Sasha said.

They already had one, of course, on their display, but now the deep-sea rigs appeared, and their support structures on the coast.

"That must be it," Sasha said. "But why oil?"

A line traced itself, an arc between the western part of the sea and the oil platforms.

"That's your Miracle Mile, Cherno," a new voice – not

Scriabin – told them. Sasha recognized it as belonging to Marshal Pentecost, just recently promoted to his new post at the Hong Kong Shatterdome. She trusted Pentecost; unlike their last presiding Marshal, he had actually fought in a Jaeger, and acquitted himself well.

She – they – did not want to disappoint him.

"Affirmative, Marshal," she said. "We will hold the Mile."

*This time we will hold it.*

The Miracle Mile was the line in the sand, the border that Kaiju could not be allowed to cross. It varied, depending on when the monsters were sighted, where they seemed to be going, and the depth of the ocean. Usually, it meant not allowing them to make landfall. This time it was more complicated.

So far, more often than not, the Kaiju had crossed that line.

Not today.

The Jumphawks dropped Cherno Alpha well west off the Miracle Mile, not too far from where the oil slick began, and there they waited.

It began to sleet, and visibility dropped to nothing, if all you were using were human senses. Fortunately, Cherno Alpha had more than that; it had eyes in the sky, radar, sonar, and some relatively new technologies that could sense the strange, otherworldly energy emitted by the Kaiju themselves. Cherno adjusted its position as the readings grew nearer.

To Sasha's finely tuned sense of him, Aleksis was becoming steadily more excited. He was a big man, a strong one, and accustomed to the fear his appearance generated in weaker persons. He drew emotional power from that fear, and although he did not say it, he was confident – determined – that Raythe would fear him. Fear Cherno Alpha.

After all the waiting, it happened very quickly. The sea level suddenly rose before them, water mounding up like a rapidly rising wave, but then the water couldn't keep up, and began sheeting off – and Raythe emerged. He had been swimming along the bottom, as some of them did. But now he was lifted up on his hind legs, to his full height, which was right about head level with Cherno.

What it really looked like, they still didn't know. All Kaiju were different, though they tended to have parts that resembled creatures natural to the Earth. All Cherno could make out in the dark and the sleet was something huge and vaguely humanoid in shape.

But she did see its eyes. Blue, like lightning burning through ice.

Unreasonably long arms swiped at them from the darkness, but Cherno stepped into the blow, blocking the attack with its massive right arm. Then they punched with the left.

Without feedback from tactile senses, it would be difficult if not impossible for a man to walk successfully, much less brawl. Pilots needed feedback that would allow their minds to comprehend what was happening to their "body" – so they felt Raythe's arm crash against the side of Cherno's massive cylindrical head. It might have been a random choice for the monster, but analysis of earlier Kaiju battles suggested that they – like most earthly animals – had a sense that the head was a sensitive area, a vulnerable spot.

Not so in the case of Cherno: her "head" was the most massively armored part of the Jaeger, and also a tremendous power core, half again the capacity of any other Jaeger on the planet. And unlike other Jaegers, there was no room in the head for pilots. Sasha and Aleksis steered from the middle, with their Conn-Pod housed in Cherno's chest.

They felt their return blow land, and it was like punching a basalt cliff padded with six meters of rubber; Raythe made a sound that was almost too low to hear, a bone-shuddering roar that hummed through Cherno and their bones. Two sets of claws grasped Cherno Alpha around the head, and again they charged forward, throwing another punch.

That was a mistake. The Kaiju's rear legs suddenly exploded from the water and hit them right in their line of sight; if Cherno had had a solar plexus, all of the wind would have been knocked out of her.

As it was, Aleksis cried out at the pain of feedback, and the sound of tons of metal flexing under the force of the blow was terrible to hear. The lights flickered, briefly; Raythe now had both feet against their chest and his claws wrapped around their power source.

"It's trying to pull our head off," Sasha said.

Aleksis didn't say anything, but she felt what he wanted to do.

They grabbed Raythe's head, and as they pulled it into the beams of their floods, she finally got a look at it. Its wide-set eyes were sunken in an immense, tri-lobed skull armored in overlapping plates and spikes that extended into a beak something like that of a snapping turtle, and its surprisingly long neck squirmed with fleshy tendrils. Almost instantly the head snapped back, out of their grasp, its neck sinking back into its body so the head lay between its heavily plated and spiked shoulders.

Without pause, Cherno pushed both arms up and spread them out, breaking the monster's grip on her head and then, grabbing one of Raythe's lanky, sinewy arms and a leg, twisted it over and slammed it into the sea.

Cherno stepped back, floods stabbing about. The beast was nowhere in sight.

Instinct – largely Aleksis's instinct – had them turning just as the Kaiju came at their back. Claws raked their head, but Cherno stepped in with the counter-punch, and this time Raythe fell back, its nearly subsonic roar shaking their bones. Cherno had no intention of letting it get back up; she lifted one massive leg and stomped down on the supine, half-submerged Raythe with a satisfying thud.

"Foot spikes," Aleksis snapped.

The Jaeger tremored as the earth-piercing spikes in each foot explosively fired; they had been designed to anchor Cherno Alpha in one place, to make an immovable object of the great machine.

It half-worked. The foot in the sea bottom was suddenly tightly anchored; but the spike intended to punch through Raythe's gut and pin it to the seabed failed to pierce the monster's hide. Still, for the moment, Raythe couldn't go anywhere, so Cherno bent and began to deliver crushing double-fisted blows to its exposed torso and shoulders. But the Kaiju's head was still withdrawn between its shoulders, and it was hard to get a solid punch there, and the monster's arms kept battering up at them, trying to get purchase once more, as all the while it squirmed like a snake – almost all of its joints seemed to bend more than one way.

Then it struck at them, very much like a snake, the neck rocketing the Kaiju's head toward them. The neck was even longer than when they had first seen it; the beaked head hit them like the point of a spear, just between their chest and head. An alarm shrieked.

"Hull breach," Sasha reported.

Cherno lunged for the neck, but the Kaiju pulled in as fast as it came out, and as they leaned forward, Raythe managed to get its legs up again and *kicked*.

Cherno hurled up and back, but because one foot

was firmly anchored to the sea floor, they also spun, off balance, and came down on one knee.

Before they could do anything, Raythe was on their back, all of its limbs wrapped around them, quite literally trying to tear them in half. Servos whined, and half the systems indicators started warning that they were fast moving into a red zone.

"No," Aleksis roared. "No!"

He was almost overbalanced, Sasha knew. If he lost it, *they* lost it, they ran the risk of Cherno becoming a mindless berserker. She tried to calm him, but there was only so much she could do, especially as she was starting to feel something akin to panic herself. It was on their back!

They released the deep-earth spike, reached back, grabbed Raythe by one arm, torqued their gargantuan hips, and sent the Kaiju flying.

"I thought you didn't like judo," Sasha said.

"Not judo," he said. "Wrestling."

"Whatever works."

They shifted, watching their feed: Raythe was once again out of sight.

"Guys," Scriabin said. It was startling – Sasha had almost forgotten that anyone was listening. It felt like they were very alone, and any possible help very far away.

"What?"

"It's gone around you. Toward the oil platforms."

# 14

AS IT TURNED OUT, IT WOULD BE NEITHER KWOON nor Kaiju education. After their run, they got quick showers and suited up.

This morning it was Burke instead of Lambert.

"Good morning, fresh meat," he said. "You'll be happy to know we've got something new for you today. We're going to start Pons training."

Suresh raised his hand, Vik rolled her eyes, and Renata stifled a giggle.

"Yes, Khurana?"

"Ranger, I thought we weren't to start Pons training until the second trimester."

"That's the usual progression, cadet," Burke said. "But K-Science has developed a theory that early acclimation to Pons technology can make your later training go more smoothly. Guess who gets to be the lab rats in their little experiment?"

He looked around and chuckled. "The looks on your

faces. Listen, if you're worried about washing out in the first trimester, don't be – that still won't happen until the second trimester, however well or poorly you do. It's true that Drift compatibility can't be taught – you have it or you don't – but some cadets freeze up or freak out even if they are compatible. We're hoping this early exposure will prevent that. If it works out, we might initiate Pons training in the first trimester as standard practice."

The first three hours were all talk. A science instructor named Singh went over the technical aspects of Pons – how it was developed, how it worked. What Jinhai found interesting about that was that at a certain level, they didn't know exactly *why* it worked, or why some people could do it and some couldn't. Only that it *did* work.

Then Burke gave them a run-down of what to expect.

"You can't imagine what it's like to be in someone else's head until it actually happens," he told them. "To suddenly have memories that feel like your own, but aren't. It's not always pleasant. In fact, it usually isn't pleasant. The nastiest memories often come up first, the darkest secrets, the things you never imagined could be in another person. And they're seeing that same stuff about you. It can be hard. But it can also be amazing."

Jinhai got it then. They weren't doing Pons training in the first trimester because anyone thought it would make things go more smoothly later. They were doing it so the PPDC could see inside of their heads, maybe find out which one of them had a big, awful secret.

He remembered what Ryoichi had said about implanted commands and memories.

He looked at the other cadets, wondering how many of them had caught on. Did anyone else look worried?

All of them did, of course, and he was sure he did as well. That was normal.

They left the classroom and went down the corridor until they reached a door labeled DRIFT TRAINING – CADET LEVEL 1.

On their first day tour, they had seen the Mock-Pods, the battle simulators where cadets practiced fighting Kaiju. But this room they hadn't seen before. It was divided into several cylindrical booths, each with a set a pair of headgear connected by wires and cables depending from the ceiling.

They passed through this room to a second room with a big table in it.

"This is the waiting room," Burke said. "This whole process can be embarrassing enough without everyone watching, so we'll go two at a time. I'll be in there, and a technician, and that's it. The J-Techs have paired you up by how compatible you seem to be in the Kwoon based on Ranger Lambert's observations, so let's see." He looked at his chart.

"Ou-Yang and Malikova," he said. "You're the lucky winners of device number one."

Of course.

When they reached the booth, the tech Burke had been expecting wasn't around, so he told them to wait while he hunted him up.

"Left or right?" Jinhai asked.

"Right is dominant," Vik said. Then she smirked. "I told you, didn't I?"

"What, that we're compatible? I still doubt it. I know what compatible looks like, and we're not it."

"You mean your parents," she said.

Again, she surprised him. How had she gotten to that so quickly? It wasn't that Vik didn't have empathy, he realized; she was pretty quick to figure out what the other person was feeling. She just didn't have any *sympathy* in her.

He nodded, reluctantly. "Yes. They are so, so compatible there doesn't seem like that much room left for me."

He was shocked, even as he said it. He wasn't sure he had ever admitted it to anyone exactly like that. Why Vik, of all people?

He braced for the retort.

Instead, he thought she looked almost sympathetic, shooting down the very theory that had just formulated.

"I, ah – well, we're about to be reading each other's minds, right."

"True," Vik said. "You know, my parents…"

"What?"

She shook her head. "Nothing. Never mind. You're just lucky you know your parents. I would like to have known mine."

It floored him for a moment.

"Vik," he said. "I'm sorry. I didn't know."

"Well, you would have found out in a few minutes anyway," she said.

"What happened to them?"

She shrugged. "Kaiju."

"Oh. I am lucky, I guess. I remember when my folks were fighting. I was just a kid, but I was so scared they wouldn't come back to me. Then they did, but it wasn't the same. It was…"

"They came back," Vik snapped. "You should be grateful. You have no idea."

She was mad at him again, right when it seemed like they might actually be able to get through a normal conversation.

That's how things stood when Burke returned, a female tech in tow.

"Honestly, I don't know where Jan got off to," she said. She checked the machine. "He set everything up, though," she said. "There's that, at least." She glanced at a small screen connected to the device, and then at them. "Malikova and Ou-Yang, right? So I won't have to calibrate the thing."

She pulled the caps down onto their heads and fastened them under their chins. Holo controls sprang into being, which the tech began to manipulate.

"I think I saw this in an old movie," Jinhai said. "You're not going to make us switch bodies, are you? With hilarious but predictable results?"

"No, we do that later, but we switch you with a chicken," Burke said. "Which is even more hilarious and predictable. Okay. Close your eyes, and take deep, slow breaths. The calmer you are, the easier this will be."

Jinhai shut his eyes and did his best to follow Burke's advice, but his heart felt like it was doing the climax of the *Rite of Spring*, the part where a young girl is sacrificed to the Earth by forcing her to dance to death – all heavy rhythm and dissonance.

"Initializing neural contact," he heard the tech say.

There was an instant where he felt like he was turning inside out, and then:

*Sitting on a log freezing thinking about the sea mother and father dancing together, with them Cherno Alpha beat it to death with an iceberg, the awful rush behind her, the skin of her legs blistering watching the Firebird with his parents Huo Da, man on the television saying oh my God it has wings Grandfather's things do we have to leave them here taste of pastry something hard, and dark, something he couldn't see through but terrible, a woman with eyes tattooed on her face calling Kaiju angels a shape rising up in the dusk, blocking the whole sky, a woman's face, someone calling her name from deep in the heart of the dead Kaiju . . .*

It came for them, but they couldn't see, couldn't look at

it. They were running, but not with their own legs. People were screaming. Jinhai looked over and saw a baby with blue eyes, carried in the arms of someone he couldn't see. Something screamed so loud it made the earth shake, and suddenly the screams stopped in his throat, and he felt his heart go strange, and something was pulling, pulling him out of his skin as something bigger than the sky blotted out the sun…

He was suddenly alone again, and his lungs and throat were working again, because he and Vik were both hollering like lost souls.

He ran out of breath, coughed. Burke had his hand on his shoulder. "Easy," he said. "Easy, Ou-Yang. It's not real. None of it's real."

But Jinhai knew that wasn't true. It was real, or had been. And despite the horror of it, there was something – something he needed to know, that he had almost understood – but it had all ended too quickly.

"Hang on," the tech said. "I want to take your vital signs."

She did more than that. She scanned their eyes with something, and then she turned the Pons machine back on.

"You're not drifting again," she explained. "Just want to have a quick look at your brain function."

"There's not much to look at in my case," Jinhai nervously quipped.

After about fifteen minutes of poking and prodding, the tech finally turned to Burke.

"They're okay," she said. "Physically, anyway."

Burke looked relieved.

"You two go back to the barracks," he said. "That's enough for you today."

They went back in silence and each took to their own bunk.

"Vik," he said, after a moment.

"No," she said.

But he felt he should persist.

"What the hell happened to you? That place, those caves or whatever, the weird smell . . ."

"Shut up," Vik said. Then she suddenly sobbed. "Just please. No."

Reluctantly, he nodded and lay back down.

"It wasn't like I thought it would be," he murmured, more to himself than to her.

He closed his eyes, but he kept seeing the images. The old woman talking about Kaiju like they were something wonderful. The big, dark place inside of Vik he hadn't been able to enter at all.

Was it her? Had she sabotaged Chronos Berserker and killed Braga?

He had been inside her head, and he still didn't know.

"Was this also sabotage?" Mako asked.

"It's not like they were in Mock-Pods," Burke said. "You can't program a scenario into a simple Pons device."

"And the subsequent Drifts by the other cadets?"

"We used a different machine for each pair, just in case," Burke said. "The rest drifted about as expected; some well, some not at all, some weakly. But none of them reacted like Jinhai and Vik."

"What do you think happened?" Mako asked.

"If you ask me," Burke said, "we're overthinking this. It was just a bad Drift. It's not the first time, and it won't be the last. They both have some serious issues and they got hung up on each other's memories. You can see it in the recording. It's nothing like what happened with Chronos Berserker."

"What there is of the recording," Mako said. "Much of it is garbled. But yes, they have issues – Malikova in particular has not had an easy life. And although the two are certainly Drift compatible, they are also antagonistic toward one another, which can have unpleasant side effects. But there is something else I observed in the recording, even as imperfect as it is. They are each hiding something. From each other, maybe from themselves. Certainly from us."

"You think one of them is guilty?" Burke asked.

She shrugged. "They are certainly the two most likely suspects," Mako said. "And even in so imperfect a recording, there was one other thing I noticed."

"What?" Lambert asked.

"The smell of Kaiju blood," she replied.

As Lambert left the meeting with Burke and Mori, something was bothering him, but he didn't pin it down until an hour later, when he remembered something Burke said — about the tech who was supposed to be handling the Pons training never showing up. He went back through the logs and found the name — Jan Sokk. He had been at Moyulan Shatterdome for a little over a year — had just returned from leave a couple of days before. Lambert tried to call him, but it went straight to message. After that, he went looking for the man's supervisor, Julia Reyes.

When he saw her, he realized he had noticed her before, working on Gipsy, moving on the giant mech like a high steel worker — as if she'd had the normal human fear of heights surgically removed. She also had the damnedest eyes, even at a distance, but up close they threatened to render him mute. She smelt of lavender, and grease.

"Jan?" she said, when he managed to get the question out. "I haven't seen him today. Did you check log to see if he called in sick?"

"He didn't," Lambert said. "He set up a Pons trainer

this morning, circa 0300. He was on an early shift – supposed to work until 1200."

"That sounds right. That means he's off now. Did you check his room?"

"No."

"Come on," she said. "I'll walk you there. Maybe one of his bunkmates has seen him."

"Okay," he said. "That's nice of you."

"Sure is," she said. "I hope you remember – one of these days I might need a favor from a Ranger."

She smiled, and he suddenly found himself wondering if she was just being friendly or if she was actually *flirting* with him. Because it felt a little like the latter.

"I guess you weren't born in the Shatterdome," he said, after a few steps.

"No, actually I was," she said. "Parthenogenesis, they call it. I just grew out of the side of a Jaeger."

"Umm okay," he said.

"But if you're asking where I'm from, I was born in Puerto Rico, but my parents transplanted to Acapulco when I was little. And they did volunteer as techs in the Panama City dome. Puma Real was my dad's baby. Well, other baby. Fourth. I've got a brother and two sisters. But you're a California boy, right?"

"I – how did you know that?"

She shrugged, and came to a sudden stop.

"What?" he said.

"We're here. Jan's quarters."

He realized he wasn't fully aware of covering the last fifty yards or so. They were standing in front of a door.

Jules pressed the buzzer.

"Who is it?" someone asked.

"It's Jules, Benny. Are you decent?"

"As decent as I get. Come on in."

There were four bunks in the room; only one was occupied, presumably by someone named Benny. He was a young guy, with tattoos of circuitry on his forearms. It looked like Jules' knock had probably awakened him.

"Have you seen Jan?" she asked. "The Ranger here is looking for him."

"No," Benny said. "He was supposed to be off a while ago, wasn't he? Maybe he went out to Fuding."

"He didn't sign out," Lambert said.

"Don't know what to tell you, then," Benny said. "Odd guy. Doesn't talk a lot. Kind of does his own thing."

"I'd noticed," Jules said. "I hope he's okay."

"If he reports in – if anyone sees him – would you let me know right away?" Lambert asked.

"Sure," Jules said. "You got a number?"

"Ah. Yes. Yes, I do."

He gave it to her, and she nodded.

"By the way," she said. "I've got some ideas about Gipsy. A few little modifications you might appreciate. Maybe we could talk them over some time."

"That sounds – yeah," he said. "But right now, I've gotta…"

"Sure," she said. "And listen – if you hear anything about Jan, let me know too, okay?"

He smiled. "You got a number?"

"I already sent it to you," she said. Then she turned and walked briskly down the hall.

"Yeah," Benny said. "Ranger, you should move on that business pretty quick, you know what I mean?"

"Thanks," Lambert said, dryly.

By the end of the day, it was official: Jan Sokk was a missing person. It was as if he had simply vanished.

# 15

THE CAR WAS A BLOCK AWAY. DUSTIN DIDN'T SAY anything on the walk there, but he handed Jinhai a couple of pills when they got in the car, then gave him his water bottle.

Jinhai took the pills.

"That was great," Jinhai said, once he had washed them down. His whole body seemed to be on fire now. "You know, I really think I had a shot at that girl. Had that whole 'wounded bird' thing going on."

Dustin still didn't say anything. He just looked straight ahead.

"Aw, come on, man," he said. "I was just having a little fun."

"English," Dustin said. "The deal is, when you're with me, you speak English."

"Fine," he said, switching languages. "I was just messing around."

"No," Dustin said, quietly. "You were trying to commit suicide."

Jinhai tapped his chest; it made a thudding sound. "Nobody gets killed," he said. "We wear masks and body armor."

"You're not wearing armor on your legs. You get hit in your femoral artery, you could bleed out in under a minute."

Jinhai saw he was serious.

"Okay," he said. "I did not know that. But I'm not trying to off myself. I'm just, you know, trying to..."

Dustin finally turned to look at him.

"Trying to what?"

"You know," Jinhai said. "I don't know. I guess I'm just trying to be me. Just me."

"Look, J, I'm not your therapist. I'm your bodyguard. Why do you need a bodyguard, you ask? Because the PPDC thinks you're at risk from Kaiju-worshipping wackos – and if you're at risk, so are your parents. If you're taken prisoner or something, your folks might—"

"What, abandon their principles? Betray the PPDC? For me? You've been around long enough to know that's not gonna happen. The Kaiju wackos could string me up on live video feed and threaten to cut off my head, it wouldn't make any difference to them."

"So you're trying to get their attention with these dumb stunts of yours? You know love and attention are two different things, right?"

"I thought you said you aren't my shrink."

"Yeah, I did," Dustin said. "It's just – you're making my job much harder than it should be." He sighed. "Let's just get you patched up, and hope you don't have any damage that will keep you out of the Ranger program."

"What if I don't want to be a Ranger?"

"Then don't. Come up with a viable alternative."

"I'm Ou-Yang Jinhai," he said. "There is no viable alternative."

"That stunt you pulled with the transponder. That was pretty cool. Why not go into the tech side of things?"

"You have no idea what you're talking about," Jinhai said. "My parents – you just don't understand about that."

"Whatever," Dustin said. "Just don't pull that trick or anything remotely like it again, okay? When you're off the grid, I can't protect you."

"But you said it was pretty cool," Jinhai reminded him.

"Yeah. And then it was pointed out to me that I don't know what I'm talking about."

Jinhai suddenly yawned. "I think those painkillers are kicking in," he said.

"Good," Dustin said. "Maybe we can both get some sleep."

He dreamed of a day when he was five. A lot of his friends couldn't remember much that far back, and there was probably a lot he didn't remember either, but that day – that day was stuck deep in him. He remembered how the sunlight made the water look like gold, and his dad told him that it was at this very place, at this time of day they had named him – Jinhai, "Golden Sea". They told him one day it would be his to protect. There had been more: walking in the woods, a picnic, ice cream in a park later, a long ride in the car singing songs. He remembered being able to feel their love like the sunshine, feeling connected to them in every way.

He remembered it. In his dream, he remembered it.

He woke to laughter, far off, in another room. He sat up, and winced as his two stab wounds reminded him they were still there after – what, four days? He rubbed his eyes and took the antibiotic Dustin had given him. He'd had a doctor come to the house, so no hospital would have an admissions record, of course. Wouldn't do to embarrass Mom and Dad.

Speaking of which, he was pretty sure that was them he heard. The house was out in the country, and things were generally pretty quiet when they weren't around, unless he was the one making the noise.

He pulled on a long-sleeved shirt to cover his injuries and then found some pants.

They were in the kitchen, of course, cooking. He stood in the doorway, watching them, the way they moved. Each always seemed to know where the other was, even without looking. They chopped and diced and cleaned up after one another; now and then they touched, gently, a stroke on the arm or shoulder, intentionally bumping into one another, but only enough to make contact, never enough to cause a spill. Effortlessly attentive. Even with her prosthetic leg, his mom moved with incredible grace. A handful of something went into the wok and began to sizzle fiercely; an instant later he smelled ginger and onion.

And now the ache deep in the pit of him hurt worse than the puncture wounds.

Eventually they noticed him.

"Son," his father said. "Good morning. Or early afternoon, anyway."

"Well, it isn't a school day, so, you know."

His mother summoned him over for a hug. It was a little awkward, as usual.

"So?" she asked.

"So what?" he said. Did they know something? Had Dustin told them? Had it made the news?

"So, what's going on?" she asked.

His father clapped him on the shoulder. That would have felt awkward, too, if it hadn't hurt so much.

"What's wrong?" his mother asked. Then she glanced at

his father's hand on his shoulder. "Did that hurt?" she asked.

He remembered one time his father had accidentally knocked the heavy stone pestle off the counter, and it had landed on his bare toe. He hadn't made a noise – maybe the slightest sharp inhalation, but nothing more. But his mother was there immediately, also without making a sound, checking to see if it was broken.

"Is your shoulder tender, son?" his father asked.

"Yeah," he said. "Fencing injury. Just a bruise. One of the beginners thought he was a pirate. Didn't get the point."

"Funny," his dad said. "The point. I get it. Well, that's fine. You got another year before you need to be a hundred percent. Have you given any thought to training in another martial art? Boxing, maybe, or mixed martial arts?"

"I was gonna look into that," he said.

"Everything you take with you helps," his mother said.

"Yeah," he said. "I know." He had heard it often enough.

Stir fry was not forgiving, and they were soon back at it. They started eating in silence, although if you watched his parents, you would think they were reciting poetry to one another. Their knowing little glances, their private smiles.

When he couldn't take it any longer, he began talking, although he knew it wouldn't help.

"So how long are you guys home for?" he asked.

"Three days," his father said. "After that…" He took a bite of kangkong.

"…we'll be flying to Anchorage," his mother finished. "We'll be gone three weeks. But we should be here for your big recital."

"That sounds great," he said.


His father surprised him two days later by asking if he wanted to go cycling. Without Mom.

It was pretty weird, so he agreed. They weren't entirely alone, of course – Dustin and a couple of PPDC agents were on the scene, but they stayed discreetly out of sight.

They went on and off trail in the national park. Jinhai's muscles throbbed, but he was enjoying himself when his father called a halt. They sat down on some rocks by a little stream.

His dad's face tried on a few expressions. He seemed to want to say something, but he was having a hard time coming out with it, to the point Jinhai started to worry. Was it something horrible? Did Mom have cancer?

"Dad," he finally said. "What is it?"

His father sighed. "Jinhai, do you want to be a Ranger? Do you want to pilot Jaegers?"

Jinhai was so surprised it took him a few beats to reply.

"You know I do," he finally answered.

"No," his father answered. "I don't. That's why I'm asking."

"Sir, I don't think I've ever given you reason to doubt my sincerity."

"Not directly, no. I know your mom and I aren't around enough. I'm sorry for that, but it means we have to rely on the reports of others—"

"Dustin, that rat…"

"Dustin? No, Dustin hasn't said anything to us. Should he have? What am I missing?"

*Damn it*, he berated himself. Sometimes he was his own worst enemy.

"No, nothing – he, uh, caught me having a beer the other day."

His father shrugged. "That's not what I'm worried about. But some of your teachers say you've been acting out. Smarting off in class. Getting in fights—"

"One fight. And he took a swing at me."

"You didn't have to swing back."

"You swung back at the Kaiju, didn't you?"

"And that, of course, was different," his father said. "Mrs. Jian thinks this is all because you don't want to go to the Academy. That you would rather be something else. A dancer, perhaps, or a scientist. Is that true?"

"I want to be a Ranger," Jinhai insisted.

"I don't care if you become a Ranger," his father said. "Neither does your mom. What we do care about is that whatever it is you do, you do it with excellence. Do you understand? Excellence. If you do so, we will be proud of you – whatever you choose."

For a moment, his words felt stuck in his swollen throat, and tears threatened.

"Then I will be an excellent Ranger, sir," he said. "I promise."

"Then work through whatever this is. I don't want to hear any more of this behavior next time I get reports."

"You won't, sir, I promise."

# 16

HUO DA JETTED TOWARD SHAOLIN ROGUE, throwing out its tentacle-like forearms so quickly they couldn't avoid them. They wrapped around the Jaeger, closed behind them, locked together, and tightened. At the same time, Huo Da's entire lower jaw suddenly shot out like the tongue of a frog or a lizard, wrapping around their left arm like a blood pressure cuff. And like a cuff, it began to squeeze, hard, and pull them toward the meat grinder of its serrated lower limbs.

They pumped their left fist into Huo Da's face once, twice, three times, but it wouldn't let go.

"There is a reef, five hundred meters off at two o' clock," Suyin said, more for Tendo than for him, because Ming-hau already knew what her plan was.

"Bringing turbines online," he said.

They bent forward as their Hydropulsers kicked in, driving them forward and the Kaiju relentlessly back. It kept at them with its claws and struck with its tail, but at last they were in deeper water and they could turn fully horizontal and detach the Kaiju's hold from the seabed. It thrashed its body, trying to find any sort of leverage, but its grip didn't relent, and the powerful tentacles and jaw pulled them closer and closer to its head.

The reef loomed, a dark wall in the water, and they slammed Huo Da into it with so much force that huge chunks of it cracked away and Shaolin Rogue's own pressure tolerances hit a red line.

Huo Da's weird jaw finally retracted, and now they used both fists to batter the monster against the reef, returning as they did to a standing position, shifting ballast to reorient their center of gravity. An uppercut lifted the monster's head up—

—and then its entire body followed it, flexing up until it towered above them, so they could see the myriad of tiny suckers on its belly, just before it arched over and fell, latching onto them like a leech, and then used its own water jets to drag from across the sea bottom while the sharp, stubby legs beneath its head clawed viciously at the junction of Conn-Pod and collar, trying to decapitate them.

"It's starting to cut through," Tendo warned.

Desperate, they tried to wrap their legs around Huo Da's midsection, but as a machine they weren't quite that flexible; the best they could achieve was a scissor hold. But that was good enough to allow them to pull free of the suckers, flip the thing onto its back, straddle it, and begin whaling at it again.

But Huo Da was basically one big muscle, and before long was able to thrash hard enough to buck them off. They quickly rolled in the water and landed back on their feet, ready to fight. But instead of attacking, Huo Da backed off and began to circle them a little more warily.

"Rogue, how are you holding up?" Tendo asked. "We've got a few red lights here. Nothin' gone cold, but your underwear is showin' a little bit."

"We're still here," Suyin replied. "I'm not sure we can say more than that. This thing is tough. I'm not sure we've hurt it much at all."

"You'll have some company in about twenty," he said. "Crimson Typhoon is on the way. If you can just hold on until then, things should get a whole lot easier."

"It's not getting by us," Suyin said.

It didn't, but it did come at them again, darting forward under the power of its water jets, aiming directly toward the Conn-Pod, as if it had figured out where its true enemies were. They battered it back, but it came again, and each exchange pushed them a little closer to the mainland, into shallower water. They were also starting to tire a little. In training, they had been able to keep the neural handshake stable for hours. The Kaidanovskys still held the record, but Ming-hau and Suyin had been creeping up on them.

But training wasn't combat, as they were discovering. Shaolin Rogue itself was holding up pretty well. LOCCENT reported they were building up some stress fractures here and there, and Huo Da had managed to finally pierce their armor in a few spots, but water incursion was quickly contained – none of their systems were seriously compromised yet.

Still, they needed to end this before Huo Da pushed them back to the mainland. A fight in Shanghai would be utterly devastating.

"Let's use the lance," Suyin said.

He remembered his earlier misgiving about releasing Kaiju blood in the Yellow Sea, but she was right. So far nothing they had done had injured the beast.

"Worth a try," Ming-hau said. "The next time it shows

its underside, I'll try for right under the head."

"Starting compression," she said.

Predictably, the monster came at them again, and again it reared up, going for the Conn-Pod, trying to wrap them with those extensive arms.

"There," Suyin shouted.

Driven by a hundred thousand psig of compressed gas, sixty feet of sharpened tungsten carbide spike sprang out of their left arm and locked there, like a giant switchblade. They felt the impact all the way to their toes, and the water around them was suddenly swirling blue with Kaiju blood. They shouted in triumph as they saw the lance had driven completely through Huo Da.

Their victory, however, was short lived, as the Kaiju twisted completely around, flipping them over by their lance arm, and jetted off, dragging them along. They tried to withdraw the lance, but its housing had bent under the pressure and was now jammed. Between the Kaiju's blood and the roiled-up ocean floor, their visibility dwindled to almost nothing. Rogue flailed about, trying to get a foothold, or land a solid punch. But Huo Da was shaking them back and forth and rolling so hard it was difficult to concentrate.

Finally, the lance tore out of the arm, taking a good chunk of the anterior limb with it. The feedback pain was nearly blinding.

Ming-hau felt the neural handshake weaken for a moment, but then Suyin was there, firmly back in his head, calm, fearless. He grinned, partly because of the pain, mostly to spite it.

"Maybe that wasn't the best idea after all," he said.

"Hey," she said. "It has a hole in it now."

"Right." They tried Rogue's left arm. It still worked, but only at about thirty percent.

"Where is it?" Suyin asked, as they circled, slowly,

trying to see in all directions at once.

"We have it moving away from you, Rogue," Tendo reported.

"Toward the mainland?"

"No, it's headed almost due south. Wait – there's something down there, too. Something big, under water."

"A submarine?"

"It's not metal," Tendo said. Ming-hau thought he detected an odd tone in the controller's voice.

"Another Kaiju?" he asked. That was a terrifying thought. The Kaiju were coming more and more frequently, but there had never been a double event.

"Can't be sure," Tendo replied. "Too much Kaiju blood in the water to get a clean signature."

"We're giving chase," Suyin said.

"That's going to use a lot of power," Tendo said. "If it's not headed toward Shanghai right away, best wait for Typhoon."

"I don't like this," Suyin said. "It's up to something. We're going."

"Agreed," Ming-hau said.

The hole in Huo Da didn't seem to have slowed it down much, and soon the trail of blue blood played out, the visible part of it anyway. But they had a lock on it, and soon the thing Tendo was picking up on his instruments was on their sonar. Like Huo Da, it had a long silhouette, but it was less than half of the Kaiju's size. As they watched, approaching on turbines, the two signatures came together.

When they finally caught up, ten minutes later, it was already clear what was happening.

The water was dark with blood – not the blue blood of a Kaiju but the iron-based blood common to earthly vertebrates.

Huo Da was eating a whale.

A wave of anger and revulsion swept through Ming-hau. They were far too late to save the poor beast, that much was clear.

Huo Da looked up at them warily.

"Let's hit it with shooting stars," Suyin said.

"Excellent suggestion."

They hadn't tried the stars earlier because they had been too close, but now they had a motionless target a fair distance away. They fired both shooting stars at once. The torpedoes must have looked insignificantly tiny to the Kaiju, just two little fishes swimming its way. It didn't make any effort to avoid them and they both hit the creature head on. Their magnesium-laced warheads detonated and shone very briefly like the meteorites they were named for, so bright that it overwhelmed their sensors.

"Two direct hits," Suyin said.

Now they couldn't see anything, and the sonar was confused as well, as chunks of whale and hopefully Kaiju expanded out and away from the twin explosions, pushing Shaolin Rogue back like a breaking tsunami.

So they didn't know Huo Da was there until the instant before impact. It knocked them over, backed up, rammed them again. It seemed to be missing a limb or two, but that didn't appear to deter it very much.

"We just made it mad," Ming-hau said. At least the poor whale was no longer suffering. That in itself had been worth spending them.

"Let's make it madder," Suyin said.

# 17

MAKO GLANCED UP AS VIKTORIYA MALIKOVA came into her office for the second time. As usual, she seemed to have a look of slight irritation on her face.

"Malikova," she said. "Please have a seat."

The girl settled in the chair and placed her hands on her knees. She looked very stiff.

"I hear you had a difficult first Drift," she said.

"I suppose, Secretary General," the girl said. "I have nothing to compare it to. But I would not call it an enjoyable experience."

"Don't make too much of it," Mako said. "You're Drift compatible – that's what counts. Things will smooth out."

"Thank you, Secretary," she said. "I hope you're right."

Mako nodded. "I'm looking at your records," she said. "You're very persistent."

The girl looked defiant. "You mean I failed the entrance exam two times," she said.

"I mean you failed it twice and took it again anyway," Mako corrected.

The girl made a little face. "That's one way to look at it, I suppose."

"You were determined. Persistent. I expect you to show the same qualities now that you have actually arrived here." She cocked her head. "Do you know why you failed?"

"I do not, Secretary General," Malikova said. "That information is not available to us."

"You passed the written tests," she said. "It was in the practical that you lost ground. For lack of control."

Malikova reddened, but didn't say anything.

"You failed the third time, as well," Mako said. "I intervened."

For the first time, the girl's guard slipped enough to show how utterly astonished she was.

"I... I didn't know that, ma'am. And... I don't understand."

"No, how could you have known? But I make a point of personally reviewing anyone who applies more than twice. Sometimes it means the applicant is delusional. Sometimes it turns out that the persistence comes from their parents, rather than the applicant. But sometimes it shows true resolve. In your case I felt you had potential. Was I wrong?"

"I like to think you were not," the girl said.

"Have you ever met any Kaiju worshippers, cadet?" Mako asked.

That caught her by surprise, too. For a moment she seemed frozen, unable to speak.

But then she nodded her head.

"Yes," she said. "Yes. When I was a little girl, in Yuzhno Sakhalinsk. There was a dead Kaiju there, so there were some who hung around. I met some of them." She shifted from looking uncomfortable to angry. "I didn't like them," she said. "I hate Kaiju. I would never be like them."

"It's okay, cadet. I wasn't trying to imply anything. But there were some things in your Drift record that I was curious about. A woman, talking about Kaiju."

"She was sort of a preacher," Vik said. "She was crazy, and I did my best to avoid her."

"Very well," Mako said. "You may return to barracks, cadet."

When Malikova was gone, Mako sat back and rubbed her eyes. She was tired, but she had been having trouble sleeping.

Malikova still wasn't telling her everything. There was something she was keeping buried, possibly even from herself. But she didn't want to push too hard, not yet. Better to keep an eye on her.

Sleep eluded Jinhai – his mind kept replaying the Drift obsessively, trying to tease out what was him and what was Vik. Even the memories he knew for a fact were his weren't exactly how he normally recalled them: they had been refracted through the lens of Vik's mind, been turned at a different angle, gotten tangled in a different point of view. He was not entirely *him* anymore. He'd thought that was what he wanted, that thing his parents had, where they knew each other so well they hardly needed to talk. Instead, he felt like he had swallowed someone else's illness when he was already sick with his own disease. Some of the stuff in Vik's head was pure horror show.

Except for him that was sort of a dark pun now; in Russian, *horosho* meant "good".

He was really starting to wish Ryoichi hadn't said anything. What if Vik wasn't who she seemed to be? What if *he* wasn't? Once you accepted the possibility that a whole other personality might be implanted in you, insanity was already breathing down your neck.

No, it was ridiculous. He was just confused, and frightened. And let down.

And worried. Did this mean he wasn't even Drift compatible? Was he going to wash out?

"Hey, Ranger."

Lambert turned at the familiar voice and saw Jules standing outside of the door of his little office. He pushed his chair back and quickly stood. Too quickly, he realized. It made him seem over-eager.

"Is this a bad time?" she asked.

"No, no, not at all," he replied. "How can I help you?"

"I think I have something you might be interested in," she said.

He froze up for an instant.

"Umm," he finally said.

"Here," she said, handing him a pen drive. "It's tracking data from Mechspace. I think we've figured out how someone got inside Chronos Berserker's Conn-Pod without being surveilled."

"Oh," Lambert said. "Great. That's great."

"Now you owe me twice," she said. "Don't forget."

As she left, Burke stuck his head out of his office.

"You know," he said. "This is not a situation where you ought to drag your heels."

"I get that," Lambert said. "And now, kindly shut up about it."

He synched the drive to his station and started looking at the contents. When he understood what he was seeing, he grinned. He had a meeting with Mako Mori in an hour, and now he had something to tell her.

\* \* \*

"That's interesting," Mori said, after he'd finished his explanation. "It certainly opens up new possibilities, as far as suspects are concerned."

"It makes it less likely that a cadet sabotaged Chronos Berserker," he said.

"True," Mori said. "It does seem to lead away from the cadets. Or at least not toward them. But then, there is Ou-Yang's pen drive."

"What about Sokk?" Lambert said. "If you ask me, he's our man."

"Sokk certainly seems guilty of something, but that doesn't rule out Vik or Jinhai or both of them being involved, whether they are aware of it or not."

"How could they not be aware they were committing sabotage?" Lambert asked.

"A few years ago, we found one of the nastier corners of the criminal underworld was using Pons technology to implant commands into people. Something like hypnotism, but far more effective. They used one such person to assassinate a corrupt police official. We managed to get custody of him – he had no memory of what he'd done. We think it might be possible to plant an entire hidden personality in someone, a personality which would emerge at predetermined times."

"You think this might have been done to Vik and Jinhai?"

"They both have gaps in their pasts, Vik more than Jinhai. In fact, much of her childhood is a black box to us. She grew up on Sakhalin, where records were sketchy after the Kaiju Wars. But what little we do know points to a rough childhood. And you saw from their attempt to drift that both have something walled away, hidden. I don't know what a repressed personality would look like in the Drift, but it might look like that."

"Are you going to question them?" he asked.

"No," she said. "I think it would be better to watch them for a while. Let them continue training. Move Mock-Pod work up; the more they drift, the more likely we are to see if something's not right with either or both of them."

# 18

LAMBERT WATCHED THE STUDENTS BOARD THE transport helicopter. They were excited, as any group of cadets were before their first liberty, but they also were understandably subdued due to not only the tragedy of Braga's death, but also the realization they must have all come to by now – that they were suspects. The way this played out varied from one cadet to the other; Suresh and Renata played several variations of a slap-fighting game; Tahima, Ryoichi, Meilin, and Ilya made nervous jokes, laughed a little too loudly, and engaged in horseplay. Jinhai and Vik avoided each other. He let a few things go by he might ordinarily have put a stop to. They had been through a lot for first-trimester cadets.

He wasn't sure liberty was a good idea, if someone out there was looking to hurt the PPDC. But the city of Fuding was no Hong Kong, rather a modest place of about three hundred thousand people. A port city that had escaped major depredation by the Kaiju, connected to Shanghai and other centers by high-speed rail, it was otherwise in the middle of nowhere. The city itself was in the mountains but laced through with inlets from the sea. It reminded him of Seattle in its situation, if not its climate. Like any city, it had an underbelly of crime: black market and general nastiness, but because of the Shatterdome and its quick response time, Fuding was a pretty safe place – and security had been stepped up in the wake of the sabotage at Moyulan.

A boat ride could get them there, but it would take most of the day, and first-trimester cadets did not get overnight liberty. So, they flew.

They landed at a PPDC helipad at the port, where everyone was imaged, scanned, and provided with pass badges before entering the city itself.

A few moments later Lambert had them line up.

"Groups of two or more," Lambert told them. "Keep your pass badges with you at all times. I will also remind you that some parts of the city are off-limits to you. If you go into any of the restricted areas, your liberty will come to a swift and certain end. Are there any questions?"

"Yes, Ranger," Renata said. "Where's the closest decent pizza?"

"New York," he replied. That drew a chuckle from a few of them.

"But, if you're not too picky, there's some pretty good pie on Haikou Road, just south of the big circle." He looked at them a little more seriously. "Be careful," he said. "And behave. Cadets are generally liked around here, because they don't cause trouble. Remember what you represent and uphold our standards. If I hear poor reports of you, I will not be pleased. Above all, be respectful – this is their city, not yours. I'll meet all of you back here at 2100 for the chopper ride back. Remember, early is on time, on time is late, and late is unacceptable. Do you all understand?"

"Yes, Ranger," they all answered.

"Good," he said. "Have fun."

With that he walked off, leaving them there.

"I'm after the pizza," Renata said. "Who's with me?"

"Tahima and Ryoichi and I are going to the art museum, and to see one of the old temples," Meilin said. "But we can meet up with you later."

"What about you, Vik?" Renata asked. She sounded as if she wasn't that enthusiastic about the Russian tagging along, but was being polite.

"Another time," Vik said. "I'm going to hunt for dumplings."

"You need a buddy," Renata said. "Who's going with you?"

"Dumplings sound good," Jinhai said. "I'll be her buddy."

"Just don't stand too close," Vik said.

Jinhai could feel the suspicious gazes of the other cadets as they left, and knew that he and Vik were maybe digging themselves in a little deeper with them – making themselves look guiltier. But the two of them needed to talk, and this seemed like a good time for it.

Once they were clear of the group, Vik, who was in the lead, glanced back at him.

"You don't have to babysit me," she said. "I just said the dumpling thing to get away from the others."

"To do what?" he asked.

"Meet up with my Kaiju-worshipping friends," she snapped. "What do you think?"

"Hey," he said. "Hold on. I wasn't saying –"

"No," she said. "No one is 'saying'. No one is implying anything. Not you, not Mori, not Lambert."

"Look, they suspect me too," he said. "Somebody stole my pen drive. I think it must have been involved in the sabotage."

She stared at him.

"Were you?" she demanded.

"No!" he said.

"Well, neither was I," she said. "Now shove off."

He touched his badge. "These are tracking devices," he said. "They'll know if we split up. Look, why don't we just get some dumplings, like you said? Now that you've brought them up, I can't get them out of my mind. And I'm starving."

She didn't exactly look happy with the idea, but she nodded. "You know where to go?" she asked.

"I speak the language," he said. "I'll ask somebody."

A nice-looking man directed them to a market square where several street vendors had set up; one was hawking pork-and-cabbage dumplings. They bought some, found a bench and began gobbling them down.

"These are pretty good," he said. "Not exactly what I'm used to. Some different ingredient."

She nodded. "I've never had this. It is good."

"You've never had *jiao-tse*?" he asked, incredulous.

"No," she said. "We had something like this back home called pyanse, but it was more of a bun – puffy."

"Oh yeah," he said. "I remember. In the Drift. And that weird old lady..."

She frowned. "We're not going to talk about it," she said.

"I just want to know what happened to you, Vik. I feel like it was something awful."

"It was something I got through," she said. "Okay?"

"But –"

135

"I guess my English sucks, or yours does," she said. "Because I'm *really* sure I already said I didn't want to talk about it."

"Fine," he said. "Okay, wait here a minute."

He went back to the vendor and bought two spicy fried rolls made with tofu sheets wrapped around pork, fish, and water chestnuts, generously seasoned with five-spice and mustard. He also purchased two zongzi: sticky rice dumplings wrapped in bamboo leaves.

"As long as you're trying new things," he said. "You can get dumplings anywhere. These are sort of regional specialties."

"Thanks," she said.

They munched for a bit in silence.

"How do you know the badges are tracking devices?" she asked.

"One of my hobbies," he said. "I've had a microchip transponder in me most of my life, so my caretakers and teachers and bodyguards – or the police – would always be able to find me. So I've gotten creative about this kind of stuff over the years."

"Why do you have an implant?" Vik asked.

"You really want to hear about this? It involves my parents."

"Go ahead."

"Remember how I said my parents weren't the first to pilot Shaolin Rogue?"

"I knew that already," Vik said. "The first were Hong and Patel – they were murdered. I remember all of this. You said your parents got death threats."

"Yeah," he said. "But what I didn't tell you was that the death threats weren't just directed at my parents – they were directed at me, too. The PPDC started a protection program for the families of Jaeger pilots. But my mom and dad took the extra step of having me tagged."

"I see," Vik said. "They were trying to protect you. You should be happy about that."

"Maybe," he said. "But being tagged like a piece of property isn't so fun, especially when you have things to do. So I figured out ways to beat it. It's probably one of the reasons I'm a suspect."

"Because you might be capable of disabling their security systems."

"Maybe."

"Could you?"

"I don't know," he said. "Something minor, maybe, but nothing like it would have taken to sabotage a Jaeger. If they think I could do that, they're overestimating me by a lot."

They were finished with their food. "What now?" she asked.

"Well, seeing as how we're stuck together for a few hours, we might as well explore the town. There's a place I was thinking about going to later on that's supposed to serve a mean Buddha Jumps Over the Wall."

"That's some kind of food?" she asked.

"Oh, yeah."

"Is that all you ever think about?"

"I wish," he said.

# 19

MAKO WENT TO THE KWOON EARLY, ALONE, IN her sweats. She inspected the armory, and after a moment, chose a bō staff. She took a deep breath, and then began moving, turning the staff in her hands, shifting stances, just warming up. She did the first kata she had ever learned, a formalized fight against an opponent that wasn't there, designed to perfect form and timing. Then she did another, closing her eyes. She didn't need sight for any of this.

And then, as always, he was there. Raleigh. She blocked his blow and cut toward his feet. He jumped over the pole and swung at her overhand.

She saw him now, in the dark behind her eyelids. And not just him, but the pale fragments of his memories, of practicing in the Kwoon with his brother Yancy, Yancy who had been yanked out of Gipsy Danger by the Kaiju Knifehead, leaving Raleigh incomplete. He hadn't been complete again until he and she drifted together, piloted Gipsy as a single mind.

But now he was gone, and she was the one who was now incomplete. He was her ghost, the thing on the other side of the kata she was making up as she went along, trying to find a way to live, to be – without him.

But he was always there. And so they drifted, in a sense. Every day, every hour, but sometimes, times like this, the Drift was strong.

She thought about Vik and Jinhai. She had thought if the two were guilty they might do something during liberty to give themselves away – to connect them to whatever malevolence had entered the Shatterdome – but they hadn't done anything unusual, according to their tracking badges. That didn't mean they hadn't done something, of course – just that they hadn't been caught at it. According to many sources, Jinhai in particular was pretty good at fooling babysitters, human or electronic. He might well have manipulated their badges somehow. And that in itself suggested he might have also sabotaged Chronos Berserker. Feeding a badge false data and convincing a Jaeger crew that they were under attack were on the same spectrum of praxis, both in terms of conception and technology. She made a mental note to have their badges examined by an expert.

And Vik – she had pursued the Academy with a single-minded determination that was rare even among recruits. She was driven by pain and trauma and revenge, which Mako understood all too well.

Jinhai's pain was subtler, but just as deep, and she wasn't entirely sure what it was. But she thought she saw bits of herself there too. The child of a famous mother and father, held back, prevented from fulfilling his potential because his parents were afraid to risk him. Like her adoptive father had tried to hold herself and her adoptive brother back.

When you had faced a Kaiju, stared into the eyes of the walking death of thousands, you did not want your child to have to face that as well. She understood her father's reticence, now.

But she hadn't then, had she?

Maybe Lambert was right. Maybe it was Sokk who had committed the sabotage. His disappearance certainly added weight to that explanation. But even if Sokk was guilty, Vik and Jinhai may have played their parts as well. All three could have been involved. She hoped it wasn't true for several reasons, not least of which was that she was starting to feel that if she could somehow help the two cadets come to terms with their mental wounds, it might help her to make peace with hers. She wasn't quite sure why she believed that, but that was often the nature of belief, wasn't it?

She finished, bowed to Raleigh, enjoyed his smile one more time. Then she opened her eyes.

He was, of course, not there.


Lambert backed quietly from the entrance to the Kwoon. He'd come down to set it up for the day's training; he hadn't expected to find the Secretary General working out. He almost stayed and waited for her to finish, but something about the way she moved and carried herself suggested that she was in the middle of something intensely personal, and he didn't want to interrupt.

They had never exactly been friends, but she had helped train him, and she was the sister of his best friend and first Drift partner.

Ex-best friend. Ex-Drift partner. Those days were long gone. But having her here reminded him. And he would rather not be reminded.

As he walked away from the Kwoon, he ran into Burke.

"All set up?" Burke asked.

"No," Lambert said. "The Kwoon is in use. By someone way above our pay grade."

"Oh," he said. "Her. I saw her in there the other day. Interesting moves. Almost like she's fighting *with* someone. A little spooky."

"Yeah, well she's been that way since I've known her. Losing a Drift partner is... hard."

"Well, especially when they die, I would guess," Burke said.

"I'm sure that's harder," Lambert said. "I wouldn't know. But to have one just walk away from you – that's tough too. The loss is still there. And you start to realize that even though you've been in each other's heads, you still don't share the same values..."

"Brother," Burke said. "You have very high standards when it comes to values. Anyone would have a hard time living up to them."

"What's wrong with high standards?" Lambert said. "It was men and women with high standards who got us through the Kaiju Wars. People who understand sacrifice and serving a higher cause."

"The higher cause was fighting the Kaiju," Burke said. "Last time I checked, there weren't that many of those around."

"Ten years is a blip for them," Lambert said. "A pause. A reset. They'll come back – and when they do, we'll be ready."

Burke clapped him on the back. "If you're right, we'd better get this fresh meat into shape. They're the future, not us."

"Right," Lambert said. "Because we're such old men."

"As Jaeger pilots go, we're two of the oldest," Burke pointed out.

Well, that made him uncomfortable.

* * *

Ranger Lambert seemed determined to make them pay for whatever fun they might have had on liberty. He and the instructors worked them in the Kwoon until Jinhai felt he couldn't keep his legs under him anymore. Suresh and Meilin actually did have to take time outs, but there was no way Jinhai was going to do that until Vik did.

Today it was less about bonding and more about learning, and the specific topic was upper-body wrestling, the sort of things a Jaeger could do at close quarters while standing waist-deep in water. Grappling, pushing, pulling. Shifting the hips, changing the balance of the situation with minimum footwork. As an added bonus, they spent the last three of their fourteen-hour session learning to fight two opponents at once.

For twelve years the Kaiju had attacked the world, and they had come one at a time. They got bigger, better adapted to fighting the huge machines that met them when they emerged from the depths, but in general one Kaiju faced one or as many as three Jaegers.

But in 2025, Leatherback and Otachi changed all of that when they appeared together in the first double event. Working together, they destroyed Crimson Typhoon and Cherno Alpha and temporarily disabled Striker Eureka in what seemed like a few heartbeats. Not long after, Striker and Gipsy had been forced to confront three Kaiju, one a category V. They hadn't had a chance in a straight-up fight; only by detonating the nuclear bomb it carried had Striker Eureka been able to clear the way for Gipsy.

When the Kaiju came back, they might begin coming in the same way, one at a time. But what if they came in twos, threes, fours?

Toward the end of the day, trembling with fatigue, he

and Vik got matched against Tahima.

Tahima had good chops; he was a well-rounded fighter, and his grappling skills were particularly good.

Tahima took the initiative, jogging quickly to Jinhai's flank, probably hoping to deal with him quickly and then move on to Vik. He had earlier done this very thing against Renata and Suresh, and it had worked well.

Jinhai didn't turn fast enough to meet him, but he did so intentionally. Tahima took him by the arm, slipped his foot behind Jinhai's ankle and prepared to take him down. Jinhai lifted his foot and flipped backward with the force of the throw, and felt a grin turn his face when Vik came through where he had just been, sticking her leg behind Tahima and clotheslining him with a front-hand-ridge-hand. Both of Tahima's feet left the floor, and he landed with a thud on his back a second after Jinhai stuck his landing.

He grinned at Vik, who almost – but didn't quite – grin back.

But it hit him, then – he had known what to do, because he had known what *she* would do.

Tahima got up, slowly, and offered each of them his hand.

"Nice," he said. Everyone else was quiet, and Suresh wouldn't even meet his gaze.

Lambert stopped Jinhai and Vik as they were leaving practice.

"I don't know if you felt that," he said. "The connection you had. But I saw it. I don't know what's going on between you, but you need to work it out. Remember what we're doing here – preparing for the job of defending humanity. If you have personal problems more pressing than that, I'd sure like to hear them. Or anything else you might like to get off your chest."

Jinhai looked at Vik out of the corner of his eye.

"Truth is, Ranger," Jinhai said, "I do have something to admit. I'm kind of ashamed of it, but, well – I actually kind of like old school seventies disco. It's super catchy, you know? Even Barry Manilow."

For the first time since they'd met, Lambert actually looked angry. He stepped forward, right into his face, and more than anything, Jinhai wanted to step back. But he stood his ground.

"Making a joke was the wrong call, son," Lambert said.

"And thinking I'm a traitor is your bad call, Ranger, sir... I might be a screw-up, I might be a smart ass, but I am not a traitor. My parents—"

"I don't give a damn who your parents are," Lambert shot back. "It's who *you* are or aren't that matters to me. Or maybe who you *could* be. And to be clear, I haven't accused you of anything."

"No," Jinhai said. "You haven't. Not to my face. But I believe you think it. Either me or Vik, right? Or both. Well I can tell you for sure, it wasn't Vik. So you can leave her out of this, right?"

"What are you saying?" Lambert demanded.

He stood straighter. "Permission to shower, Ranger, sir."

Lambert glared at him for what seemed like a great while.

"Permission granted," Lambert finally said.

He and Vik walked back most of the way in silence. But before they reached the showers, she did ask him a question.

"Do you really think I'm innocent?"

"*Da*," he said. "*Ya dumayu, chto.*"

She blinked and then stuttered out a little laugh.

"What?" he asked.

"That's not quite right," she told him. "But I appreciate the effort."

# 20

2025
JANUARY 6TH
CHRISTMAS EVE (RUSSIAN ORTHODOX)
SAKHALIN ISLAND
RUSSIA
VIK

IT WAS COLD; OUTSIDE THE SNOW STOOD IN drifts up to a meter deep. Inside it was cold, too. Their apartment was heated by warm water pipes in the floor, which was cheap and efficient, but not as niçe as gathering around the ceramic heater they'd had back home. Seeing her shiver, Babulya gave Vik her Christmas present early: a black luftgel coat with lots of pockets. She was warmer the second she put it on, and when she closed the seal in front, it was like being wrapped in six blankets. It wasn't one of the fancy ones, but it must have cost her grandmother half a month's pay.

On Christmas Eve, they didn't usually eat anything until the first star appeared in the sky. Vik was starving, and it was overcast, so as soon as it seemed dark enough, they ate what she had been smelling for a while – sochivo, a mush made from rice boiled with poppy seeds, honey, and walnuts. The first bites were heaven, but by the third she was starting to feel a little guilty, remembering the far richer, tastier paklava. She should have shared the last of her money with her grandmother, or at least bought her a present. As it was, she had nothing to give her but a picture, but she had worked on that all day. When she saw it, Babulya smiled and cried at the same time. She'd drawn a picture of her grandfather, inside a border of flowers.

"It's beautiful, Vik," she said. "I'll put it on the wall, just over there."

"It's not as good as a coat," Vik said.

"No, it's better," her grandmother said. "The coat warms your body, but this warms my soul." She looked again at the drawing.

"I miss him so," she said. "Did I ever tell you how we met?"

She had, of course, but Vik listened to the story anyway, hoping this time it would go past the point where she accepted his half-drunken apology and proposal. Grandmother was half drunk herself by the time she finished, from a mixture of lemon soda and vodka.

"What about my mama?" Vik asked. "How soon after you were married was she born?"

She had asked that question before, but her grandmother had never answered it. She didn't seem like she was going to this time, but after taking another drink, she smiled sadly.

"Hard-headed," she said. "Like you. Always trying to push ahead, to be seven before he was five."

"He?"

Babulya looked a little flustered. "I'm drunk," she said. "I meant she. Do you want to hear this or not?"

"I do."

Her grandmother took another drink.

"I couldn't keep up with her. I tried, but I couldn't. And

she just – slipped away from me."

"What do you mean?"

Babulya's face cleared, and her eyes sharpened. "She was just so young when she left home," she said.

"And she ended up in jail," Vik said. "That's where she met Papa."

Grandmother frowned. "You shouldn't believe everything you see on vidiot," she snapped. "Your mother was a good girl. They make things up, these people. And some of them…" Her voice lowered, became conspiratorial, and her eyes got that strange, faraway look they did sometimes.

"All Kaiju are not gigantic," she whispered. "Some of them are no bigger than you, and they can look like anything – anyone. They come, and they lie, and they twist things; twist our hearts if we're not careful."

Her hand suddenly shot out and gripped Vik's wrist. Surprised, she tried to pull away, but Grandmother's fingers tightened, and it hurt.

"Have you been talking to them?" she asked. "Have you been with them? Are you still my Vikushka?"

She had always been a little scared of Babulya; but now it was dark, and the wind outside sounded like ghosts moaning, and her arm hurt. She felt trapped – and for the first time, truly terrified.

"Babulya," she said. "It is me. It *is* me."

Her grandmother stared at her for several long heartbeats, her expression like nothing Vik had ever seen before. It was like Grandmother wasn't real anymore, but some sort of large doll made of plastic, with eyes of glass.

But then she let go, and leaned back, and poured some vodka – this time without the soda.

"You are my Vik," she said. "Of course you are. I've done things, you know, things to keep the apartment safe. They can't come in here. Even if they look like one of us."

She suddenly smiled again, and seemed completely normal.

"I almost forgot," she said. "I have something else for you."

She went into one of the cupboards and brought out a long, tall bag, the kind vodka came in, and set it on the table.

"It's really from Dedulya," she said. "He was working on it when – well, open it."

Vik took the bag, and felt something heavy in it. She reached in and lifted it out.

"Cherno Alpha," she gasped.

It was carved from wood, and some of the details weren't finished, but it was clearly the Jaeger her parents rode in, with its huge cylinder of a head and massive arms.

"*Mater bozhya*," she breathed.

"Don't swear, girl," her grandmother said.

"Sorry," she said. "I love it."

"True love goes beyond the grave," Babulya said. "Always remember that."

"Yes, Babulya."

They put the lights out early and went to bed. Vik kept the carving with her. She thought about Grandmother at dinner, and worried. Grandfather had always been there when Babulya was at her worst: when she started screaming for no reason, when she threw the pots and pans around – and he had also been there to reassure her when Grandmother took to her bed for days.

Now he was gone. Had he known he was going to die? Had he carved her Cherno Alpha to protect her after he was dead?

She finally drifted off to sleep, but a commotion woke her. At first she was afraid it was Grandmother, but although she was awake, too, the noise was coming from outside – sirens were wailing. She looked at the clock and saw it was a little after three o'clock. Christmas morning.

"They're here," Grandmother said. "They've come."

By the time they went outside of their apartment, everyone in the building was awake. They went down the hall to the little common room, with its vid screen; it was packed.

"That's in Hong Kong," Mr. Azhakov grumbled. "Why sound the alarms here?" He was an older man, and seemed like a tall tree the wind had spent years bending.

"Because there are two of them!" Ms. Hong shot back. "That's never happened before. If there are two, there might be a dozen. They could be everywhere."

The Kaiju were named Otachi and Leatherback. It was nighttime in Hong Kong, just like it was here, and the K-Eye images were blurred and hard to follow. Otachi looked something like a horned frog, with a bulging phosphorescent blue throat sac. Leatherback wasn't anywhere to be seen.

Two Jaegers were on the scene, and everyone cheered when they saw one of them was Cherno Alpha. She also recognized Crimson Typhoon, a Chinese Jaeger with three arms, piloted by identical triplets: the Wei brothers.

Once there had been Shatterdomes everywhere, with Jaegers guarding their home territory. But the Vladivostok Shatterdome had been closed when she was three, and Cherno Alpha moved to Hong Kong. Other closures had followed, and now Hong Kong was the only Shatterdome in the world.

And two Kaiju were attacking Hong Kong.

They were after the Jaegers, after Cherno Alpha.

She thought it herself, but she heard plenty of people saying it as well.

She watched in disbelief as Crimson Typhoon was torn apart, only minutes into the fight. But then Cherno Alpha was there, and she knew things would go differently.

Except they didn't. Otachi's throat sac suddenly

swelled huge, and it spit blue liquid all over Cherno. The image fluttered for a moment. Then the reporter said that another Jaeger, Striker Eureka, was on the way, and when the view cleared up, Vik saw it, running through the waves toward Cherno, which was still fighting, despite the fact that the blue stuff was burning through it. It was going to be okay.

And then something burst from the water, a thing like a giant gorilla with scales, and everything got really confusing. She thought she saw Cherno Alpha decapitated, torn in half, but she knew that couldn't be true. It was dark, so much was happening, it couldn't be what she saw.

Her parents couldn't be dead. It wasn't possible. Cherno Alpha never lost. They were supposed to come back for her one day…

Where there had been cheering before, now everything became very quiet, and Vik suddenly couldn't watch anymore. She went back to her bed. When she woke in the morning, it would all be sorted out. Everything would be fine. It was Christmas, after all.

Gipsy Danger won the fight, but the news the next day was that there were no survivors from Cherno Alpha or Crimson Typhoon.

Vik sleepwalked through the next few days. Grandmother went to work, like always. Vik went to the market. They heard from the school and were informed that there was no room for her until spring, but she hardly cared.

She wasn't alone. Everyone seemed to feel not that the world was coming to an end, but that it had already ended. That nothing mattered anymore.

That night, there were fires burning in the park she could see from her house. Kaiju worshippers, her grandmother said, praying for the end of the world. Vik had heard of Kaiju worshippers, but had never seen one, at least as far as she knew. This looked like a lot of people.

But she didn't care about that either.

That night Babulya got very drunk, and very angry. She shouted at things that weren't there. Vik took her carving of Cherno Alpha and a blanket down to the common room. She wasn't alone – several others were there, watching the video stream, although nothing was really happening. A few more were curled up with blankets on the floor. She did the same.

Grandfather was gone. Cherno Alpha was gone. All of her protectors were gone.

She woke to a babble of voices, and at first didn't know where she was. Then she remembered. The room was full now, and everyone was cheering.

She came groggily to her feet.

With all the commotion, it took her a while to understand what was happening.

The Jaegers had won. Somehow the two remaining Jaegers – Gipsy Danger and Striker Eureka – had sealed the breach in the ocean the monsters swam up from. The world was saved, although both Jaegers were destroyed.

Vik almost didn't care, partly because she didn't believe it. Whatever had happened, the Kaiju would be back. They would always be back. And there were no Jaegers left to stop them.

But there would be. They would build more. And when they did, she was going to be in one, just like she'd told Eun.

But that meant she had to train, and she had to learn. And that meant money.

All of her protectors were dead. Fine. She would be her own protector.

The next day, she found the van where Eun lived and knocked on the door. A different girl answered, but when she asked for her, Eun came out.

"I'm ready to work now," she said.

Because Jaegers fought, and they either won or lost, they lived or died. They didn't feel fear, or pain, or loss, or shame. They did what they needed to win, whether that meant beating a Kaiju to death with an iceberg or digging around in the guts of one.

She would do what she needed to do.

Vik had seen dead things before, and she had seen the things that ate dead things. Ravens, maggots, feral dogs.

But nothing had been eating the Kaiju. No carrion birds circled above, no worms were in evidence – only people in funny yellow suits that covered even their heads, although she could see their faces through clear plastic plates. There was a terrible smell, but it was not like rotting meat. More like chemical sewage with a sort of fishy odor thrown in. The Kaiju was so big, she wasn't sure whether she was looking at its belly or its back, and the hundreds of holes that had been hacked through its blue-black scales didn't help at all. She thought it was probably best to try not to think about what it was; just to pretend she was going into a cave to collect stones.

Eun found her one of the yellow suits. Before she could put in on, Andrei arrived.

"Most of the good stuff was harvested right away," Andrei explained. "The living tissue, the liquid blood. The stuff that really pays. Some guys came from Hong Kong to do that, with all kinds of fancy gear. Pumped it full of carbon dioxide, and all of that. When they were done, they sold me the contract for what was left. I'm telling you this, kid, because these guys from Hong Kong – they aren't to be screwed around with, ever. I work for them, so I am also not to be screwed with. Whatever comes out of there, it comes to me. It doesn't go in your pockets. It comes from your bag, to my hands. Work hard, don't steal, follow the rules, and you'll be okay. Do you understand?"

"I understand," Vik said.

"Great. Come on, I'll introduce you to your crew."


The central cavity of the corpse had been hollowed out, forming a cavern large enough to hold a village. Light came through the various holes cut through the outer hide, but strings of LEDs provided most of the illumination when they got deeper in.

Her "crew" consisted of Aleks, a boy of about fifteen, a girl her own age named Kora, and Ji Su, who was maybe ten. Ji Su had a long scar on her face. Vik couldn't help looking at it.

Ji Su noticed.

"Kaiju blood," she said. "Hong Kong got most of it before it spoiled, but what was left dried out. It forms crystals – it's one of the things we look for. But if water hits it, it can get gloopy. Some idiot thought it would be a good idea to drill a hole in from the top of Vodyanoi. That was in midwinter. It snowed. In the spring all that snow thawed out and worked its way down. A big glob of it dripped on me."

"I'm sorry," Vik said. "It burned through your mask?"

"I wasn't wearing it," Ji Su said. "Sometimes we have to get up in some spaces so small, masks get in the way."

"What kinds of places?"

"Don't worry. You'll see."

Soon after that they left the gutted central cavity and began climbing through what turned out to be an empty blood vessel. It was big enough that they could walk in it without stooping, but smaller vessels branched off at regular intervals.

"Most of these have been pretty well cleaned out," Aleks said. "We have to go further in every time."

He wasn't kidding. She wasn't sure how much time had passed. The only light now came from the lamps on their masks, and the air felt heavy, like syrup sucking in and out of her lungs. The suits had filters, but no independent air supply.

At last they reached a place where the wall of the blood vessel had been cut away, revealing a network of what looked something like honeycomb, or the inside of a sponge.

"These are the marrow nacelles," Aleks said. "They're connected by little tubes, most of them. The ones you see have been hollowed out; you'll have to crawl back in there to find any marrow."

Vik didn't like that idea much at all. But she was a Jaeger, wasn't she?

"What does the marrow look like?"

"Blue-grey. Fills the nacelles completely. The bone is really, really hard. We take those out with explosives, but that messes up the marrow. So we get that out first. It's softer than the bone, but you'll still have to use your multi-tool. Got it?"

"Yeah," Vik said. "At least I think so."

"I don't like *novichoks*," Aleks said. "They're slow, and they whine a lot, and they never make quota. We need to make quota. You got that?"

"Got it," Vik said.

And with no further comment, she climbed up into the nearest nacelle.

The connecting tubes were tight, all right, and she had to crawl though about ten of them until she came upon one still filled with marrow. Fighting a growing claustrophobia, she began hacking at the stuff with the tool. It might be softer than the bone, but it was still hard, and after half an hour she'd only managed to dig a hole a little bigger than her head. Digging in the confined space was awkward at first, but soon became painful, and by the time she heard the faint sound of Aleks calling a halt, her whole body was sore.

She scrapped what marrow she had into her bag zipped it, and started back out. The nacelle she was working in wasn't big enough to turn around in, so she had to back out, blind, which was so claustrophobic it nearly put her into a panic, but she pushed it down to where she kept every other hellish thing in her life.

Aleks looked in her bag. To her surprise, he didn't seem angry.

"You'll have to do better," he said.

"Tomorrow?"

"Tomorrow?" he snorted. "It's only noon."

He and the other three started unpacking lunch from plastic boxes.

"I didn't know to bring food," she said.

"That's too bad," Aleks said. But after he'd eaten a little more than half of his rice, he handed her the lunchbox.

"Here," he said. "I need you strong. But bring a lunch tomorrow."

"Thank you," she said.

She ate in silence for a little while, realizing just how hungry she was. Then it hit her.

"We're having a picnic inside of a Kaiju," she said.

Kora laughed. "Yeah," she said. "That's what I thought the first time, too."


The first few weeks were the hardest, but by her second month in it became routine. Her body adjusted to the torturous positions; her mind found places to go. She saved her money, so when a position at the school opened she could afford to go, and worked when she could. As her nest egg grew, she thought about other kinds of training. Jaegers fought; she would need to learn to fight. Karate, boxing, maybe some kind of sword. Digging her way through the Kaiju corpse was horrible work, but she wasn't doing it for nothing, wasn't doing it just to survive, but to move on.

It was the least she could do for her parents, for their memory.

But as the pain and fear of the work faded, she began having the dream. It was almost always the same; a darkness, rising up to blot out the sky, a cloud with a face, and then she was alone, deep in the Dig. Someone was calling her name – not Vik, but her full name, Viktoriya. She was afraid; she remembered what her grandmother had told her about hiding her name from the Kaiju. Yet someone knew her name, someone she did not know. So she followed the voice, deeper and deeper, farther from the light, until she saw a faint, pulsing blue glow ahead. She could see it was coming from inside of the wall, within of the dried tissue of the Kaiju. She bent to look more closely.

Eyes opened, staring at her. A woman's face appeared.

And then, each time, she awoke shouting, tears pouring down her face.

# 21

JINHAI WAS NOT EXACTLY LOOKING FORWARD to Pons training, not after how the first one had gone. But he'd spent the night steeling himself for it between fitful moments of sleep, and by morning he had begun to see it as an opportunity. He felt in his bones that the unanswered questions about his Drift with Vik were important – he needed the answers to them, even if he couldn't quite say why.

But when they arrived and got their assignments, he was paired with Ryoichi, not Vik.

He knew that – given the circumstances – he should be relieved. Instead he found himself disappointed.

This time, when the tech started the Drift, he wasn't sure anything was happening at all; he glanced up at the meter and saw it was just barely over the red line.

"Concentrate," Burke said. "Both of you."

After a moment it started, but not like it had with Vik;

Ryoichi's memories were more controlled, less chaotic, but at the same time to Jinhai they seemed far more ephemeral. Ryoichi was a little boy, being bullied by some bigger kids because of a small speech impediment; he was ten, and his grandmother died, one he loved so deeply that he didn't speak a word for almost a month; gathering in the Kaiju refuge in Sapporo, watching as Tailspitter wreaked havoc; the smell of sake on his father when he came home drunk one night...

The needle on the dial dipped up and down, always at the lowest end of Drift strength, until at last, it stabilized at a minimal level.

"Now," he heard Burke say. "Just try to be. Let the memories flow past."

Jinhai took a deep breath, let it out slowly.

It was working. His memories mingled with Ryoichi's – not violently, although perhaps a little indifferently. The meter rose toward the middle, and stayed there.

He understood a lot about Ryoichi, now. But one thing stood out clearer than anything else.

The other boy didn't trust him. It was hard to blame him, especially after being in Ryoichi's head. He had problems with trust that ran far deeper than Jinhai's own. Add to that recent events, the consensus forming among all of the other cadets... Ryoichi looked at him apologetically when they unhooked.

"It's okay," Jinhai said. "I get it."


"They all think we're guilty," Vik told him, that afternoon, after mess. They were outside, on the dock, watching the billow of crimson clouds fade beyond the low mountains of the coast.

"Yeah," Jinhai said. "How was it inside of Renata's head?"

"Crazier than you would think," she replied. "Lots of drama. Daddy issues."

Jinhai laughed. "Ryoichi too, with the daddy issues anyway." He paused. "We're probably not supposed to be talking about this."

"You can be sure they're talking about us," Vik said. "They're also withholding things."

"What do you mean?"

"Your missing pen drive. You were right. They found it in the Conn-Pod. They figure it was used to upload the code that made Chronos Berserker go ballistic."

"That's dumb," Jinhai said. "That's a completely rookie mistake. I mean, we are rookies, I guess…"

"But it isn't a mistake *you* would make. Is it?"

"No," he said. "Leave an incriminating pen drive right after uploading a murder-virus? Hell no."

"Okay," she said. "I believe you."

"Believe what?"

"That you didn't do it."

"You mean you just now came to that conclusion?"

She shrugged. "I thought you might be leading me along, for some reason. I haven't had the best of luck with people. In my experience, most of them want to use you for something or other. Maybe you've been the one trying to lay the blame on me all along. Someone is trying to frame me."

"Frame *us*," Jinhai corrected.

"Don't go on and on about it," she said. "I just told you I believe you. That's not what's important right now. After we left the Conn-Pod, some techs went in right behind us, didn't they?"

"Yes."

"And none of them noticed anything wrong, or found a misplaced pen drive?"

"Apparently not. Of course, one of the techs could have put it there."

"Sure. But it would have had to be more than one of them – it would have to be all of them, or the others would have known. How many people do you think are in on it? One or two I can imagine – but the whole team?"

"Maybe one of them came back later."

"Anyone could have come back later," Vik said. "But they suspect us, cadets. Why? You lived in a Shatterdome, do you know?"

"I'm not sure," he said. "There is surveillance in the really sensitive areas. That can be messed with, of course, but not easily, and not without leaving a trace, unless you were really, really good. Way better than me."

"What we need to figure out," she said, "is not how they *didn't* do it, but how they did."

He had an idea then, and a kind of wild idea.

"You know," he said. "I think I might know where to look. It's a long shot. And it will probably get us in trouble."

"Yeah," she said. "What else is new? Let's go."

"No, it's not that easy. It could be a while before we get a chance."


They certainly didn't get a chance the next day; that was when they started training in the Mock-Pods.

"We've paired you up," Lambert said. "Each team will get a different scenario based on a fight that really happened in the past. You will be awarded or deducted points depending on what choices you make and how resourceful you are. If you lose your Jaeger – if you 'die' – big deduction. Civilian casualties count against you. I leave it up to you to figure out the rest. Now go to your pods."

* * *

Jinhai paused at the entrance to the Mock-Pod. It was shaped a lot like a Jaeger's head, with a large curved window in the front. But what caught his attention was inside.

"Well, that's interesting," he said.

"It's old school," Vik said. "A Pinocchio rig." She seemed almost excited.

"I know what it is," Jinhai said. "It's like the one my folks used, more or less. But why? Do they think we might actually ever fight in one of these?"

She shrugged. "They built Mark-5s for a few years after the Breach was closed. I think a few of them are still in service. So I guess it *could* happen."

"Yeah," he said. "Or maybe it's just a history lesson."

She frowned, but didn't say anything.

A couple of techs came in to help them clip the boots of their drivesuits into the mechanical actuators and otherwise get them situated.

*Whatever this is, it won't be real*, Jinhai told himself. *Whatever happened to Vu and Braga won't happen to us.*

And he believed that. The Mock-Pods were built for simulation. They didn't have the same intense feedback loops as real Jaegers. They were safe. Nobody had ever been killed in a simulator, and since the sabotage of Chronos Berserker, he knew every piece of equipment had been gone over ten times. But it was a worry he couldn't quite put out of his mind. All he could do was push it down and try to focus on the checklist as they prepared to drift.

"Engage neural handshake," someone said.

For an instant, nothing changed; and then everything did. He gasped involuntarily as memories that weren't his suddenly flooded through him, but this time they were more familiar, memories that almost seemed to belong in his head. The hard, dark, hidden place in Vik was still there, but it felt more relaxed, somehow. He wouldn't quite call it trust, but it was better than before.

And then he felt big. That hadn't happened in Drift training. He heard Vik bark out a little laugh, and he knew why; because with the impression of size came a feeling of power, of invincibility.

Around them, beyond the holo-controls and instruments, the world came alive; they were standing in a shallow sea, beneath a bright morning sky, gazing out toward a large city. Off to their left, giants were fighting.

One of them was instantly recognizable by its massive cylindrical "head".

"Cherno Alpha," Vik gasped. "It is Cherno."

It was indeed the Russian Jaeger, and it was in bad shape. Steam was boiling from a crack in her energy refinery, and one of her arms hung as if it didn't work anymore. She was still fighting, though, leaning into her Kaiju opponent, her good arm trying to get a lock around the monster's neck, not quite managing it.

"No!" Vik shouted.

"It's not real," Jinhai said. "Focus. What Jaeger are we in? What are our capabilities?"

He was trying to stay calm, but despite his words, it *felt* real, and it was all happening too fast. Shouldn't they have at least been briefed on what Jaeger they were piloting?

And Vik already had them in motion, slogging through the water toward the fight.

*Crap*. He desperately ran his eyes over the unfamiliar controls.

"The Kaiju is Reckoner," Vik said. "I think the city must be Hong Kong."

For an instant, he looked out at the city skyline.

"Yeah," he said. "It is. We're just southeast of the Island. That's Cape D'Aguilar over there."

Reckoner was a crouching heap of ugly. At first glance it resembled a bat on all fours, with long, webbed forelimbs that rose and bent above its bunched shoulders and shorter, thicker reptilian hind legs set just behind.

There was nothing bat-like about its head though, which was a horrifying mish-mash of crawfish, gar, and crocodile. Two grasping claws grew from its mandibles.

He tried not to look, to keep his eyes on the instruments. He used his hand to visually scroll through their weapons systems.

"We have Cryo-Cannons mounted on our shoulders," he realized. "I think we're Horizon Brave!" A Chinese Jaeger. He'd met the pilots before they died – was this the fight they got killed in? No, no, that was Bangkok, not Hong Kong. But this was a simulation. They could be destroyed, which Lambert said would result in massive deductions from their point total.

Probably best to avoid that.

They hadn't reached the fight before the damaged Cherno Alpha dropped to one knee. Reckoner spun with amazing speed and slammed the Russian Jaeger with its thick tailfin. Cherno toppled, and the Kaiju pushed past it and sprinted for the city, trailing sea-spray.

"Good you're here," a woman's voice said. "We held it at the Miracle Mile as long as we could…"

Jinhai felt a little chill. The voice was that of Sasha Kaidanovsky, now ten years dead, drowned in the waters off Hong Kong.

"We've got it now, Cherno," he said. He felt slightly ridiculous, talking to a simulation, but he was getting into it.

Vik, on the other hand, seemed to be struggling a little; he felt her anger, and sadness and something he didn't quite understand. She rattled off a few sentences in Russian, which he was pretty sure contained at least a few obscenities.

"Vik," he said. "Snap out of it and let's go kill a Kaiju."

"Yeah," she said. "Let's do that."

Horizon Brave was a Mark-1 Jaeger, the same as Cherno Alpha, powered by a nuclear reactor and not nearly as versatile as later models. But whereas Alpha had been designed to be an immovable object, Horizon Brave had been built to optimize maneuverability. They pushed the Jaeger to full speed and began gaining on the monster, but even from here it was clear that it would reach the city before they caught up.

"Use the Cryo-Cannons," Vik urged.

"I don't think we're close enough," he said, "but it's worth a try."

He sighted in on Reckoner as the cannons powered up. Then he cut loose.

Two jets of super-cooled liquid blasted out ahead of them, and for a moment, Jinhai felt jubilant. But as he'd feared, they were out of range.

Worse, their energy level plummeted, and Horizon Brave dropped from a fast run to a moderate jog.

Vik muttered again in Russian. "Stupid," she said. At first he thought she meant him, and was about to remind her that it had been her suggestion, but then he realized it was self-recrimination.

Their power came back up after a few minutes, but by that time Reckoner had made landfall on Shek O Beach and had already begun plowing a trail north, through the beachside condominiums and hotels. Fortunately, the eastern half of the Southern District was lightly populated compared to where it was headed. They needed to stop it before it got much further. If they could turn it uphill, onto the high, rocky ridge known as the Dragon's Back, they might be able to keep casualties pretty low.

Reckoner seemed oblivious to their approach, and he thought they might actually catch the Kaiju unawares, but the thing had eyes scattered all over its head, and some of them apparently looked backward, because as they drew near it slammed them with its tail, cutting through a twenty-story condo in the process. Brave tried to side-step, but they still caught most of the force of the blow, and their hydraulics whined as they fought to stay on their feet. They punched the monster in the back, but that was nothing but a mass of muscle, and he wasn't sure the Kaiju even felt anything. They reached for its head, but it suddenly sprang up half their height, stretching its not-quite wings high before hammering down onto their shoulders. One of their Cryo-Cannons exploded, sending a spray of subzero fluid all over the beast. It trilled out an awful, alien scream as ice formed over half its body.

"Jettison the cannon," Vik shouted. He did, but they had already lost a lot of their cryogenic solution. Meanwhile, they punched Reckoner in the face, hard, and then brought a double-fisted blow down on its iced right limb, hoping to shatter it.

The ice broke and fell off in huge flakes, but Reckoner seemed undeterred, and with another spinning blow of its tail, sent them backwards off of their feet to destroy several buildings.

"How do we kill it?" Vik asked, as they pushed up from the rubble. "How did Horizon Brave kill it?"

"Electricity," Jinhai said. "Remember? The 'Blackout Knockout'? They threw it into the Fong power plant."

"Where is that?" Vik asked. "You lived here, right?"

"Yes. It's where the Bone Slums are now. North and West of here."

"Let's get it there, then."

"But this is before the fight. That's the Kowloon district. Lots and lots of people. Unless we can keep it in the water, or drive it though the hills, so it doesn't have waterfront to chew up the whole way."

"We've got to try something," she said. "And it seems to be headed that way anyway."

"Yeah. It's worth a try."

So now they had a goal; each engagement was intended to drive the Kaiju toward the power plant.

Reckoner didn't want to play along. No matter what they did, they couldn't get it to climb up into the highlands. But when they reached the juncture between the Junk and Kowloon Bays, where everything opened up, they were able to force it West, toward Kowloon.

It wasn't easy, and it seemed to take forever, but the Kaiju wasn't all that bright; it didn't seem to know it was being herded, nor had it picked up on the fact that Horizon Brave wasn't really able to inflict any damage on it. They punched, wrestled and even threw the beast a few times. Jinhai surrendered to Vik's instincts in close-quarters fighting. They slammed it in the side of the head with their Sub-Zero sucker punch, but as when their cannon exploded, the cold didn't seem to bother the thing.

But they were doing a good job of staying in one piece, too. The only thing he was worried about was how long he and Vik could keep their connection; they had never been tested beyond a few minutes, and it had been two hours now. If they lost their handshake, the whole thing was over.

"There it is," Vik said, as they fought the monster to the top of the hill.

They were squarely in the Kowloon District now, the old part of Hong Kong that lay on the mainland, and the trail of damage they'd left behind them was horrific. But they had reached their goal. The Fong power plant lay below them.

The plant had been built as part of China's coastal defense, powering not only most of the city but also providing back-up power to the Shatterdome, if necessary. The reactor was deep in the rock of the hill, but the site was surrounded by a vast field of transformers and high-tension lines, circumscribed by reinforced concrete walls eighty feet high to protect it from storm surges.

"Come on," Jinhai said.

They took five explosive strides forward, ducked down, and crashed into the Kaiju, pushing their arms beneath and lifting its forelimbs off of the ground. Its hideous face was almost all they could see; its mandibular claws struck furiously at their head, but they were too small to have much effect. They heaved, and sent the monster flipping toward the power plant.

It landed on its back and skidded, but stopped when it hit the wall. As both of them shouted, Horizon Brave charged down the hill and landed a haymaker that lifted the Kaiju up and sent it over the barrier and thrashing into the transformers. Sparks engulfed it, and again it bleated out its harrowing call – but this time it was a death scream. It blackened and split; blue blood spurted, and dark smoke rose. It struggled to rise, leveling the retaining wall, and dragging itself into the city beyond, not understanding that it was already dead.

For a moment, they stood there, watching its last feeble movements.

"Well," Vik said, after a moment. "That was satisfying."

He nodded, as he felt their connection begin to dissolve. The drill was over: they'd won.

\* \* \*

"How was that?" Jinhai asked Lambert as they stepped out of the simulator. He felt drained and weak, ready for a shower and a meal and his bunk, in that order, but he felt good.

"You failed," Lambert said.

"What?"

"How can that be?" Vik exploded. "Ranger, we killed it."

"That you did," Lambert said. "Go outside and run twenty laps around the deployment platform. I'm docking you each two rec chits. Tomorrow you can tell me what you did wrong. If I like your answer, you get to try again. Now, go."

"Yes, Ranger," they said in unison and then started toward the Ocean Doors. Jinhai had serious doubts as to whether he could do one lap, much less twenty.

# 2 2

WHEN HE FINALLY MADE IT TO HIS BUNK, JINHAI was about three steps away from crawling. It was early, and he was alone in the barracks – the rest were doubtless out cashing in the rec chits he didn't have. Of course, Vik had been shorted, too, and he wondered briefly where she was before closing his eyes.

He was nearly asleep when someone nudged him.

Vik.

"Hey," she said. "What are you doing?"

"Is this a trick question?" Jinhai murmured. "Go away."

"We have to figure this out," Vik said. "If we don't, we're screwed."

"I'm too sleepy," he said.

"I brought coffee," she told him.

"So thoughtful," he replied.

He wasn't fond of coffee, but with a fair amount of sugar it was bearable. And it did wake him up, a little. He watched Vik, sitting cross-legged on Tahima's bunk, right next to his, working at her pad.

"So I went back and got our sim data," she said. "We maintained Drift for more than two hours. The real fight took more like three – we finished faster."

"Sure," Jinhai said. "Because we had the cheat sheet. The original pilots probably didn't really plan what they were doing the whole time. More likely they spotted the plant after they'd been fighting for a while and got inspired. We just copied what they did. Obviously, that wasn't the right answer for Lambert. What was our casualty count?"

"Right around seven thousand killed, four times that many injured," she said.

"And in the original attack?"

"About the same," she said. "At least initially."

"What do you mean by that?"

"A lot of the injured died in the next week."

"I'll bet some of that was from lack of power, right? They had to do everything on generators at the hospitals."

"Yes," she said. "So obvious."

"What?"

"Lambert probably knew we would recognize the scenario. I mean, you lived in Hong Kong, you knew where the power plant was and what happened. Clearly, we weren't meant to repeat the old fight. We were meant to do better. Fewer casualties. No damage to the power plant."

"How?" he said. "Nothing else we did made a dent in that thing."

She took a sip of her coffee.

"Well," she said. "We've got all night to figure it out."

He suppressed a groan and nodded.

Lambert listened to their explanation about what went wrong in their drill with a face so neutral that at first Jinhai thought they must have blundered again. When they finished, he continued to stare at them for a few moments.

"Okay," he said. "You can saddle back up. Try not to disappoint me this time."

"Yes, Ranger," he said, relief flowing through him like a cool stream.

Once more they were Horizon Brave, standing in the waters of the South China Sea, facing Hong Kong, watching Reckoner beat down the worn-out Cherno Alpha. Jinhai had looked up the fight the night before; what they were seeing here was the tail end of a magnificent effort by the Russian team. Fighting alone, Cherno Alpha had managed to keep the Kaiju at sea for nearly six hours, first by slugging it out and finally, as some of her systems began to fail, by grappling with the beast and anchoring herself to the sea floor with spikes deployed from her legs, enduring the constant punishment for more than an hour before the Kaiju finally damaged one of her arms and broke her grip. Historically, that was when Horizon Brave had arrived, and that was how the simulation was set up.

This time there was no hesitation; they started their run at Reckoner immediately, opening with a volley of shells from their chest-mounted guns. Jinhai knew from experience that wouldn't do anything but distract the beast, but that was all they wanted. The Kaiju turned from the disabled Jaeger and charged at them, dealing Cherno a blow from its tail in what seemed to be either an accident or an afterthought. Jinhai saw the Jaeger stagger as it came unpinned from the continental crust, and despaired. Then he couldn't see the Russian machine; Reckoner's incoming bulk blocked the view.

"Now!" Vik shouted.

They fired both Cryo-Cannons – not at Reckoner, but at the sea it moved through.

The water instantly seized up in sea ice several meters thick, trapping Reckoner. They continued to fire the cannons until they had discharged most of their cryogenic solution.

It worked, but not for long: Reckoner flexed its immense muscles and pulled first one, then the other forelimb from the ice, writhing back and forth, causing it to begin cracking. Brave charged in, fists swinging, knocking it back, getting up under the thing's belly, wrapping her arms around it and locking them in place.

"Cherno Alpha," Vik said. "If you can hear me, bring the lightning."

"We're starting to lose hydraulic pressure in our left arm," Jinhai said. "I'm switching to auxiliary pressure. It might buy us a minute or two."

The ice was almost all shattered by then, and Reckoner was bucking like a bull.

"We might have to rethink this," Jinhai said. "We have to let go, back off, stay between it and the city…"

"If it gets past Cherno, we have no hope of stopping landfall," Vik said. "We're not built for it. They will come. I know it."

"It's just a simulation," Jinhai said. "What if Cherno is just a prop? What if it doesn't have any AI guiding it?"

Several red lights were flashing now, and the schematic display of their Jaeger showed systems on the verge of failure. They were losing pressure in both arms, and there were no more back-up drivers to compensate.

"I think we're about to learn what it's like to die in a simulation," Jinhai said.

But then Reckoner's struggles became more spasmatic, and they were thrown clear; sky and undersea alternated as they rolled through the shallow water.

"We're not dead yet," Jinhai said, reading the instruments. "Get up, we can still win this."

When they managed to get to their feet, however, it was to behold a wonderful sight. Cherno had limped up behind the monster while they held it and grabbed it with its huge Tesla fists, jolting it with all of the electric a small nuclear reactor could produce. Smoke was pouring out of the Kaiju's eyes and mouth as it slowly sank into the bay.

"Lightning brought, Horizon Brave," the resurrected voice of Sasha Kaidanovsky said.

This time, when they came out of the simulator, Lambert gave them a nod of approval. It was the best feeling Jinhai had experienced in a while.

The director of K-Watch was Rajen Lokman, a round-faced, rather humorless fellow who took his job very seriously. Gottlieb approved of him – usually. But today he was being a bit obstructionist.

"I have already tasked two hundred man-hours to this matter," Lokman said. "I've diverted three Amberjack Mark-2's from their accustomed duties. I have redirected several of our instrument arrays. At this time, I see no point in adding more of our equipment and expertise to research this... supposition."

"I'm telling you," Gottlieb said, "if I'm right about this – and I think you will recall I am very often right – then we may be about to experience the greatest Anteverse event since the triple event ten years ago. An event I predicted, I might add."

"Dr. Gottlieb, I am well aware of your expertise. Your proofs were required reading at university..."

"Then you will also have read the earlier equations worked out by Dr. Ysabel Morales," he snapped. "And that is exactly who brought me the base data for my 'supposition'. So if you would kindly do your job—"

"I'm doing my job, Dr. Gottlieb," Lokman said. "Here, let me show you something."

He walked over to a console and waved his hand. A holographic projection of the Pacific Rim appeared.

"These are the readings from today. Here, along the Kuril Trench, there, near the Philippine Trench – that's from the Amberjack submarine I sent down at your request."

Gottlieb frowned and bent nearer. "What's this?" he asked. It was a tiny blue dot highlighted on the map, just at the edge of the Philippine Trench.

"That? It's incidental."

"It has an Anteverse radiation signature."

"We figure it's some bit of junk from one of the nearby battles. A Kaiju bone or something. It's tiny."

"It doesn't have a fixed position," Gottlieb said. "As if something is blurring the signal. Don't you find that odd?"

"Whatever it is, it's incidental," Lokman said. "None of your data – pardon me, Dr. Morales' data – involved the Philippine Trench."

"No," Gottlieb said. "You're right. I want to see if the pattern is in keeping with the other points of information."

"My point is," Lokman said, "the geo-energetics aren't as predicted by your model. The same as everywhere else we've looked."

Gottlieb studied the map, trying to see how the patterns fell together, what would make it all make sense.

"It's really quite impossible," he said.

But he'd thought it impossible that he and Newt could have drifted with a Kaiju, much less learned anything from them.

In his field, "impossible" was a suspect concept, and very often the harbinger of very bad things.

* * *

"What do you think they'll throw at us this time?" Jinhai asked, as he and Vik did a final check of their drivesuits. "I heard Renata and Suresh got Taurax last time."

Vik nodded. "No one else got the Reckoner scenario," she said. "But so far as I know, everyone has been handed a fight that really happened. Of course, not everyone is talking to me."

"Join the club," Jinhai said. "Amazing how shabbily people treat you when they think you might have murdered a couple of people."

"Yeah," she said. "Funny that."

He'd thought to lighten the mood, but it seemed his comment had the opposite effect as Vik fell silent.

"Anyway," he said, "I've been brushing up on my Kaiju fights."

"Didn't do us much good last time," she said.

"Maybe. But maybe we'll know what *not* to do."


As they prepared to drift, Jinhai realized that Vik might have a point; it was probably best to try to go into the next simulation with no expectations, to judge the situation as they found it, the way they would have to if they met a real, unknown Kaiju. As the neural handshake began, he tried to clear his mind, to be ready to accept whatever they were faced with.

A good thing, too because when the lights came up, he didn't have the slightest idea where they were.

There was no water, for one thing, not in any direction. Instead they were in a valley surrounded by mountains. And in the middle of a city, much of which was already in ruins. The city too was unfamiliar – he could see modern-looking skyscrapers, but the part they were in was mostly one- and two-story buildings, white, with rusty brown tile roofs. He didn't hear or see any Jumphawks, so they hadn't just been deployed – they must have walked here; they were in the middle of a fight.

And they were also damaged, although not badly. Their power cell was down to about half capacity.

"We're in Striker Eureka," Vik said. "Look, the fight's over there."

He saw it, maybe half a mile away. It was daytime, but there was a lot of dust and smoke, so all he could make out were two very large creatures, grappling.

"Yeah," Jinhai said. "Looks like we were in it, and maybe got knocked down. This simulation is starting after Striker got back up."

"Let's go," Vik said.

"Watch out for civilians," Jinhai said,

He needn't have worried too much. A clear path of leveled buildings led from where they had "appeared" toward the ongoing battle.

"Power levels are dropping, LOCCENT," a voice crackled in their ears. "We're right near empty."

"I hear you, Specter," Control shot back. "Just hang in there. Striker Eureka is back up and on the way."

"Vulcan Specter," Vik said.

Specter was a Mark-3, and like Striker Eureka, Australian built.

"We're coming, Specter," Jinhai yelled.

"Aw, no," one of Specter's pilots said. A heads up on the holo display identified him as Joshua Griffin. "Please, take your time. We're having a great time here."

They could see the Kaiju now as well.

The monsters from the Breach were never pretty, but some of them had a sort of majesty, looked at the right way.

This thing was just nasty. The massive, bony skull was what they saw first, long-jawed with ragged teeth and three pairs of slitted eyes; it looked sort of like the head of a hairless opossum, albeit with a jumble of spines jutting from its skullcap and running down its back and tail. The head rode on a sinuous neck; the body was balanced on a pair of long, scaly, birdlike legs, so in silhouette it was a little like an emu or cassowary, although the two sets of upper limbs diluted that impression. Each of these ended in hands with extraordinarily elongated, bony-looking digits, which were currently clutched around Vulcan Specter, wrenching at its Conn-Pod. It wasn't looking good for the other Jaeger, and they were still a hard jog away. It almost seemed like a replay of the situation with Cherno Alpha.

"We have missiles," Vik said. "Let's use them."

"We'll hit Specter," Jinhai pointed out.

"No, they're built to tunnel into and explode inside the Kaiju"

"Okay."

An instant later, a pair of missiles jetted out of the launchers on their chest; one struck the Kaiju just above one of its walking legs and the other a little higher in its chest. The detonations came a few heartbeats later, and they were rewarded by the sight of blue Kaiju blood spraying freely from both wounds. It hesitated, craning its head around to see what had injured it.

Vulcan Specter didn't let the pause go to waste. One of its fists came down on the Kaiju with a horrible crunching sound that seemed to fill the valley. The Kaiju's head dropped under the blow, and Specter instantly raised its other hand, from which protruded what looked like a narrow, blurry cone.

"Have my Atomic Drill for breakfast, mate," Griffin yelled.

Then the cone went straight into the top of the Kaiju's skull with very messy results.

The monster collapsed without so much as a whimper.

"Well," Jinhai said, after a moment. "That wasn't so hard."

"Yeah," Vik agreed. "That was easy. Too easy."

They eased up on the scene. Vulcan Specter hadn't moved since the kill.

"Specter?" Jinhai asked.

"No worries," the pilot said. "That was the last of our juice, but the job is done. Thanks for the assist."

"Glad to help," Jinhai said.

"What's that?" Vik asked.

Jinhai saw it, too. Vermin's dead body was slowly slumping down; blood had ceased pumping from its wounds. But the Kaiju's skin seemed to be – moving, like it had a life of its own.

"Specter, can you see?"

"Hell!" Specter's pilot yelped. "Yeah, we see, Striker. There's littler ones coming out through its hide. God, there's hundreds of them."

"Magnify," Jinhai said. Their view zoomed in on the beast. All over, things were wriggling from its skin, leaving empty holes behind.

"I knew it was too easy," Vik said.

"Some kind of parasites?" he said. "Babies?"

"Parasites," Vik said. "This must be Colombia. Medellin. They swarmed all over the city, killing and contaminating everything in their path."

"How did Striker Eureka stop them?"

"I don't remember," she said. "I was never all that interested in that fight. Step on them, maybe?"

By the time they reached Specter and the dead Kaiju, the "littler" monsters were everywhere, spreading out in a rough circle into the city.

Kaiju had parasites – that was well known. The most

common were skin mites, which were about the size of a small dog; Burke had showed them a preserved one early in the trimester. Whatever these things were, they were not skin mites. They were bigger, for one thing, about a meter long, shaped like fat, smooth snakes, and moving something like serpents as well, but instead of merely slithering, they also coiled and sprang into the air, over walls, onto rooftops. Their heads were grenade-shaped, and when Striker snatched one up to examine it, they saw that instead of a mouth, it had a trilobed beak covered in hundreds if not thousands of tiny serrated teeth set in a tight spiral pattern. The head didn't spin all the way around like the drill bit it resembled, but it could twist its head back and forth with great speed. A collar of four clawed limbs probably pulled it forward as it burrowed into its host.

Stepping on them killed them; they exploded like engorged ticks, spraying Kaiju blood everywhere. They couldn't use their missiles, because the parasites were now all over the town. Vik finally came up with the idea of overcharging their Sting-Blades. These were weapons set in Striker's hands, like knives, but which could be heated to incredible temperatures by carbon nano-tubes. When overheated, they could be used to mortally burn bunches of the things; they didn't have to actually touch them – coming close was good enough. Even so, it was tedious work, finding the things, all too often after they had already burrowed into some hapless dog or in a few cases, human stragglers. Obviously Medellin had had time to evacuate – the coast was miles away – but there were always holdouts and left-behinds.

LOCCENT clocked in with their analysis as they chased one of the things down a street, trying – without complete success – not to destroy any more buildings. Jaegers were built to fight behemoths, not to chase fleas. It seemed to Jinhai they might end up doing as much damage as the Kaiju.

"We've got good news and bad news," LOCCENT reported. "The good news is that these parasites are blind – they don't have eyes. The bad news is that we think they have a heightened sense of smell, or something. Satellite feed shows a whole bunch of them converging on a Kaiju shelter."

"That's actually good news," Vik said. "I saw a gas tanker a few blocks back."

"What – oh," Jinhai said. "We have to be quick, though. If those things can burrow through Kaiju skin, concrete isn't going to keep them out."

They picked up the gas tanker and traced the path LOCCENT painted for them through the hilly, winding streets until they reached the location of the underground shelter. The parasites were collected there in a swarming, hopping mass. They tore the  tank open, splashed the whole area liberally with gasoline, and set it ablaze with their Sting-Blades.

As it turned out, the little monsters could scream.

That wasn't the end of it – there were plenty more. But with satellite support they were making pretty good headway.

But after an hour or so, the simulation just – stopped.

"I wonder what we did wrong?" Vik sighed.

But this time, Burke had an approving look.

"That was good," he said. "I shut you down because otherwise you would have been at it for the rest of the day. Five chits for each of you. Take a break."

# 23

WHEN HE WAS ALONE, SOMETIMES JINHAI TURNED the music up approximately to the volume of thunder. Their house was in the dead center of twenty hectares of nowhere, so there were no neighbors to complain. The housekeepers were out, and Dustin didn't seem to care, and sometimes made suggestions. It could be anything: Robert Johnson, The Clash, the Brain Geysers, Quell, Madonna – except when he wanted to dance.

When he wanted to dance, it was Stravinsky, and he vanished into it; melody, rhythm, his blood, his muscle, his brain all one. It didn't always perfectly line up, but when it did, it was amazing. And sometimes, after, he wondered if it was anything like – if it even approached – what his mother and father seemed to have every minute of every day.

Maybe one day, he would know, if he was lucky. If things went right.

He let the thunder die away and got some water.

"Stravinsky again?"

He turned and found Dustin sitting in the corner of the kitchen, reviewing something on a pad.

"Dude's music started a riot back in its day," Jinhai said.

"That's a recommendation?" Dustin asked, mildly.

"Yeah. Because he makes you *feel* something. And not always something sweet, or fun, or pleasant. Some people didn't like that about his music. Some people said it wasn't music at all."

"Well, people said that about rock and roll, too," Dustin said. "And rap. And jazz, I think."

"There have always been stupid people," Jinhai said.

Dustin nodded. "Granted. How was school today?"

"It sucked," Jinhai said. "But I got through it. How would you like to take me shooting?"

Dustin blinked.

"Shooting? You mean like with guns? I thought you hated guns."

"Only on principle," Jinhai said. "But what are principles? Limitations pretending to be virtuous. Come on, I need to learn how to shoot."

Shooting was more fun than he imagined it would be, although there were a lot of rules. Dustin was very firm about rules.

Cleaning the guns was less fun – but that was one of Dustin's rules.

"A gun is equipment," he said. "Like all equipment, it requires maintenance."

"I guess so," Jinhai said. "Of course, if I'm a Jaeger pilot, there will be other people to take care of the equipment."

"I don't know," Dustin said. "I wouldn't trust my life to something I didn't understand. If my gun jams, I might not have the luxury of taking it to a repair shop. If you're out in the ocean, and your Jaeger pops a gasket, and the

Kaiju is right in front of you, wouldn't you like to have some idea how to fix the problem?"

"Yeah," Jinhai said. "Right. Like there's ever gonna be another Kaiju attack."

Dustin stopped cleaning his gun and set it carefully on the table, pointing away from either of them.

"You're a yo-yo," he said. "You know what a yo-yo is?"

"The cellist? I love that guy. He's like, eighty-something and he's still a complete wizard."

"No, not – it was a kind of toy – never mind. My point is this – a month ago you, so far as I can tell, you were doing everything you could *not* to get into the Ranger training program. Now you're all gung-ho about it – but you don't think you'll ever see any real action. What gives?"

"I'm complicated," Jinhai said.


The doorbell rang so seldom that Jinhai wasn't sure what it was, at first. He looked up from the calculus problem he was working on and asked the door to show him who was there.

To his surprise, what it showed him was a girl. An attractive girl, wearing a knee-length black-and-white checked skirt, a yellow pullover and stockings of the same color.

She looked familiar, but it took him a few beats to recognize her without her fencing outfit.

"Hey!" he yelped. He was starting for the door when he saw that Dustin was way ahead of him.

"No, no, no, no, no, no, no, no…" he muttered under his breath as he ran down the stairs.

Dustin was just closing the door when Jinhai got there.

"Where is she? Where did she go?"

"J…"

He yanked the door open and saw she was about ten meters away.

"Hey!" he called.

She turned around.

"Your babysitter said you weren't home," she said.

"This is not cool," Jinhai hissed to Dustin.

"And this is a bad idea," Dustin whispered back. "Very bad."

"What did you want?" Jinhai asked the girl.

"I just – I thought I would see how you were," she said.

"Would you ah, like to come in?"

"I don't know – is your spook going to shoot me?"

"No. He only shoots people on even-numbered days. Odd-numbered days he uses his garrote."

She crossed her arms. "You know what," she said, "you seem to be okay. So I'll consider my mission accomplished."

"No, wait – please come in. I'd like to talk to you."

She hesitated. "It was kind of a long walk," she said. "I could use a glass of water, I guess."

"Just FYI," Dustin said, his voice dropping to the faintest of whispers as she approached. "It wasn't a long walk. A car dropped her off just up the road."

"Go clean some guns or something," Jinhai said.

To his embarrassment, Dustin searched her for weapons, even though most anything dangerous would be detected before anyone was even close to the house.

Her name was Xia, and she took a glass of water from him.

"So this is where the famed Ming-hau and Suyin live," she said. "Impressive."

"Well, sometimes," he said. "Not that often these days. Very busy people, you know. Heroes and all that."

"Is that why you left your nice house to get your ass kicked?" she said. "Bored?"

"Something like that," he said. "Do you want to see what you did?"

"You're just looking for an excuse to take your shirt off," she said. "Impress me with your manly muscles."

"Wow," Jinhai said. "You see right through me."

"Right. On account of the holes I made."

"Ouch."

Her smile faded a little. "Seriously though – I hope you're all right. I get – carried away sometimes."

"I asked for it," he said. "Almost literally."

"Yeah, you did," she said. "I'm not sure street fencing is your thing."

"You guys must have had such a laugh about me," he said. "Little rich kid comes down into the city, thinks he's so big…"

Her eyes widened, and then she burst out laughing.

"What?" he asked.

"Those guys you saw me with?" she said. "One of them has a father who is the CEO of Xelofirm. The guy who started our fight? His mother is a neurosurgeon. What, you thought we were street kids or something? Who but a bunch of upper-class punks would come up with something as doofy as street fencing in body armor?"

That made a good bit of sense, but it took a little of the sheen off his memory of the whole thing. He actually had sort of thought they were street toughs.

"I guess I didn't think about it that much," he said. "So how long was your walk again?"

She smiled and looked a little embarrassed. "Yeah, you got me," she said. "A friend dropped me off."

"So are you still doing it?" he asked. "The street fencing thing?"

"No," she said. "Or at least not too much. I prefer the sport, really. And foil to épée."

"I can totally beat you in foil," he said.

"I wouldn't count on it," she replied. "But come to my

*salle* next week. You can bring your spook. He won't need a first aid kit this time."


Xia was better than Jinhai with a foil, too, but he loved fencing her, even if he lost, which was usually. And the more he fenced her, the better he liked it.

A lot of fencers – most of them maybe – didn't really interact with their opponents; they just sort of threw out their best chops and hoped they would stick. One fencer did his thing, the other hers, and that was sort of it.

But it wasn't like that with Xia. It was really more like dancing, an improvised ballet in which each partner was trying to anticipate what the other would do so as to respond appropriately. Winning was... secondary.

She felt it too. It was intense, and soon it was clear their feelings would not be confined to the piste.

Kissing, as it turned out, could also be pretty thoroughly interactive. He had kissed before, and been kissed, but looking back on it, he wasn't sure he and anyone had kissed *together*, to solve the kiss like an equation, to meet each movement of the lips and tongue with a suitable reply.

So fencing went to kissing, and kissing to long walks and late nights on the phone, and spending every moment they could steal from their schedules.

And Jinhai began to feel... harmony. Balance. Or at least that such a state might exist and be within reach.

And yet, at the same time, he couldn't avoid thinking about the future. He saw the year before them: a flat sea as autumn arrived, but in the distance, it began to curl up, first a little wave, then bigger, until it formed a tsunami that would – in the end – crash down upon them.

He had applied to the PPDC Ranger training program; he had already been accepted. Xia was going off to Beijing, to begin her studies toward a career in medicine.

He tried not to think about it. She never brought it up. But as the year moved on, the wave began to blot out the sky.

But they still had beautiful, perfect days, and it was on a day that was at least going that way that he decided to have the conversation he had been practicing at night, when he was alone, and the whirr of his brain wouldn't slow down, much less stop so he could sleep.

It was after a swim in the lake, and they lay on a blanket underneath the branches of a willow, looking up at the blue-porcelain sky through its leaves, where a pair of eagles lazily danced upon the winds.

"You could qualify for Ranger training," he said, as if it was something that had just occurred to him.

But she wasn't buying it. She rolled on her side so her gaze was directly on him.

"How long have you been thinking about that?" she asked. "A while, I bet."

"I love you," he said. "I've been trying to think of a way—"

"For us to be together. I know. But I'm not going to Ranger training, Jinhai. Why would you want me to? Really?"

"Because…" He tried to get his thoughts together. "Because we know each other. The way we are together. The way we fence, kiss, dance, cook…"

"You think we're Drift compatible," she said.

He felt his face reddening. He nodded.

"I've met your parents," she said. "I see how it is. And yes, I know you. I understand what you want. And I love you too, Jinhai. And if you want to stay together – if you want to do the hard work of a long-distance relationship, I'm willing to try. A few years of our lives apart, and then we could be partners for life. But I want love to be enough for you. Regular, normal, human love. I don't want to drift with you. I don't want our minds all mixed together by a machine. That should happen with time, caring. Communication. It comes with patience, and growing old together. That's what I want, Jinhai."

"Okay," he said, and he kissed her. "I'm sorry I tried to—"

She laughed. "I knew you would bring it up," she said. "That's why we don't need to drift. We already have so much more than other people have. We both know it. What we have isn't the usual, Jinhai. It's special."

And it was, and for a little while longer he was able to tell himself that it was enough.

But it wasn't.

# 24

IN THEIR NEXT MOCK-POD DRILL, JINHAI AND Vik found themselves in the legendary Coyote Tango, accompanied by Mexico's Matador Fury and their ride from the day before, Striker Eureka, right in the middle of a fight with Ceramander, a slimy, eight-legged newt with a flaring skull plate and a mouth full of razors. By this time, Jinhai didn't think he could be surprised, but when he tried to use Tango's Ballistic Mortar Cannons, he got one. They didn't work.

"We've got no missiles," one of Eureka Striker's pilots reported. It was a familiar voice, not a simulation of one of the original pilots.

"Renata?" Jinhai said. "Is that you?"

"Jinhai?"

"Yeah, me and Vik are in Coyote Tango."

"Oh no," Suresh's voice came from Matador Fury, just as Ceramander smashed into the Jaeger.

"Joint mission," Vik said. "Great."

Jinhai shared her reservations. The other cadets had barely spoken to either of them for days; they all clearly believed he and Vik were guilty. But right now, there were other things to worry about. As everyone reported in, their Jaegers all worked fine – but not any of their weapons systems or special attacks.

They would just have to slug it out, then.

Jinhai and Vik started forward to help Matador Fury, but Striker Eureka moved in front of them.

"Just – stay back, Tango," Renata said. "We'll let you know if you're needed."

*Jinhai suddenly felt a furnace light in him, and realized that it wasn't just his anger, but Vik's much brighter fury coursing through him. Ceramander and the other Jaegers faded, replaced by a man's face. The man was angry, yelling at Vik, telling her to do her job. They were running in a dark place, driven by equal parts anger and terror. Then he was in her room; she was tearing a poster of Cherno Alpha off of the wall. There was a woman, and Vik was screaming at her, demanding to know if her parents were the Kaidanovskys –*

Then everything came back, and he realized they were in the process of punching Striker Eureka in the side. It felt good, but part of him knew it was anything but. They hit Eureka again, this time lunging forward, sending the other Jaeger staggering from their path. Then they rushed toward Ceramander, which was savaging Matador Fury. Suresh was freaking out, yelling incoherently as one of the huge mech's arms came off and the Jaeger toppled into the sea. Then the Kaiju's huge maw was right in their face. They sidestepped, grabbed the monster with their left arm around its neck and the right arms under its front legs, and heaved it through the air toward an outcrop of black basalt.

Then Striker Eureka slammed them from behind. Vik let out a stream of Russian curses as they hit the same rock formation as Ceramander. They turned to face Striker.

"You don't want to do this," Vik said, her voice low and dangerous.

"What are you going to do," Renata said, "smother me in my sleep?"

"Vik," Jinhai said. "Cool off."

Then Ceramander leapt back up, and with a swing of its tail, knocked them off their feet. Sirens wailed.

"Crack in the reactor!" Jinhai shouted. "We have to –"

Then Vik was out of his mind as the link shut down. Ceramander, the other Jaegers, and Hawaii vanished, and were soon replaced by a very, very angry Lambert.

"Get out here, all of you!" the Ranger shouted.

They did as he said, trying not to look at each other.

"This is not a video game," he said. "This is a very expensive, cutting-edge battle simulator. It was not built for children to have playtime in. Are you children, cadets?"

"Sir, no Ranger sir," they replied in unison.

"Well then you fooled me completely," he said. "Because that is how you were behaving. You *cannot* have differences with your fellow pilots. You all just died right now, and because of that, so did a lot of other people. People you are sworn to protect. You have problems with someone, you leave that outside of the Conn-Pod, so you understand me?"

"Yes, Ranger," they replied.

Suresh raised his hand.

"What?" Lambert said.

"Ranger, none of our weapons were functioning."

"Exactly right, they weren't. Do you remember how Ceramander was beaten, cadet?"

"Didn't they, um, throw him in a volcano?"

"Yes, they did, cadet. Because their weapons weren't having much of an effect. But you know what they did have?"

"More experience, Ranger?" Renata said.

"Cooperation," he replied. "Even without weapons, the three of you could have worked Ceramander back to the caldera and knocked him in. One of you couldn't have done it. Two of you couldn't have done it. Three of you could have. Instead, you chose to waste my time and the precious resources of the PPDC on a playground spat. If this happens again – if anything remotely in the ball park of this happens again – those involved will be out. Done. Do you understand me?"

"Yes, Ranger," they replied.

"You all fail this one. No redo. Hit the track and give me forty laps. Your next liberty is canceled."

"What about Tahima and Meilin, Ranger," Renata said. "They weren't involved."

"They are now," Lambert said. "You can explain to them why while you run your laps."


"It's another group drill," Vik muttered the next day, as they were entering their pod.

"Yeah," Jinhai said. "I think Lambert wants us to screw up again so he can bounce us. So let's punch Kaiju and not Jaegers this time, okay?"

Vik nodded, but still didn't look happy. She didn't feel happy when the Drift started, either, but once the handshake firmed up, he felt her spirits rise. He understood why.

Drifting with Vik worked. They were a pretty good team.

What he and Vik had wasn't what his parents had, but he was starting to think that what they had was deeper and weirder than what most pilots experienced. Lambert and Burke sometimes didn't seem to like each other very much at times. The other cadets had been paired up before the Mock-Pod drills began, based on their performance in the Kwoon and Pons training, but none of them seemed to have a bond any deeper than he and Vik had.

He wasn't in love with Vik, or anything goofy like that, and he could tell that – even though she liked him better than she had when they met – she didn't have any amorous feelings toward him either. It just wasn't who they were as pilots.

He had to face the possibility that what he was looking for was something that for him would never exist.

Still, they were good together, and it made both of them feel better. But deep down he had the nagging suspicion that they could be better. She was still holding back; there was still a shadowy part of her he couldn't quite feel or see into.

Vik looked over at him and shrugged, and he realized she had probably followed a good part of what he'd been thinking.

"Clear your mind," she said. "We want to do it right this time. And yeah, I know it was me that got us off-game last time. But this time I'm really gonna try, okay?"

"Okay," he said.

They had a few minutes to get their bearings this time.

Once again, there were three of them, standing a few miles off shore. He and Vik were in Puma Real, a Mark-2 Panamanian Jaeger, as lithe and nimble as any Mark-2 ever built, a little less armored than some. She had eight missiles mounted on her shoulders, earlier versions of the anti-Kaiju rockets Striker Eureka had carried. Her torso could rotate three-hundred-and-sixty degrees, and she had retractable tungsten-carbide claws on the ends of her arms.

Renata and Ilya were in Diablo Intercept, also a Mark-2, built in Chile, the country Renata called home. She looked squat and powerful, her Conn-Pod painted dark red. Not having access to Diablo's controls, he wasn't sure what her capabilities were, although he remembered she had some sort of long-distance flame throwers that ran up her arms, which were bulky enough to hide any number of nasty surprises for Kaiju.

Romeo Blue, piloted by Tahima and Meilin, completed their trio. Romeo was a Mark-1 built in the United States, and like several of that first generation of Jaegers, a bit on the experimental side – the first and only tripedal Jaeger. Mounted on its three legs was a torso that ventured toward spherical and deeply armored. Her protruding Gatling chest could produce a withering sleet of armor-piercing rounds, but mainly she was built to stand her ground, a fortress rather than a brawler.

Something was rising out of the sea.

"This is Ecuador," Renata said. "That's Ceptid, I'm willing to bet."

"The Living Sewer," Meilin said. "This is going to be so much fun."

"They didn't really beat Ceptid," Renata said. "Diablo Intercept tried to go toe-to-toe with it and it blew up. It's basically a walking acid bomb."

"How do we handle it?" Ilya asked.

"I think –" Vik began, but Renata interrupted.

"We don't let it get close," the Chilean said. "We stay out of its range and pound it with whatever long-range weapons we have. Romeo Blue, you set up just offshore. Puma Real, flank it on the south; we'll take the north. If it makes a drive for someone, try to draw it back out to sea. But do not close with it. If we lose a Jaeger, it's bound to deduct points from the group as well as whoever buys it."

"Why is she giving the orders?" Vik asked. She wasn't broadcasting, so no one else could hear.

"They're not going to take orders from us," Jinhai

said. "They just aren't. Anyway, it's not a bad plan. Like she said, Ceptid is basically a bomb. Hit it with enough ordnance, it's bound to go off."

"It's too simple," she said. "Whenever we use what we know about the old fights, we get tripped up."

"Not the fight in Medellin. We did more-or-less what the real Striker Eureka did when she hunted down all of the parasites."

"That one was just to throw us off."

Ceptid was about two thirds out of the water now, and was certainly one of the weirder Kaiju. It walked upright on skeletal legs attached to a body that resembled a gigantic pelvis, leaving a trail of rancid blue-green in the water as it approached them.

"Let's hit it with some missiles," Jinhai said.

They launched two, watched them streak through the clear air and impact solidly on the Kaiju, blowing a pair of its weird appendages apart and revealing what appeared to be bone beneath. At about the same time, Diablo Intercept began hitting it with Hellbolts, shells full of a napalm-like substance that soon had the Kaiju covered in sheets of flame. Now a gigantic walking torch, Ceptid kept coming, burning chunks of it falling into the sea, but at last it seemed to falter a little...

"It's working," Renata said. "It'll be dead before it reaches shore."

Vik and Jinhai fired two more missiles, this time targeting its knee joints. They hit fair, and both made satisfying kabooms, digging holes in the bony substance. A few minutes later the Kaiju walked into range of Romeo Blue, which had placed itself squarely in Ceptid's path and unloaded a steel wind from its Gatling Chest, pocking and eroding the Kaiju like a steel wind.

Almost anything that looked like flesh was stripped

from the Kaiju now, and as it approached Romeo Blue, in the shallow water, Ceptid slowed to a stop.

Then the monster began to unzip, its head splitting and unfolding, its chest opening...

And then it ran. *Fast*. Straight toward Romeo Blue.

"Romeo," Renata said. "Get the hell out of there, now."

Tahima and Meilin already had the American Jaeger in motion, but it was the slowest Jaeger Jinhai had ever seen. All Ceptid had to do was veer a little, and there was no way Romeo could escape.

But the Kaiju didn't veer. It kept running, past the fleeing Jaeger and onto land.

"Crap," Jinhai said. "Let's get it."

They raced through the water, throwing up spray, firing another pair of missiles; bits of the Kaiju flew off, but Jinhai was starting to get the picture. Everything on the outside of the monster was expendable; it gave them the illusion they were damaging it, like when a lizard dropped its tail to distract a predator. But the core of the beast – they hadn't hurt that at all.

"Puma," Renata said. "You're the only one that can catch it."

"We're on it," Jinhai said.

They came up on land, firing the last of their missiles, this time targeting Ceptid's feet, hoping to upset its footing, make it trip or fall, but it just plowed on. Ahead, the skyline of a city appeared.

But they were getting close. What they would do when they got there, Jinhai wasn't sure.

Suddenly the Kaiju's back split open, and a blue-green mist boiled out, engulfing them.

"Oh no," Jinhai said. "Did it just fart on us?"

Almost immediately, their viewport started going opaque.

"We're losing all of our outside sensors," Vik said. "Some kind of acid."

"Hull integrity?"

"Weaker, but still good. But we're blind."

"Crap," he sighed.

A few moments later the simulation ended. Ceptid had reached the city of Guayaquil and detonated, destroying a quarter of the metropolitan area, killing twenty thousand instantly, dooming another fifteen thousand to slow, agonizing death in the next few days and weeks, and leaving many more scarred, blinded, and crippled by permanent lung disorders.

They expected a rebuke from Lambert, but when they assembled afterward, he didn't have anything to say about their performance – he just sent them to the showers. The next day, they ran the same simulation. They tried different tactics, but in the end it worked out the same, except with even higher casualties. Again, Lambert and Burke offered neither criticism nor advice.

In the next week they went through a series of simulated fights, none of them done as a group. The battles were against "real" Kaiju, but the scenarios differed from the historical ones. They started the week in Mark-1 Jaegers, progressed to Mark-2, until finally, by the end of the week, they were in state-of-the-art Mock-Pods – Mark-6s. No more Pinocchio rigs. Jinhai and Vik were piloting November Ajax.

"Oh, hell yeah," Jinhai said, as the simulation started. "This ought to be good."

Then he realized the scenery was all too familiar.

"Guys? Are we all here?"

Renata again. Another group drill. The other three

Jaegers were all Mark-6s as well – Gipsy Avenger, Titan Redeemer, and Saber Athena.

"It's Ecuador again!" Suresh exclaimed. "Ceptid!"

"Right," Renata said. "But we're not in antiques anymore. And there are four of us. This time we'll kick its butt."

"I don't know," Vik said, as the Kaiju once again rose from the water. "This doesn't feel right."

"No way is it getting past us again," Tahima said.

But it did. And this time twenty thousand simulated souls went down.

This time, Lambert looked them over and shook his head.

"I'm disappointed," he said. "Starting next week, we're going to start washing people out. You've got the weekend off. No liberty – you're not leaving the island. But you get a break. I suggest you take this time to get your minds together."

"I think we just got our chance," Jinhai told Vik, once they were alone and out of earshot. "The thing I mentioned earlier? How they messed with Chronos Berserker? Do you still want to check it out?"

"Yeah," Vik said. "Let's do it."


Jinhai took Saturday morning to explore the coastline alone. There wasn't a beach, but the rocks were interesting, and tide pools teemed with strange little shrimp, snails, and a few sea urchins.

He was really just trying to get his mind off the stuff he had planned for the afternoon.

Toward midday, he thought it might be interesting to climb up to the highest point of the island for the view, which was pretty spectacular. The Shatterdome itself aside, most of what surrounded Moyulan was forested mountains and rugged coastline; Fuding and its suburbs were mostly hidden by the hills to the west and across the water. He looked off at the nearby islands, which appeared serene, uninhabited, and wondered if it would be possible to just – disappear. Vanish into the forest and live off of mushrooms and bugs or whatever.

Probably not. He had hiked enough to know that – in China at least – civilization was never far away, and even if he could find wilderness deep enough, he would probably starve to death in under a month.

After a while, he noticed Vik climbing up and started back to meet her. It was supposed to appear accidental, if anyone was watching. Like they didn't have anything planned. But in the moment, it felt hideously obvious and contrived. Not that it mattered, really. As far as the other cadets were concerned, the jury was already in.

"Hi," Vik said, when they were within earshot.

"Hey," he replied. "Are you ready to do this?"

She sat down, facing east, beyond the bay and toward the sea.

"Just give me a minute," she said. "I like the ocean."

"Oh," he said. "Yeah, me too."

She kept to herself for a few minutes, shifting her gaze slowly, as if trying to make certain she could remember it all in detail.

"Did you ever see Shaolin Rogue fight?" she asked. "See your parents fight?"

"Not really," he said. "Not at the time. I was in Hong Kong, in PPDC family housing at the Shatterdome. I was about six, I guess. Anyway, Huo Da was more up this way, in Shanghai. There was this lady who watched me back then, and – well, nobody even told me it was happening. If they had never come back, if they had died…" he stopped, remembering Vik's parents *had* died. "Anyway, it was a long time before they did come back. They were messed up pretty bad. That was their first and last fight. After that they got promoted, and when the Jaeger program really started building again, they were pretty big deals. But they never piloted again."

"I always wanted to see a fight," she said. "Even if only at great distance. Especially, I wanted to see Cherno Alpha fight."

"There are recordings," he said.

"Yes," she replied. "Not the same thing."

She stood up. "Okay. Let's go."

They made their way around the northern slope, to the barge docks, where a few low-grade techs were repainting a loader. Beyond was a vast hangar whose doors were currently open. The techs glanced up at them as they approached. One, a red-headed woman who was maybe twice his age, gave them the once-over.

"Cadets in the wild," she said. "Dahlgren, Ling, take a good look. You don't usually see them out of their native habitats." She grinned. "Are you two looking for something?"

"We're just bushed," Jinhai said. "I thought rather than walking all the way around to the front, maybe we could go back through the utility corridors."

"Listen to you," the woman said. "What do you know about the Mechspace? You could get lost in there."

"Grew up in the HK dome," he said. "Spent half of my time in Mechspace."

"You don't say. Dome rat, huh?"

"Every dome needs one or two," he said.

She shrugged. "I guess there's no harm. Door you're looking for is back there and to the right."

"Thank you, ma'am," Jinhai said.

"Just remember us little people when you're riding up high," she said. "And be careful – I trust you know better than to get underfoot."

"Yes, ma'am," he said. "We'll watch out."

They passed through rows of power chugs, tool trains, convoy units, finger lifts, armored six-wheelers and all other manner of support equipment and vehicles. Some looked brand new, others were older and up on racks being worked on. They passed a gigantic head clamp with a crew swarming on it.

"Where is this?" Vik asked.

"Mechspace," he said. "It's where everything *but* Jaegers gets stored or repaired. They require tons of support equipment. That head clamp was probably dinged up when Chronos Berserker went off."

"All these people are seeing us," she said.

"Just act like you belong," he said. "If somebody looks at you, just nod. We'll be fine."

"Okay."

They reached the back of the hangar and the door the red-headed woman had mentioned.

That was one obstacle passed. This next one would be bigger.

The door popped open, revealing a long corridor.

"Come on," he said.

As the woman suggested, the one corridor quickly became several, and then a warren, allowing access to various parts of the dome's basic infrastructure. Not the power core, or anything like that, of course – but the units that scrubbed and recycled air in the event of a shatterdown, waste water management, and the various cooling systems that kept the Shatterdome from being unbearably hot due to all the various forms of energy consumed within it.

He was searching for none of that. Moyulan wasn't laid out exactly like the Hong Kong dome, of course, and his memory of even that was a little unreliable at this point but what they were looking for was so *big* it really should be hard to miss.

"Ah," he finally said, as they approached another door. "This is it."

"Where are we?" Vik asked.

"You'll see in a minute, I hope," he said.

The door opened into another hangar, much larger than the first, a cavern bigger even than he remembered at the Hong Kong dome. The main overheads were down, but as they walked along the row lights came up, and Jinhai began to recognize some of the shapes.

"Jaeger parts," Vik said. "Replacements? Prototypes?"

"Both," Jinhai said. "Welcome to Spare Parts."

"Yeah," she said. "Wow."

They moved through rows of what seemed like dismembered giants – here a massive forearm assembly, there one of the enormous motors that pulled the cables that acted as tendons inside of the machines.

The ceiling was festooned with cranes and clamps, all fastened to a track system that led off to areas where the ceiling went even further up.

"Parts ride up through the conveyance system to various parts of the bays," he said. "If Gipsy Avenger needs some new fingers, or whatever, they're retooled down here and then they go up."

"What exactly are we looking for?" Vik asked.

"There," he said, as they reached the back of the room.

"*Bozhe moi,*" she murmured.

Jinhai had once seen pictures of artifacts from the ancient Olmec culture of Mexico. The Olmecs had had a thing for carving big statues; not of whole people, but just of their heads – massive stone heads. In the near dark, that was what he was now reminded of, except these heads were way bigger than anything the Olmec had ever carved.

"Conn-Pods," Vik said.

"Yeah," he said. "I wasn't sure. In Hong Kong, they didn't always have spare Con-Pods. But times were kind of tough, then. They were scraping the bottom of the barrel. But the PPDC is pretty flush now, so I took a guess." He nodded at one of them. "That's the one we want."

"Chronos Berserker," she said.

"Yep."

"So, what now?" she asked.

"We go inside."

They climbed up through the side of the head and down the anterior hatch.

It was dark inside; the only power was in a few battery-operated subsystems, so the only light was what came in through the "face" of the Jaeger and a few LEDs on the console.

"I think I get it now," Vik said. "You think they switched the heads out."

"Yeah," Jinhai confirmed. "This is the Conn-Pod we all went into, right here. Meanwhile, the other head was down here, where someone uploaded the Kaiju attack scenario while no one was looking. During the night, they changed the heads – the sabotaged one went up, this one came down."

"That wouldn't show up on their surveillance scans? Giant heads moving around?"

"The conveyance system is separate," he said. "I'm sure it leaves a record someplace when you shift things like that around, but if you've ever been in the Shatterdome at night, things are always moving around. A lot of it is automated, and the Con-Pods are way up there. There probably was an actual order to switch out the heads that nobody had bothered to access because no one thought of it. Why would they? They have their suspects. Us."

"So how do we prove it?"

"Like I said, there should be a record if somebody looks for it."

"And how do we get the record?" Vik asked.

"You know who we could probably ask?" he said.

She folded her arms.

"Ranger Lambert," he said. "Marshal Quan. Pretty much anybody who runs this place."

"And what if they're in on it?" Vik said. "What if one of them is trying to frame us?"

"We're not detectives, Vik. It's time we stopped pretending we are."

She looked at first like she wanted to hit him, but then she closed her eyes.

"This doesn't clear us," she said. "The very fact that we got in here means we could have done it – moved the Conn-Pod and everything. Someone is trying really hard to make it look like we're guilty."

"But we aren't," he said. "So we'll be okay."

"You have way more faith in people than I do," she said. "I'm scared, okay?"

He nodded. "Yeah. It's okay."

She sidled over and looked forward. At first he didn't understand, but then he saw she was standing where one of the pilots would stand.

"I've dreamed of being in one of these," she said. "I've dreamed about it for so long…" She sighed. "You're right. We should go to Mori. If she's involved with this mess, we don't have a prayer, anyway."

Something dropped from the hatch above clanged against the deck and bounced, a silver canister about a foot long. He just stared at it in incomprehension, but Vik grabbed him and started pulling him toward the ladder, swearing in Russian.

Jinhai smelled something funny and a little familiar. He

took a deep breath and tried to hold it, but since he could smell it already, it was far too late for that. The Conn-Pod suddenly started to shrink, going pitch black as it did so. When it shrank to the size of his head, and smaller, his mind wicked out like a candle flame between wet fingers.

# 25

PAVEL OUTWEIGHED VIK BY AT LEAST FORTY pounds, so she didn't block the kick he'd aimed at her head – she ducked it and delivered a sharp, short sweep to the ankle of the only leg he still had on the ground. He yelped as he fell, but he landed well and rolled back up and came back at her again.

This time he kept his feet planted and threw a flurry of punches at her. She retreated, deflecting the blows with her arms, lengthening her steps back until he overcommitted and lost his center of gravity. Then she sidestepped and punched him in the gut. He said something like *guh*, and bent over, trying to catch his breath.

"Stop!" the sensei shouted.

She returned to a position of attention, feet apart, fists down in front of her.

Sensei walked over to her, frowning. He was a short man, not much taller than her.

"You knocked the wind out of him," Sensei said.

"Yes, Sensei."

"I asked you to spar with control. You could have made your point by hitting him half as hard."

"Sensei, I did hit him half as hard as I *could* have."

"Don't be insubordinate," he snapped back. "You know what I mean."

"Sensei, if his roundhouse kick had connected, it would have knocked my teeth out."

"So you think Pavel's shortcomings excuse your own? You know better than that."

She glanced over to where Pavel was finally managing to stand back up.

"I'm sorry, Pavel," she said, although she didn't mean it. She knew it was what Sensei wanted to hear. "It won't happen again, Sensei."

Pavel grimaced, but he put his feet together and bowed. She did the same.

"It's okay," Pavel said. "I was stupid. I let myself get mad."

Sensei didn't seem as forgiving.

"Clean up," he said. "Get dressed. Then I want to see you in my office."


The dojo was a tiny place. It had once been a shop of some sort, and Sensei had done very little to give the place atmosphere. It was, as he liked to say, purely practical. If you want a koi pond and water running through bamboo, he'd once told her, go to the botanical gardens.

His office wasn't much different, but it had a little more personality. On the wall behind his desk hung an old photograph of himself as a much younger man, with his own sensei. A glass jar on the corner of his desk held a collection of pebbles, and he had a picture of his wife and children on his desk, although she suspected that the children in the picture – two boys – were now much older than they appeared in the photograph. Sensei himself was about sixty, clean-shaven with short, bristling hair that according to the picture on the wall had once been reddish-blonde. His name was Alexander Kamaroff, but no one ever called him anything but "Sensei".

By the time the door closed behind her, he was at his desk. She started toward the chair.

"Remain standing," he said.

She stood.

"Your anger is doing you no good," he said, "and it's hurting my other students. If I ask you to hit someone full force, I expect you to do it. If I ask you to use control, I want them to think you stroked them with a feather, do you understand? In this place, it's what I say that matters, not how you feel. I won't say this again. Next time, you're out."

She took a breath. "Yes, Sensei, it's only…"

"Tell me."

"What if I'm in a real fight, and I don't hit hard enough?"

"If you're in a real fight, you'll hit what you need to hit, how you need to hit it. That is what control is about. Why were you able to beat Pavel?"

"He was too eager, and came at me too fast. I backed up just a little faster to encourage him, and he overbalanced." She dropped her head. "He was out of control, I guess."

"Correct," he said. He clasped his hands together in front of him on the desk.

"You've been coming here for what, two years?" he asked.

"Almost three, Sensei."

"That long," he mused. "You think you've learned all I have to teach you?"

"No, Sensei."

He nodded. "Do you still work for Andrei?"

She hesitated.

"I thought so," he said.

"We need money, Sensei," she said. "My grandmother barely makes enough to get by. Working for Andrei, I'm able to pay you for lessons."

"And what if I were to tell you I would teach you for free?" he said. "Would you still work for him?"

She considered that, but not for long.

"Yes, Sensei," she said. "I was delayed almost two years getting into school, so I have tutors to pay, as well."

"How old are you?" he asked.

"Eleven," she said.

"And you're still digging in the Kaiju?"

She held her chin up. "Yes. But I supervise four others, and I get a cut of what they make, too."

"You know for every ruble he gives you, he is probably making a hundred from your labor."

She shrugged. "That's how it is."

"If you keep doing it, you're going to get sick," Sensei said. "You know that those suits they give you are so worn out they're hardly any protection at all."

"With respect, Sensei," she said. "You say that in here, in the dojo, it is what you say that matters. But what I do out there is my own business, yes?"

"It is," he said. "I am advising you, not commanding you. But if you find a way to survive without Andrei, I will teach you for free."

"I could still use the break," she said.

"I know you could," he replied. "But I won't feed your habit, or help to feed Andrei," he said. "You must understand that."

"Thank you for your wisdom, Sensei," she said.

By the time she was back on the street, the anger she'd kept bottled steamed fully to life. Who was this old man who thought he could judge her? If he wanted to teach her for free, fine, but putting conditions on it made him just like Andrei. Everyone had an idea about what she should be doing, and no one seemed to understand that it was none of their *grobanyy* business.

So she was in no mood to deal with Andrei, who today of all days was at the site, and yelled at her for being late.

"What do you care?" she told him. "As long as I meet my quota? I could be an hour late and still hit my mark."

She knew as soon as she said it she'd made a mistake. She was just so angry.

"Is that true?" he said. "You've been robbing me, then. Your quota has just gone up."

"You can't do that, you cheat," she snapped.

She saw the blow coming before it landed. She almost blocked it, but he was fast, and standing way too close. His open palm slammed into the side of her face. She staggered back, stunned.

"You want to use some of your karate?" he said. "You want to show me some of that useless crap?"

She put her hand to her face. It was hot, and she thought she would probably get a black eye.

*But it doesn't hurt*, she told herself. *Nothing I can't handle.*

"I thought not," he sneered. "I don't see why you bother."

"It's only a few hours a week," she said.

"Yes, plus school," he said. "As if school will ever be any use to you. Better you stick with me."

"I still work for you, Andrei," she said. "I'm not working for anyone else."

"Oh, damned right, you're not," he said. "If you were, you would think what I just gave you was the paw of a kitten."

He tensed up, and she thought for sure he was going to hit her again. But then he gestured with the back of his hand.

"Well go on, get going," he said. "They've opened up whole new section in the spinal column. Take Mina and Lubomir for your crew."

"What about Hyeon?" she asked. Hyeon was tiny – he could fit into places she and the older kids no longer could.

"I'm sending Hyeon with Lucie today," he said. "Good luck making your new quota. You talk big, now act big."

She did make it, of course, but just barely. And he kept more of her cut than usual. But there was nothing to be done about that.

She made up another story to tell Babulya, but her grandmother hardly gave her a second glance when she came in, any more than she seemed to notice the soup had a little beef in it. She was getting worse, Grandmother. There had been some incidents at work. Her supervisor, a kindly man named Cho, had brought her home the week before.

"I want to keep her on," he'd told Vik. "But if she gets much worse, it could mean my job, too. Try and make her understand."

As much as she wanted to forget them, Andrei's words hung with her.

*I don't see why you bother.*

Sometimes she didn't either. Even with tutors, she was struggling with school, especially with math. Her brain didn't seem built for it. Maybe more to the point, she didn't like school. She didn't have much in common with the other kids – they all seemed to think everything was some sort of game, a game in which you scored points by wearing the right shoes and knowing which piece-of-crap slang phrase was current, or whether you thought K-prog sucked more than Pinoy-ScreamScream.

The teachers were no fun either, but at least some of them *knew* something.

But the bigger thing was that maybe she had been wrong. It had been four years since anyone had seen a Kaiju. The PPDC was building Jaegers again, a whole shiny mess of them, but what were they using them for? Keeping civil order? Putting down warlords in some godforsaken place she'd never heard of? That was not what she wanted to do. That was not what her parents had done. They had grappled with monsters the size of mountains, and they had put down six of them before they finally died fighting. She had studied the requirements to get into the PPDC Ranger training program, and she had spent four years trying to get a jump on all of that. Why? She was getting old enough to understand how stacked the odds against her were. The promise a seven-year-old made to her future self couldn't hold its weight against that. What had she known? Nothing. Now that she had a better – a more realistic – idea of how the world worked, maybe it was time to tell the seven-year-old where to stick it.

If she had been saving her money, she could put her grandmother someplace where she couldn't hurt herself or anyone else. Maybe she could have even gotten them out of this hell-hole to someplace decent, with better jobs. As it was, it looked like everything she'd done was for nothing.

But she couldn't think that way. She had to get into the PPDC. She had to get through this for just a few more years.

But this time, the gloom didn't lift. And that night she had the dream again. Familiarity made it worse, not better. And this time, there was more; she stood with her grandfather, looking down at two gravestones. And her grandfather, who never cried, was crying. And then the voice in the Kaiju Dig, the woman's face…

She woke up, as always. She looked at the clock and

realized she had only been asleep for an hour. She turned on the light, clutching at her statue of Cherno Alpha. She looked at her old poster of them, on the wall.

Then she got up. She went into the tiny living room where Babulya was still awake.

"Who am I?" she demanded.

"What?" her grandmother said.

"Who am I?" This time she screamed it, and her grandmother's eyes widened. Vik saw she was drinking again, but she didn't care.

"Don't you raise your voice to me," the old woman said.

"Am I a Kaidanovsky?" she said. "Am I really?"

That stopped Babulya. She actually stumbled a step back as if the words had made a physical impact.

"Why would you ask that?" she whispered. "Who have you been talking to?"

"No one," Vik said. "It just doesn't make sense. It's never made sense. Why have you been lying to me?"

She was crying now, as despair replaced her anger.

"Vik," her grandmother said. "I want you to be great. Like your parents. To do something with your life. Your grandfather wanted the same. So we told you –"

"So you lied to me," Vik said. "All of these years. How stupid do you think I am?"

"You're not stupid," her grandmother said. "You're special. But you have to believe you're special."

"Shut up," Vik said. "I hate you."

"Vik, your father, your mother –"

"Stop it!" she screamed. "No more lies. No more."

She stormed back into her room, tore the Cherno Alpha poster from the wall and threw her grandfather's carving into the corner.

She realized she had known for a long time, but had refused to face it. She wanted to be a Kaidanovsky, be someone important. After they died, it had been even easier to believe. No one could tell her she was wrong.

No one but Babulya.

And as she lay there, a new understanding began to take shape in her, all of the misgivings from earlier that evening coming into focus.

She wasn't born to be a Jaeger pilot. She never had been. She was just a girl with a crazy grandmother and no real prospects. Andrei was using her, but he was right. School, training, all of that really was a waste of time. Better to be realistic, to live in the world as it was, not as a little girl once thought it should be.

The next morning, she found Babulya passed out on the couch, her vodka bottle empty. She stirred at the smell of porridge heating in the stove, and rose to regard Vik with bloodshot eyes.

"Vik," she said.

"I'm sorry I yelled at you last night," Vik said. "I don't hate you."

"Did we have a fight?" Babulya asked. "I don't remember. What was it about?"

Vik studied her for a moment to see if the old woman was serious, and saw that she looked genuinely puzzled. That wouldn't be unusual. When she drank that much, Babulya sometimes didn't remember the night before.

"It was nothing," she said. "Never mind."

She didn't go to school that day. Instead she went to the Dig and took an early shift as well the usual one. There was still time. If she went to work full time for Andrei, set some realistic goals, she might still salvage her life, for what little it was worth.

A week before her twelfth birthday, she arrived at the Dig to Andrei waiting for her.

"Look," he said. "I'm sorry about last month. You ticked me off. I have a bad temper. So I'm sorry I hit you. And I'm sorry for the stuff I said. Truth is, I admire you. All this stuff you're doing, to improve yourself – that's great. One day you'll be somebody big, and I'll just be some guy saying hey, I used to know her. She worked for me once upon a time."

"I... thanks," Vik said. It was so unexpected she wasn't sure how to respond.

"So, look, I think I can help you out. You've been working real hard, and the money – for what you want, it's not that much. Especially if you have the babushka to take care of, and everything. What I'm trying to say is – I'm promoting you."

The way he smiled made her feel cold. Promotions were not always a good thing.

But what did she have to lose?

# 26

LAMBERT GRIMACED AS HE LOOKED AT THE corpse.

"That's Sokk," he said. He had looked at enough pictures of the man,

"Was Sokk," said Aubrey, the forensic biologist examining the dead man. She had a heavy French accent. "He's been dead for days."

"What killed him?" Mako asked.

"There's no sign of a wound," she said. "But if you look here at the edges of the eyes, in the fingers under his nails, there is some hemorrhaging. I suspect a poison of some sort. Given that there is very little putrefaction, I would guess the poison was toxic enough to wipe out most of the bacteria in his body as well."

The body had been discovered a few hours earlier, crammed into a canister meant for toxic waste. If the techs involved had been a little less observant, he might have made it to the furnaces near Fuding where such rubbish was disposed of.

"This dust on him…"

"Probably Kaiju marrow powder."

"Right," Lambert said. "Wouldn't that keep him from rotting?"

"Well, it would deter external microorganisms from entering his body, and that's probably why it was put there. But, Ranger, surely you know that more than half of the cells in your body aren't human, but bacteria."

"I did *not* know that," Lambert said. "I'm not sure that information will improve my life tremendously."

"It's the case," she said, standing up.

"If he's so well preserved, how can you tell how long he's been dead?"

"There are other signs," she said. "He's already moved into and out of rigor mortis, which tells me he's been dead for at least two days. But there is also a good deal of dehydration – you can see it, yes? He's well on his way to becoming a mummy."

"So he might have died as long as a month ago?"

"Yep," Aubrey said. She pulled off her gloves. "We get him to the lab, and I can tell you more. Very exciting. I've only seen a few deaths from Kaiju-related toxins, back when I was an intern."

"You think this was a Kaiju-based toxin?"

"Oh, I would bet," Aubrey said. She started to depart, but then she turned back to Lambert.

"And, Ranger?" she said.

"Yes?"

"That Jules business – you better move on that fast. Don't dilly-dally."

He watched her leave the autopsy chamber.

Damn it. Did everyone in the Shatterdome know about this?

With a sigh, he turned back to the body.

"Why Sokk?" he murmured. "What else were you up to?"
Because this all felt – incomplete, somehow.

A half hour later, Jinhai and Vik were declared missing.
They weren't anyplace they were supposed to be, and no
one had seen them since before noon, when Renata and
Ilya had noticed Jinhai up on the high hill the Shatterdome
was built into.

Marshal Quan renewed the lockdown of the island
and ordered a complete review of any comings or goings.
None of that showed anything to do with the cadets
specifically, but in the process, they made the discovery that
one of the patrol boats was missing. They hadn't noticed
immediately because once again the security system had
been subtly tampered with.

The boat was discovered a few hours later, near Fuding.

Marshal Quan paced like a caged tiger. Mako waited
patiently for him to settle down.

"Malikova has no living family," he said. "Her
grandmother died last year. But Ou-Yang…"

"If his parents learn of this, it could lead to a great deal
of trouble," Mako said. "For that reason, I advise against
releasing the names of the cadets. This should be handled
quickly and quietly."

"They've vanished," Quan said. "Eventually it will
become known. It will also become known that we
admitted two cadets who committed sabotage and at least
two murders. Then we will be accused of covering up, and
it will be true. It could endanger the whole program."

That wasn't likely, Mori thought, but it could well
endanger Quan's position as Marshal, and her own
credibility would be called into question. Neither of those

things, in her opinion, really mattered. What mattered were the cadets and crimes in question.

"I do not believe the two cadets are guilty," Mako said.

"There is a great deal of evidence that they are," Quan said. "Including their DNA on Sokk's clothes."

"Which could have been planted there," she said. "It is all far too convenient for me. Whether they fled or were abducted, it is the first few hours and days which matter most in investigations like this. I would like to continue the investigation unhampered by the press and parents for at least that long. I will take the responsibility for any unpleasantness that may result."

Quan's lips pressed together. Then he nodded curtly.

"I respect your judgment, Secretary General," he said. "For the time being, we will continue the search as quietly as possible. But if this goes on for much longer, it will be out of my hands. People talk – even my people."

Mako watched Quan leave the room, ran her hand over her forehead, and then returned to her investigation with renewed urgency. She feared that if Vik and Jinhai weren't found in the next few days, they would never be.

It was not unusual for Dr. Gottlieb to be agitated. But when Lambert and Mako arrived in his lab, he seemed unusually so; pacing, muttering, scribbling at his chalkboards and then blotting things out with the sleeve of his white coat. In fact, it took him a few moments to become aware that they had arrived.

"Yes, what is it?" he asked, once he did notice them.

"You asked for me, Dr. Gottlieb," Mori said. "You said you had further analysis concerning Sokk's autopsy."

He stared at them blankly for a moment.

"Oh, yes," he said. "I had forgotten. Well, it's just as

Aubrey surmised. Sokk ingested a fatal dose of a toxin derived from Kaiju blood."

"Purposefully?" Lambert asked.

"Well, there's no sign he was forced to take it. But it might have been introduced into his system in food or drink. It is very nearly without taste, and what taste it does have is easily disguised."

"This poison," Mori asked. "Does it act quickly?"

"Not particularly," Gottlieb said. "You wouldn't know anything was wrong for a number of hours, maybe even up to a day depending on the dosage. By the time you did notice it, however, it would be too late. Catastrophic kidney and liver failure, accompanied by internal hemorrhaging, followed rather quickly by heart and lung failure."

"It seems a strange way to commit suicide," Lambert said.

"It is used for suicide," Gottlieb said, "but usually with a great deal of accompanying ritual, and often in the company of other Kaiju worshippers. They believe in the victim's last moments they become one with the Anteverse, and possess the ability to communicate with their gods. Sokk, however, was in his work clothes. And his body was moved, yes? So in this case, I rather doubt suicide."

"This would lead us to consider murder," Mako said. "But by whom? Jinhai or Vik or one of the other cadets? Where would they get the poison? No, I think we're looking for someone else. Is there any way to trace the source of the toxin?"

"I have its chemical signature," Gottlieb replied. "If you were to find another sample that shared that signature, we could probably say they were produced in the same batch. Although I'm not sure how that would help."

"Anything else?" Mori asked.

"Well, not concerning any of that," Gottlieb said. "I've

got a rather knotty problem here, though. I shan't worry you with it, however."

"This concerns the deep-sea trenches?" she asked. "The possibility of a new breach?"

"The data I got from Dr. Morales, yes," he said.

"I remember you were very concerned with it."

"Yes," he said. "Very. The more I worked with it, the more certain I became that a new breach is imminent, if not something of an even greater magnitude. But the data from K-Watch not only doesn't corroborate anything in my data set, in many instances it flatly contradicts it. I find it impossible to reconcile the two. It's like quantum and Einsteinian physics, but actually worse."

"Maybe it was some sort of collection error, bad instrumentation, or something on that first set of numbers," Lambert said.

"I find that hard to credit," Gottlieb said. "It came to me from Dr. Morales. I'm sure she vetted the collection methods before handing it off to me. It would be unthinkably unprofessional if she didn't, and truly I don't think she's capable of such behavior. It would be just as likely if she…" he trailed off and stalked back over to his chalkboards.

"What, Doctor?" Mori asked.

"Well, I just – it's ridiculous – but it's almost as if she *faked* the data. But why would she do that?"

"Are you telling me she sent you on a wild goose chase?" Lambert said.

"No," Mori said, slowly. "Not a wild goose chase. *Kunsei nishin no kyogi.* In English, I think this is 'smoked herring fallacy'."

"You mean a red herring?" Lambert asked.

"Red herring," Mako said. "Yes. Misdirection. Morales – when did you meet with her?"

"Just a day or two after she arrived," Gottlieb said.

"She sent me a message that she wanted to come by for a visit. So I cleared her through security. In fact, it was the same day as the incident with Chronos Berserker."

"The same day?" Lambert asked. "Are you sure?"

"Quite sure," he said. "We were in here, and we were talking, and then I heard the commotion in the bays. And of course, I rushed to see what was the matter."

"Did she come with you?" Lambert asked.

It was dawning on Gottlieb now. Lambert could see it on his face.

"I don't know," he said. "I don't think so."

He was instantly in motion, moving from this workstation to that, frowning, looking for something, obviously.

"No," he muttered. "Not that, not that either..." He kept going, and little by little he began to seem more relieved. But then something seemed to occur to him, and he walked briskly across the lab, away from his calculations and holographic models and toward the preservation receptacles, K-scanners, and autopsy chambers, the stuff they had once used to preserve and analyze Kaiju tissue and organs – which, for the most part, now stood empty and unused.

He bent over a terminal there, and his face quickly soured.

"What's wrong?" Mori asked.

"It's Newton's – Dr. Geiszler's – database," he said. "Someone logged into it." He looked up. "It could not have been done remotely. This isn't connected to anything outside of the room – it was his personal hard storage."

"You think Morales broke into it?"

"The time-mark matches up," said Gottlieb. "The same day, the very hour. When I left the lab, she must have stayed behind."

"She knew no one would be paying attention to her," Mori said.

"Because she created the distraction. Or used Sokk to," Lambert finished.

"And then kept me sidetracked with this bloody fake data, so that it didn't occur to me to check up on anything."

"Dr. Morales," Mori said. "Where is she now?"

"Her contract job finished yesterday," Gottlieb said. "She's already gone home."

# 27

VIK GRUNTED AS SHE TRIED TO GET THE DRILL TO the right angle, not easy to do in the cramped space, but absolute precision wasn't necessary either. She pressed the switch and the little engine whined to life, cutting into the Kaiju bone with a combination of a diamond tip, solvent, and high heat. It took almost ten minutes to drill the twenty-centimeter hole.

"Got it," she said, when she was done.

"It's on the line," Mina's voice came up from below.

Mina was fifteen, and too big to crawl around even the larger nacelles. Vik almost was, and she certainly couldn't make into the dense, deep mass they were attempting to tunnel into at the moment. They were burrowing their way up the equivalent of a femur, nearing one of the hip joints of the Kaiju. She had two other kids, farther along where everything got denser and tighter – they were also drilling holes.

She pulled the line up, which had a shaped-charge

explosive at the end, and tamped it carefully into the hole. She knew intellectually it wouldn't explode no matter how roughly it was treated – it needed an electrical charge to set it off – but knowing what it could do, it was hard not to treat the thing with respect.

"How's it going up there, Anna?" Vik asked.

"Good," the girl called down from above. "I've got three set up."

"Great. Pull up your charges."

They got done about an hour before quitting time and made the long trek back down to the belly of the beast. They were about halfway there when Vik felt the charges detonate by the way the floor quivered under their feet. She frowned, but didn't say anything. Protocol was to make sure everyone was accounted for before setting off explosives, but less and less did Andrei seem worried about protocol. They had lost more diggers to injury and death in the last year than in the other three she had been working for him. He seemed in a hurry to mine as much of the Kaiju as he could, as quickly as possible.

When they reached the outside, Andrei was there, having an animated discussion with Chandra, one of the few real scientific types that worked for him. Uncharacteristically, his excitement seemed motivated by cheerfulness rather than his more typical anger or disappointment. The two were staring at the screen of a scanner.

Andrei noticed them after a moment.

"Good work," he said. "You get a little extra today. But I need you back here an hour early tomorrow, yes?"

They went into the chemical shower, still in their suits, and when they came out, Andrei was gone.

She went over to Chandra, who was a pretty decent guy. He was new, so that would probably change.

"What's all of the excitement about?" she asked.

He smiled, and tapped up an image.

"This," he said. "I suspected from some of the earlier readings, but that last round of charges you set enabled us to get our best resonance image of the hip yet. You see that?"

Vik examined the image. She could see the leg bone they had been digging, and then a massive shadow which must be the pelvis. But inside of the pelvis was a largish, irregular light spot.

"It's hollow?" she guessed.

"I think it's an auxiliary heart," he said. "Most Kaiju have them – they're far too big for a single heart, no matter how massive, to keep blood moving up and down more than two hundred feet. Different Kaiju have different solutions for the problem. In some, the major arteries also contracted and relaxed to accelerate the blue fluid on its journey. Others had a sequence of smaller, heart-like muscles that acted like pumping substations. This one – well, this pelvis is larger than the other, larger than it needed to be, but there weren't extra muscle attachments to the outside to suggest it needed to be. So I guessed it might be doing double duty as a hip and as a vault, protecting something. In this case, I believe a heart. It will be long dead, of course, but that doesn't matter to the people who think Kaiju heart will promote longer life and… ah… virility. An ounce of dried heart will fetch more than a hundred pounds of bone powder. Imagine the bonus you'll get."

She was trying to. If Andrei stuck with his usual percentage, that could be something. But he probably wouldn't. He had always paid as little as possible, and she didn't see that changing just because he got a windfall.

She shucked off the Dig suit, hung it back with the rest, and started home. Anna was waiting for her, as she had been for the last several days. She was nine, with mussy red hair and big dark eyes. She lived in one of Andrei's "accommodations", an old hotel that was so dilapidated it was almost as dangerous as the Dig.

Why she had latched onto Vik, she had no idea. She hadn't gone out of her way to be friendly with her, or with anyone else, for that matter.

As they were walking along, she actually heard the girl's stomach growl. Anna looked embarrassed.

"I notice you didn't have much lunch," Vik said.

"No," Anna said, "rent was due this week, so Andrei just took it out of my pay."

It was a neat trap Andrei had a lot of his workers in. He gave them money which they had to give right back to him. He made sure they never earned enough to save anything. Workers with savings might leave, try to find a job somewhere else. If you were always about a meal behind, that wasn't possible.

Vik wasn't in that trap at least. Not yet. She and Babulya still had their place, and Andrei didn't own it. But if grandmother lost her job, they could very well end up like Anna.

After another couple of blocks, she saw a woman selling *pyanse* from a cart on the street corner.

"Hang on," she told Anna, and bought two of them and offered Anna one.

"Don't get used to it," she said.

Anna looked like she didn't understand at first, but then took the steamed bun and bit into it, closing her eyes as she chewed the filling of pork and cabbage.

"That's so good," she said.

Vik agreed. She didn't usually buy anything from street vendors. It was too expensive. But sometimes a small extravagance was called for.

* * *

When she approached the Dig the next day, Kaiju worshippers were there, blocking the road in. It wasn't the first time; they gathered periodically, sometimes just a few of them sometimes a lot of them, like today. Andrei didn't tolerate them on the site, of course, but they were a nuisance anyway. Vik kept her gaze down, trying not to make eye contact. Some of them were chanting a song in a language she didn't know. Many of them had tattoos of Kaiju, and despite the chill that still lingered in May, were half-undressed to show them off. Others were burning incense; the smoke smelled a lot like burnt Kaiju, and probably was.

She shouldered her way through half of the crowd, but then someone grabbed her by the shoulders and spun her around, bringing her face-to-face with an old woman. For a second Vik thought she had four eyes, but then she saw that two of them were tattooed in dark blue, and didn't have pupils. The rest of her face was tattooed as well, and she came to the sickening realization the markings and the weird headdress she wore were meant to make her resemble a Kaiju, probably Karloff.

"You have been within the Sea Angel," the woman said.

"Yeah," Vik said. "Let go of me."

"They came for us. They came to rid the Earth of inequity. To save us and make us one. And yet look what they did! Killed this beautiful, worshipful god so you can crawl around in it like a maggot. But your days are soon to end, little worm. Righteous justice will not be delayed forever!"

"Let me go!" Vik said, bringing her hands up and out, breaking the woman's hold. She felt unaccountably frightened; they were all around her, chanting, some yelling almost in her ears.

"You will die and become dust and never know their embrace!" the woman shrieked.

That was more than enough for Vik. She fought her

way clear of the crowd and ran for the Dig.

They were just idiots, she knew. Losers. Crazy. She knew she shouldn't be scared of anything the old lady said.

But she found it hard to shake off her words, for some reason. The horrible, loving tone of her voice when she talked about Kaiju had rattled her more than any of it.

But there was work to do, and despite having a generally bad feeling, she got to it, climbing back up into the monstrous body and planting more charges in the bone. The night crews had been cleaning out the shards liberated by the previous explosions. Chandra figured it was going to take another two sets of blasts to reach the heart cavity.

After donning her suit, she saw Andrei and went over to him.

"Someone set the charges off early yesterday," she told him. "Before we were clear."

"You're in one piece, aren't you?" he said. "So obviously you were clear."

"Well, but the charges aren't supposed to blow until we're completely out of there, right? That's the rules."

"Who do you think makes the rules?" he asked, angrily. "Don't worry about it. You'll be safe. Go do your job and stop thinking you can tell me how to do mine."

She knew better than to push him any farther. At least he'd heard out her complaint.

Once more, they set the charges, then started back down. The warning klaxons began, and soon diggers from other parts of their section began filtering into the thoroughfare behind them.

They were just about halfway there when she noticed a streak of blue on Anna's protective suit.

"What is that?" she asked.

Anna glanced at it, then lifted her hands. The fingers of her gloves were also blue.

"I dunno," she said. "It was kind of wet up there."

"Wet?" Vik said. "But – oh, crap. Anna, run." She turned to shout back at the other crews coming out, some of which were pretty far behind them. "Everybody!" she shouted at the top of her lungs. "Run!"

Anna had taken her at her words, and was already twenty yards ahead of her. Vik ran after.

*Don't set off the charges early, Andrei*, she thought. Just once, let him listen to her, to anyone but himself.

She caught up with Anna, and almost ran past her. If she reached Andrei in time, warned him what was about to happen, she might prevent it.

She never found out what she would have decided, because at just that moment, the charges went off.

"Faster," she told the other girl. "Faster."

Anna tried. The concentration was clear on her face. She was going as fast as she could.

Maybe she was wrong. Probably. What did she know about these things?

But then she heard the screams behind her, sounds she didn't know a human voice could make, and without another thought she grabbed Anna's hand and practically dragged her along as the shrieking continued, and now she heard a rushing sound, like the sound of water going down a storm drain, but louder. She looked back and saw blue light racing down the walls.

They made it to the great cavity and halfway across it before the cyan flood reached them; the smell was incredibly strong, so intense she thought her breath would close up in her chest. Her eyes were burning. And then it hit her in the back of the legs, and she knew they were done, but she slogged on, anyway, still holding the screaming Anna by the hand, expecting at any moment to be overwhelmed.

But then she realized that the gut hollow was big enough

that the flow had spread out, and was now no deeper than her calves. Still, she felt a tingling sensation beginning, and ran for the exit.

Outside was bedlam; crews were suiting up, vac hoses that hadn't been used in years were being prepped. She saw Andrei arguing with Chandra and several foremen as she struggled to get the hysterical Anna into the chemical shower.

Stripping out of her own suit, Vik saw blisters were developing on her legs, and on Anna's as well.

"You saved me," Anna said. "I would have died."

"Come on," Vik said.

"Where are we going?"

"Away from here."

"But my pay..."

The run after the explosion had been the most sustained panic of her life. But something was coming out of the other end of it.

Anger. Certainty.

She was nothing to Andrei, and working for him – or someone like him – she would always be nothing. Even if she kept getting promoted until she *was* Andrei, she would be nothing, because in the grand scheme of things, Andrei was nothing. A user. An exploiter. He contributed nothing to the world, and neither did she, as things were now.

It had been easy to quit, once she was certain she was not a Kaidanovsky. Easy to think she was nothing. But now she remembered the conversation with her grandfather, the night she nearly froze to death, the night the Kaiju she had just come out of had been slain by Cherno Alpha. How he had reacted when she said her parents were the Kaidanovskys. How it seemed he wanted to tell her it wasn't true. He hadn't, because – like Grandmother – he thought if she believed, she might rise to excellence.

But she didn't need to be a Kaidanovsky to be somebody.

Her grandfather had been somebody. She needed no more than that.

She wanted to pilot a Jaeger. She wanted to be someone of consequence.

As she stood there, thinking that, it was like she was in the eye of the storm. Andrei was mobilizing his people not to search for survivors, but to capture the blood before it lost its potency. Was it really Kaiju blood, preserved in that heart, sheltered in a vault of bone? Or was it merely water that had collected from snowmelt and become toxic?

She didn't know. She didn't care. But she noticed that the door to Andrei's office was ajar.

She didn't even try to sneak. No one was watching. She just walked in, went through his desk, came up with a double handful of rubles, and walked out. She took Anna to her mother, gave her a hundred rubles, and told her to leave town if she could.


Sensei came to the door, looking sleepy and cross. She had been pounding on it for several minutes. When he saw who it was, his eyebrows rose. He evaluated her for a moment.

"This is my home," he said.

"I didn't know what else to do," she said.

"Downstairs," he said. "In the dojo."

She went back down the stairs and waited as he unlocked the dojo. It wasn't warm inside, but it wasn't freezing either.

He listened to her story without comment. When she finished, he sighed.

"What do you want me to do?" he asked.

"When I don't come back, Andrei will figure out it was me," she said. "If he doesn't know already. If someone saw me. And he will kill me, I'm sure of it. I must leave town.

And I must take my grandmother with me. But I don't know where to go, or – or how to get there. I've been on one train in my life."

He nodded, and stared off at nothing for a minute or two.

"How much money did you take?" he asked.

She handed it over to him.

His eyes sharpened. "Well, that will help," he said.

"I'll get your grandmother," he said. "In case Andrei already knows. What can I tell her? How can I get her to leave?"

"Tell her the Kaiju know her name, know where she is, and they're coming for her. Tell her Vik sent you to help."

In a way, she thought, it wasn't even a lie. Maybe her grandmother wasn't as crazy as she seemed.

# 28

THE KAIJU GRAPPLED ONTO THEIR INJURED ARM and began to torque. Metal screamed in protest; renewed pain knifed into Ming-hau's shoulder. Deep inside of Shaolin Rogue, cables began to strain and then snap, as the tail struck the Conn-Pod repeatedly, until cracks began to spiderweb across the viewport.

They fought for control, but were overwhelmed by the sheer savagery of the attack.

Then, suddenly, above, the water broke as something plunged through – and the Kaiju was off them. Gone.

"Hope we didn't need an invitation," a new voice said. It was one of the Wei brothers, he couldn't tell which.

"No, please," Suyin said. "Come in, sit down, have some tea."

Crimson Typhoon had arrived.

It was good timing; as Shaolin Rogue came back to her feet, they could clearly see the towers of Shanghai. They hadn't realized how far toward shore the fight had taken them.

Crimson Typhoon was a Mark-4, and one of the most technically advanced Jaegers in existence. It was the only Jaeger with three pilots – triplet brothers, Cheung, Jin, and Hu. They were intense, standoffish toward strangers, extremely competitive among themselves.

And incredible Jaeger pilots.

Typhoon had been tailored to the Wei brothers, to take full advantage of their abilities; she had three arms, and all of them were now in motion; they had deployed their vortex blades – essentially gigantic circular saws – and were now in what the triplets called Thundercloud Formation. Huo Da submerged as if trying to avoid the attack but then exploded from the sea, wrapping its remaining limbs around the Jaeger. Typhoon chopped its vortex blades down on the heavily armored back; they sparked and sheared off.

This was the first time Ming-hau had had a clear view of the Kaiju out of the water – it was thicker than he thought, closer to cylindrical than flat.

"No," Suyin said, in response to his unspoken observation. "It is changing, blowing up like a balloon."

The Kaiju whipped out its two long tentacle arms in another attempt to grapple Typhoon, but with almost blinding speed the three arms whirled and the vortex blades keened through armor and bones, and one of the Kaiju's arms fell writhing to the ocean.

"Why is it inflating like that?" he wondered. "To fight better out of water? If so, it's not working too well."

Any speculation on that had to wait, as Typhoon kicked its knee up into Huo Da's underside and the Kaiju suddenly lunged low, toppling the crimson-and-gold giant with pure mass.

Shaolin Rogue's left arm remained connected but was

now useless. But their right arm was still fine.

"Meteor Chain!" Ming-hau said, aiming the arm. From the center of the fist, a steel ball shot forth, pulling a chain of titanium alloy a hundred and fifty feet long at maximum extension. Rogue whipped it in a circle over her head, three times, then sent it arcing toward Huo Da, just as the Kaiju reared up to crash down upon Crimson Typhoon again. As intended, the ball went past the monster but the chain caught it below the head and then spun to wrap around it. Rogue deepened her stance and heaved.

The razor-sharp titanium chain went tight enough to sing an almost subsonic note. Huo Da fought the pull, straining back until blue stripes appeared on its armor. It jerked back and forth, like a fish on a line, yanking them toward it, but as they drew nearer, motors inside the Jaeger pulled the cable in to keep it from going slack.

Crimson Typhoon rose back up from the sea, got back in Thundercloud Formation, and charged.

Huo Da suddenly leapt high, pulling Shaolin Rogue off her feet, and twisted contrariwise to the pull of the chain, unwinding in midair before splashing back into the sea, sending minor tidal waves out to push both Jaegers back a step.

Now free, the Meteor Chain began retracting.

Crimson Typhoon turned about, searching for the Kaiju.

"There," Suyin said, pointing toward shore, where Huo Da's back was just visible above the waves. Confronted by two Jaegers, it seemed to be running.

Typhoon went after it, taking long strides, emerging from the water as the continental shelf grew ever shallower. Shaolin came after, although they weren't quite able to match Typhoon's speed. When the water was a little more than knee deep to a Jaeger, Typhoon leapt free of the water, the rocket assists on her legs blazing. She came out of the water with such grace, Ming-hau was reminded of a dancer. She landed just behind the Kaiju, gripping it with two hands on the right flank with digits designed specifically to latch onto Kaiju, and delivered an enormous blow with the much bigger, heavier third fist.

Shaolin Rogue was catching up, but it looked like the battle might be over before they got there. The sea bottom rose up to form a shoal; they were now only a little more than ankle deep.

Huo Da wasn't looking so good; it was bleeding in many places, and its long torso was now bloated and misshapen, as if it was hemorrhaging massively within, its guts ruptured and rearranged by Crimson Typhoon's savage punches. The Mark-4 lifted the beast out of the water and hurled it – not directly at them, but in their general direction, toward the shelf they stood on. The shallow water did nothing to cushion the Kaiju's fall; it landed with a jarring crunch, then struggled to rise back up.

Shaolin deployed the Meteor Chain again, and this time just swung the heavy weight into the Kaiju's head as it tried to recover. It went down, hard, and with a ragged cheer they started toward it.

The water was too shallow for Huo Da to completely submerge; its water jets were more or less useless, so it was reduced to crawling with its remaining forelegs. Ming-hau wondered how it had planned on attacking Shanghai in the first place, when it was so thoroughly aquatic. In general, the Kaiju seemed to have been getting better, adapting somehow to Jaegers and other human technologies.

This one seemed more like a mistake.

It lay there, writhing, probably dying. Typhoon started forward for the kill.

Before the Jaeger got there, Huo Da split open, blue ichor spurting from the rupture.

"That's right," one of the Weis said. "Go ahead and die. You don't want any more of this."

Ming-hau relaxed in his harness. He glanced over at Suyin, feeling her relief as well. He breathed in slow, out slow.

But then something pushed up out of the Kaiju, wriggling through the blood and bile, unfolding into the atmosphere, like a cicada coming out of its skin, or a butterfly from its cocoon – but much more quickly.

Before either Jaeger could react, three pairs of wings opened to the sky. In any other context, he might have thought them pretty; they were translucent, shot through with faint blue strands, reminding him very much of dragonfly wings. Eight long, clawed legs unfolded beneath it as it stood from its discarded skin. The rear pair were particularly enormous, resembling the jumping legs of a grasshopper, and it now used them to leap forward and kick Crimson Typhoon in the face.

Shaolin Rogue was still retracting the Meteor Chain, but they nevertheless rushed forward to aid Typhoon. Huo Da saw them coming and climbed into the air, the wind from its wings rippling the water, then dove down at them. Rogue threw up their arms to block the attack. Even as they did so Ming-hau saw that the powerful legs each ended in a foot with six clawed toes, two of which were opposable.

The first ever flying Kaiju. What luck.

Huo Da caught Rogue's good arm; they pulled back, but they'd never imagined how strong its wings were; Shaolin Rogue felt herself pulled up; for a moment, the inertia of their considerable mass kept them in place, but then one foot came up from the sea bed, and then another.

And then, impossibly, they were airborne. They saw Crimson Typhoon splashing desperately toward them, but the other Jaeger was too late; in moments, they were far out of reach.

"Shoot it down," Suyin yelled. "Typhoon, use your plasma cannon!"

"We might hit you!" Crimson Typhoon replied. "Fight free, give us a clear shot."

Huo Da was holding them by their only good arm, so it was impossible to punch or grab it, so they tried to swing up and kick it, but they simply didn't have that much mobility in their waist.

"We can jettison the arm," Ming-hau said. "Use the explosive bolts."

"Shaolin Rogue," Tendo broke in. "You won't survive the fall."

"We might, if we do it now," Suyin said. "The sea will break our fall."

"It's less than fifty feet deep, where you are."

"We have to give Typhoon a clear shot," Suyin said.

Their eyes met. They didn't have to talk. There was no argument to be had.

"Firing the bolts," Suyin said.

The jolt of the explosions was tiny, but they were instantly in free fall.

"I love you," he told his wife.

"I love you, too," she said.

He remembered the first time he had ever seen her. They had been twelve, the first day of school – she was the new girl in class; everyone thought she had a funny accent, because she was from Yunnan. He wanted to put his arm around her, shield her from the others, but he had been too scared of what they might say. The other boys also said she had a big nose and thick legs, and she wasn't very pretty.

But she was to him.

Four days later, when he finally worked up the courage to sit next to her at lunch, she looked at him, and then leaned forward.

"It's about time," she whispered.

Ming-hau closed his eyes.

# 29

JINHAI WOKE IN A BOX, OR PERHAPS THE DREAM of a box. His mind seemed to float in and out of being, as if he was stuck at the fine edge between sleep and waking. He knew he ought to be freaking out, but it was as if his emotions were wrapped in a big, fuzzy blanket. It wasn't dark: the walls of the box glowed softly.

Time blurred away from him. He slept. When next he woke, the box was opened, and someone pulled him out of it. He realized that his vision was hazy; he couldn't quite make anything out. Faces moved before him as ovals with dark patches for eyes and mouths. Now and then someone said something, but not in English or Mandarin.

Eventually, his sight began to sharpen. As everything gradually came into focus, he saw someone sitting, back slightly turned toward him. In front of her – he saw it was a woman – was a hologram display. As he watched, she manipulated some of the images.

Then he became much more concerned with his condition. He was in a chair – well, not just in it, but strapped to it with narrow plastic bands. He didn't seem to be in the Moyulan Shatterdome, either, or at least no place he had been. The room had an odd shape, with one curved wall, and was painted an unpleasant pale green.

He turned his head and saw Vik was there, and likewise restrained. He also felt a sharp pain in his ribs.

"Ouch," he said. "What the hell—"

The woman turned at the sound of his voice.

"Ah," she said. "There you are." She pointed at his side. "I hope that doesn't hurt too much. We had to remove your transponder, of course. I wonder why you even had one. Very peculiar."

"Help!" Jinhai hollered.

"Don't get hysterical," the woman said. "If yelling would help, do you really imagine I would have left you the ability to speak?"

"Who are you?" Vik demanded.

"That's not all that important," she said. "You two. You're the important ones."

"You know us?"

"Only recently," she said. "You've been a very convenient distraction."

"You're the one who framed us? You killed Braga?"

Her face fell, slightly. "Of course I didn't mean for Braga to die," she said. "All of that was merely a diversion, you know. Since he did die, they made more of a fuss, so it worked to my advantage, but it wasn't my aim. But these things happen, and we move past them."

"Distraction from what?" Jinhai demanded. "Why did you frame us? What are we doing here? What's happening?"

"What must happen, of course," she replied.

"Wait," Vik said. "If you wanted the sabotage blamed on us, why kidnap us?"

"At the moment, you seem guiltier than ever," she said. "You've killed again and fled the Shatterdome by boat. By the time the truth is discovered, no one will really care who reprogrammed a Jaeger or killed a minor-grade J-Tech. Least of all the two of you."

"What, you're going to kill us too?" Jinhai asked. He jerked at the plastic bonds, knowing it was hopeless.

"Among other things, yes."

"Something is wrong with you," Jinhai said.

"Something is wrong with all of us," the woman said. "We're all born broken, already dying, and if that were the end of it, all would be well. But instead we're taped and wired together with lies and gibberish and false hope and turned out into the world with mutilated senses. We see beauty in all the wrong things, the things that don't last: the soap bubble in the sun, the cherry blossom in the wind, the flare of a shooting star. Illusion. But there is an underlying reality. You can see it in the numbers. You believe the quantum fields that make you possible care that you believe you have a soul? You are nothing, Jinhai. I am nothing. We are nothing. Epiphenomena. But we can be made real. Through Them. Fighting Them was our biggest mistake. Fighting Them took my love. It took my life. I wanted to die for so long – but then I realized I could do better than die. I can deliver myself to them. Deliver everyone to them. Give them their world. I will rectify our mistake."

He thought he was going to vomit. She sounded so sincere, so absolutely sure of herself. He had once seen a guy on a train telling everyone that his fingers were talking to him. He asserted it with utter conviction. He even did the voices of his different fingers, so everyone could hear.

His pinky had been a baritone, which was surprising.

He had also been sporting the round part of a banjo for a hat, wearing boxers with no pants, big yellow boots, and an old Quell t-shirt. The whole package. It made sense.

But this woman didn't look crazy. She looked normal, just a regular person dressed for work.

But maybe that was because he wasn't really looking at her. Dustin had told him once that usually you only *looked* at another person's face once, so you'd know it next time. After that you recognized it by a sort of neural shorthand that sorted salient features. And his neural shorthand was telling him something was seriously wrong.

And now that he was really looking at her, when he let his gaze extend beyond the surface of her expression – which was sort of sincere and almost serene – her eyes looked like holes drilled into stone, empty and without bottom.

He fought down his panic and tried to think.

"They'll find us," he said desperately. "Lambert and the rest."

"They may," the woman agreed. "Anything is possible. But our voyage is almost complete."

"Voyage?" Jinhai said.

"Of course," the woman said. "We left Moyulan more than a day ago, by helicopter, with you in the cargo area. It was a scheduled flight, nothing that will attract attention. Just a respected scientist, her job complete, flying home. And yes, now we're on a ship."

"Where are we going?" he asked.

She smiled. "The future."

Then she turned back to her work.

When the woman stopped talking to them, Jinhai tried to reassure Vik that things would be okay, but she had slipped into herself, and for a time it was as if he was alone. After a little while the woman excused herself and left. A moment later, a bald guy with a gun took her place. He wore a sleeveless shirt, probably to display the various Kaiju tattooed on his arms.

"What's your name?" Jinhai asked the guy. The man smiled slightly.

"Don't bother," he said. "No matter what you say, or do, our course is set. If you only knew what glory awaits, you would be content."

"Why not explain it to me then?" Jinhai asked. "I wouldn't mind being content."

But the man just shook his head, gave him a pitying look, and went to stand in the corner.

"I'm sorry about this, Jinhai," Vik said, after a few minutes.

"Hey," he said. "Glad to see you're back with us."

"Not for long, I think," she whispered.

Time passed, Jinhai wasn't sure how much. Then more men came, and unstrapped them from the chairs. Vik snapped into action the instant she was free, punching one of the men in the jaw. Jinhai tried to do the same, but he didn't even manage to connect – there were far too many of them, and they clearly knew what they were doing. In moments, they had also subdued Vik. Then the two cadets were more or less carried through the metal corridors of the ship.

After a few turns and some steep stairs, Jinhai found himself on deck.

Jinhai didn't know a lot about ships; he thought it was probably some sort of freighter, maybe a few hundred feet in length. It had a battered, worn, twentieth-century feel to it.

Around them was – nothing. Ocean all the way to the horizon. The sky was cloudless, the air hot. A few gulls followed them and perched now and then on the rails. He thought that meant they weren't too far from land, but again, his nautical knowledge was pretty limited.

The woman said that they had left the Shatterdome in a helicopter, but not how far they had flown. What distance could the ship sail in a day?

What he should probably be focusing on, he figured, was what was happening on deck, but he really didn't want to. Whatever it was it seemed kind of religious. Smoke floated up from several tall censers, and an altar of some sort had been set up close to the bow of the ship. The altar was oddly irregular – it took him a moment to realize that it was a vertebra, maybe six or seven feet across; way bigger than any vertebra ought to be.

Around all of this, a crowd gathered; a lot of them wore robes of one sort or another, and Kaiju tattoos seemed to be a pretty standard feature. Two women and a man stood behind the altar, singing; now and then the crowd chimed in. The music was shrill, weird, and discordant.

"*The* bloody *Rite of Spring*," he muttered aloud.

"What's that?" the woman said.

"*The Rite of Spring*," he said. "It's a ballet, by this Russian composer—"

"I know Stravinsky," she said. "I just wasn't sure I heard you right. Most people don't appreciate that sort of music anymore. But yes, this is very much like that, although you won't be forced to dance to death. That would just be cruel."

# 30

JINHAI WAS A COWARD WHEN IT CAME TO THE break-up. He couldn't find the words to tell Xia that it was over, that it had to be over. Instead he just started finding excuses not to see her. It was easy – he was busy after all. He thought that eventually she would break up with him. That would be great, because he wouldn't feel guilty about it.

Only she didn't do it. But she wasn't happy. Their time together became less and less pleasant as their connection frayed.

"I know what you're trying to do," she said one evening. "But I won't let you."

She started kissing him, and for a few hours he convinced himself it would all work out. He told her he loved her, that he was sorry he had been distant.

But he knew better, and he knew, finally, that he was going to have to say the words, no matter how hard or unpleasant it was.

When he finally worked up the nerve, a few weeks before leaving for the Moyulan Shatterdome, she didn't even seem surprised.

But she was angry.

"I was wondering if you would even have the guts," she said. "I figured you would just leave, and I would never hear from you again."

"I'm sorry," he said.

"No you aren't," she said. "Not yet. But you will be. When you realize this drifting, fantasy lover of yours is just that, and that you pushed the one person that might have come close…" She was crying now, but she was still angry.

"Xia –"

"Don't say anything else," she said. "I'm done with this."

# 3 1

"TO BE HONEST, I FIND A LOT OF THESE formalities pointless and tiring," the woman said, as the preparations for their imminent sacrifice continued below. "It's all sort of gilding the lily. But any group needs an identity, and ritual is an important part of that identity."

While she was talking, he craned his neck to make eye contact with Vik. Vik looked more angry than scared which was probably a good thing. He wished he could say the same, but he was terrified.

He wanted to threaten the woman, to resist somehow, but despair was starting to take hold. This was all so crazy it didn't seem real.

"Why are you doing this?" he asked. "Can you at least tell me that? I mean, if I'm gonna die—"

"You are going to die," she said, a little angrily, the first genuine emotion he felt he'd seen from her. "We all are – today, tomorrow, a few decades – it makes no difference when, does it? How can it? But you, you're going to be elevated. Your life will have meant something." She paused and waved at the singing crowd below. "You know. Sort of."

He sighed. "You really are just crazy, aren't you?"

"I *was* crazy," she corrected. "When I was your age, and for years after. And for a long time after that, I lived in a pit so deep and dark I hardly remember the years passing. But then I understood what I was meant to do, found my purpose. And very soon now, that purpose will be complete. And so will I."

"Killing Vik and me is your whole purpose in life?"

It wasn't the craziest thing she'd said, but he was starting to see how hard that would be to sort into a list.

"Oh," she said. "That's silly. No. Do you know anything about western marriage ceremonies?"

"I've been to a couple," he said.

"Often a little boy and girl are chosen to participate. The girl is the flower girl, and she lays a trail of flowers. The boy is the ringbearer, and he brings the wedding rings to the couple. It is all very cute, and people like it. I mean, neither child is critical or even necessary – the marriage is the important thing. It can happen without a flower girl and a ringbearer." She smiled and patted his shoulder, and then Vik's

"But it's nice to have them, anyway."

Jinhai was about to say that he didn't recall – in the weddings he had attended – either child being *killed*.

But something else weird was happening, and he became distracted.

Just in front of the ship, a wave was rising; but it didn't break over them, it just kept going up, shining from within with golden light.

*Kaiju*, was all he could think. She bloody did it somehow. She summoned a Kaiju back into the world.

The people down below knew it, too, and just lost their minds.

Then the wave broke, and its maker stood revealed. And it was very, very large. But it wasn't a Kaiju.

People began to scream now, but not Jinhai.

Because it was Gipsy Avenger.

Coming toward them, growing nearer and taller as if walking up an underwater staircase.

"You know what?" Jinhai told the woman. "I think the wedding has just been canceled."

Once they realized Morales was behind Sokk and ultimately the sabotage of Chronos Berserker, things moved pretty fast. They discovered she had been picked up – along with some of her equipment – by a company helicopter from her employer, Geognosis. Checking the registered flight plan revealed the chopper had never reached its intended destination, so they went to satellite data, which showed the chopper headed southeast, ultimately rendezvousing with an old break bulk ship near the Philippines.

Twenty minutes later, Lambert and Burke were strapping into Gipsy Avenger and under tow of Jumphawks, following her trail. The Jumphawks had circled wide of the ship and set them down in deep water, directly in her path, and there they had waited until she was within striking distance. After that, it was a simple matter of walking up the slope of the continental shelf to take them by surprise.

It had all gone perfectly, except for one thing: from the moment they had engaged pilot-to-pilot protocol, something had been wrong. Not with Gipsy, but with her pilots.

With Burke.

For the two pilots to function as one, their thoughts

had to be joined to the point that it was hard to know who was thinking what. This was almost never absolutely true or completely stable – it was one reason why a Jaeger could only be piloted for a limited time before the neural handshake fell apart. But this time – it was rough. Burke was fighting him, for some reason. He wasn't all in or even close to it.

He was hiding something. And Burke knew that Lambert knew he was hiding something, which set up a dangerously low level of Drift – and that was causing glitches: things weren't always lined up. Once, climbing up the slope from the edge of the shelf, they had nearly stumbled.

What could be so bad Burke needed to hide it? Unless he and Morales were somehow in this together...

*Not going there.*

Because if he did, and he was right, Burke would know.

"Burke," he said, as they emerged in front of the ship. "Tighten up."

"Aye, aye, skipper," Burke said.

Lambert tried to ignore that, and instead watched with a certain amount of pleasure as the people on the deck of the ship abandoned whatever kind of Kaiju-worshipping weirdness they were up to and began to run around pell-mell. That was inevitably followed by small-arms fire which had about the same chance of stopping them as a handful of gnats had of taking down an elephant.

It wasn't impossible – just very, very unlikely.

Gipsy began wading forward.

"Any sign of big guns?" Lambert asked.

"That's probably a rocket launcher," Burke said. "Right there."

A part of the holographic display suddenly zoomed in on a largish piece of equipment that had just been unveiled from beneath a tarp.

"Yep, that would be a rocket launcher," Lambert said. "Engage Gravity Sling."

"Gravity Sling engaged," Burke said.

Gipsy Avenger was more than an upgraded version of Gipsy Danger; she had equipment that no Mark-3 or 4 could have dreamed of. One of the neatest was the Gravity Sling Gipsy's right hand immediately reconfigured to form. Just as it finished, the first of the missiles fired.

The air between Gipsy's Gravity Sling and the rocket launcher suddenly rippled as if seen through high heat as the gravitic beam reached across the intervening space. It caught the missile in flight, the launcher, and two operators. For an instant, it held them and then – as the name implied, and with a motion of Gipsy's arm to create the trajectory – slung the whole lot far out to sea. Just as it was nearly invisible with distance, the rocket exploded, a blinding flash of blue-green light that sent shockwaves through their systems.

"What the hell was that?" Burke yelped.

"I guess it's a good thing it didn't hit us," Lambert replied.

It was time to stop playing around. There was no telling what these nuts had up their sleeves.


Jinhai cheered aloud when the rocket launcher went sailing off into the air. Then an explosion seemed to fill the sky. He watched it expand, awestruck, and belatedly realized that had been his chance to try and break away. He had missed it. The Kaiju cultists all had firm grips on him again.

The woman turned to the men holding him and Vik and pointed out one of them.

"You," she said. "Go tell the captain to destroy navigation and all of the onboard computers. Everything.

Don't just wipe them, destroy them. Use the charges. We cannot let them know our destination. And tell him not to send any messages out. Our brothers and sisters will know how to act on our silence. Do you understand?"

"Yes, Sister," one of them said.

"The rest of you, drag these two up front," she said. "Make sure the Jaeger sees them. They won't destroy the ship if they know these two are on board."

The men started to pull Jinhai forward.

Gipsy grabbed the ship by the prow.

Everyone flew off their feet as the ship ground to a sudden halt.

Jinhai fell like everyone else, but he was free of grasping hands, so when he hit the deck he rolled, jumped up, and ran back down into the ship. Vik was just ahead of him, leaping over his captors as they made a grab for her. He felt a sudden rush; gravity went strange and a wind rose; a backward glance showed him Gipsy was lifting the ship completely out of the water. He also saw one of the Kaiju worshippers coming after him, a red-headed guy, almost on top of him.

His natural instinct was to back up, get some distance and look for an opening, but the little bit of Vik in him said otherwise; he stepped closer, planted his feet, kidney punched the man with his left fist and drove his right fist hard into his armpit, then brought his left elbow back around, connecting with his opponent's chin.

The guy dropped like a sack, and Jinhai scrambled on as, belatedly, an alarm began to blare. The ship shuddered again, tilting wildly, but Jinhai managed to brace himself against the bulkhead to keep from falling. A quick look back showed no other pursuers; the rest of his minders must have reprioritized their life-templates or whatever.

"Vik!" he shouted. He'd lost her – she had gotten too

far ahead. There was almost no one down here, now, but the alarm was still loud enough to make it hard to hear.

He turned a corner and found himself almost face to face with one of the guys who had been holding them earlier, the bald guy with the tattoos.

Before Jinhai could do anything, something hit him in the gut, and a bolt of electricity raced through him. He stumbled back, trying to stay on his feet, but it was no use. He fell, and the man hit him with the Taser again. He fought for consciousness as his own muscles tried to break his bones; through the red filter of agony, he made out Vik in the room beyond, doubled up on the floor. Then the man kicked him in the head, and Jinhai flopped over and fetched against a bulkhead.

"It's over," Jinhai managed to groan. "That's Gipsy Avenger out there. You're done."

"No," the man said. "This changes nothing. The blood of the Sea Angels will cleanse the earth. It can't be stopped."

"You're nuts."

"The bomb isn't on board, you see," the man said, kicking him in the chest. "They won't find it in time. Or you." He turned and walked back toward Vik, brandishing the Taser.

*Stay down*, his body told him. *You're not a hero. Not like Mom and Dad.*

But it wasn't about being a hero. It was about not letting the man get back to Vik.

So, doggedly, he pushed himself up, using the wall.

"Hey, jerk," he grunted.

The man had taken a few steps away from him, but now he turned back.

"Idiot," the man said, and thrust the Taser at him again.

Jinhai blocked. Or tried to, but nothing seemed to be working right. The man batted aside his hand, and again he felt the body-jolting sting of voltage coursing through him. This time he smelled something burnt, and he bit his tongue, painfully. He began whiting out, but before everything bleached completely away, he thought he saw something behind the man. It looked like an angel, an angel with eyes of fire holding a chair over her head.


As Mako Mori's helicopter settled on the deck of the Akumagami Front ship, she saw up close what a bloody business it had been. Gipsy Avenger had carried the ship to nearby Kabani Island, where it was greeted by a contingent of Philippine-based peacekeeping marines.

Three quarters of the ship's crew had died fighting, and most of the rest were wounded. The marine colonel in charge of the mission – Ferand Ocampa – greeted her as she disembarked. She'd met him on another occasion and remembered him as someone who laughed easily. But he was frowning now.

"Secretary General," he said. "I don't think you should be on board."

"The fighters are subdued. You swept for bombs."

"We might have missed something."

"I am sure you didn't," she said, "and time is of the essence, Colonel." She swept her gaze over the carnage: medical teams covered much of the deck, and another detail was moving the bodies of those who no longer needed medical attention to a PPDC marine transport.

"Your people fought fiercely, and well," she said.

"The Philippines suffered greatly from the Kaiju," Ocampa said. "Hundun, Gyakushu, Taurax. It seemed we were cursed. When I was young Manila was such a jewel…" He sighed. "The Kaiju cannot pay for what they did to our homeland. It is a pity men and women had to die today, but for the Kaiju worshippers, I shed no tears. And my marines – they will sleep well."

Mako remembered the need for revenge. It had once driven her almost completely, or so she thought. There had always been other things – love, respect, honor. But she hadn't really appreciated that until she really understood how hollow and... incomplete revenge could be.

"What of my cadets, Colonel," she asked. "I'm told they are alive?"

"They're okay," he said. "Some bumps and bruises, but nothing serious."

"And Dr. Morales?" Gottlieb inquired, anxiously.

"She's alive," Ocampa said. "It appears that they blew up their navigation console and fried their computers. None of the survivors are talking about where they were going, or why. My suspicion is that none of them know, except for Morales. The captain and all of the officers are dead."

"I want to talk to Dr. Morales," Mako said.

"We found her in her office," the colonel said, "destroying her computer and files. We detained her there."

"If they are medically able, have the cadets brought to her office as well," Mako said.

A marine escorted her and Gottlieb through the ship to where Morales waited. The scientist seemed very calm as she watched them enter.

"Dr. Morales," Mako said. "I wonder what you're up to."

"Not very much, Secretary General, as you can see." She held up her cuffed hands.

"Good Lord, Ysabel," Gottlieb exploded. "What is this about? Why are you involved with these Kaiju extremists? Do you know the sorts of atrocities the Akumagami Front has perpetrated?"

"Yes, Hermann," she said. "I'm more than aware of the things they've done. I was involved in quite a few of them. I am sorry to have involved you too, old friend, but it was unavoidable."

"I really do not understand," Gottlieb said. "You have one of the greatest minds the world has ever known—"

"Then perhaps, Hermann, you should trust that what I've done is for the best."

"But what have you done?" he demanded.

"You will find out soon enough," she said. "I'm only sad I won't be around to see it myself."

"What do you mean? See what?" He put his hand to his chin, and looked away before swinging back to her.

"Why won't you see 'it'?"

"We call it crossing the Breach," she said. "I've taken steps to assure I cannot be questioned by more… invasive methods."

"You've taken poison," Mako said. "The same poison you gave Sokk?"

"Sokk was pitiful," she said. "His faith wasn't pure. When he learned the full measure of our mission, he failed. I had little choice but to kill him." She smiled thinly.

Mako heard a sound behind her and saw that Vik and Jinhai had been brought, as she asked.

"Cadets," she said.

Jinhai bowed, low. "Secretary General…" he began.

"There's a bomb!" Vik blurted.

Everyone turned to her, but Mako looked instead at Morales. For an instant, the scientist's calm veneer broke, and Mako saw a strange kind of anguish there. It was an expression she would never forget.

"Go on, cadet," Mako said.

"There was a guy – he called it the blood of the Sea Angels. That it was a bomb, but that it's not on the ship."

"Morales?"

"You are not the scourge," Morales whispered, her gaze

searching somewhere beyond them. "You are the salvation. We fall to our knees in your infinite shadow, and raise our hands in awe and admiration. Let the blue blood of the Archangels wash away our iniquity that we may start life anew in the world before."

She kept going, but her voice grew weaker.

"Tell us about this bomb," Mori demanded.

The scientist shook her head. "You are left with nothing," she said.

"Ysabel," Gottlieb said. "I beg you. Help us stop whatever you've begun here. Explain it to us."

She shook her head. Mako noticed a single red tear leaking from the corner of one eye. When she spoke, the strain was evident, and her words were pinched and somewhat difficult to understand.

"Our... time... is over, Hermann. I've... accepted it, as I accept my death. As I... am finally... at peace with... Sean's death."

"Ysabel," Gottlieb said. His voice shook. "I am so sorry that this is what you believe to be peace. So sorry."

# 3 2

FIVE YEARS AFTER HER FLIGHT FROM YUZHNO-
Sakhalinsk, Vik sat on the roof of a warehouse, staring
across Golden Horn Bay at the Vladivostok Shatterdome,
heart hanging in her chest like a stone. Although the
PPDC allowed the public to take extremely limited tours
of the facility, this was as close as she had ever gotten to
the place where her parents once trained and fought from;
she was determined that if she ever went in, it would be as
a Ranger, or at least a Ranger-in-training.

But now she thought that maybe she would never see
the inside of the place, or any Shatterdome.

Not for lack of trying. That last night in Sakhalin had
changed her life. Sitting in the dojo, waiting for Sensei
to bring Grandmother, she'd had a moment of clarity. It
began when she realized how ashamed Sasha and Aleksis
Kaidanovsky would be of her if they saw the path she
had started down – the path of victimhood, of being a

little person living at the whim of forces that could crush her at any moment. Both of them had had difficult lives, especially Sasha. They met in a prison, for God's sake. But they became two of the greatest Jaeger pilots to ever live. And when they died, they died fighting, not as hapless casualties of a world that didn't care about them. They might not have been her parents, but she had all but worshipped them. Not because they had been born special, but because they had *become* special, and made her believe she could do the same.

She often thought of that night. Sensei had some connections in Kholmsk, and had bribed someone there to let them cross to the mainland on a railway ferry. From there, they had taken the train to Vladivostok, where Sensei had a sister, Evgeniya, who managed to register Babulya for a disability stipend and got Vik work cleaning and painting ships and dock equipment down at the shipyards. She was technically underage for such work, but the authorities pretty much looked the other way – a lot of her coworkers were no older. It was sort of like mining in the Kaiju – kids could get into places adults had difficulties with, and they could scramble up and slide down ladders like monkeys. Some complained, but to Vik it felt like real work, something her parents would be proud of. That she was also near the Shatterdome was a bonus, and when she was fifteen she was trained in the use of scuba gear so she could work more efficiently underwater. She liked the wetsuit; she thought of it as preparation for wearing a drivesuit.

She worked weekends and summers and sometimes after school, and at school she studied hard. She learned English, even though she hated the very sound of it, because it was more internationally useful than Russian or Korean. She found a coach who taught Systema, a martial art which emphasized knife-fighting, unarmed combat, and firearms. She ran seven kilometers most mornings, before school.

"You didn't get in, did you?"

She'd heard Kolya approaching. She didn't look at him as he settled down cross-legged next to her, but she did hand him the rejection letter.

"Does it say why?" he asked.

"No," she said. "They don't tell you that. They want me to figure it out, I guess."

"You can try again."

"I can," she said. "I will."

"Crap," he said. "You're crying."

"It's just the wind in my eyes," she told him.

"Oh, that's right," he said. "You're too tough to cry. I forgot."

"You want me to push you off this roof?"

"No. Look, I thought you seemed upset. I know how hard you've worked for this; how much it means to you. Thought you might need a friend."

"Thanks," she said. "That's nice. I'm just upset, and I don't usually work through things with people."

"You want me to leave?"

She shook her head. "It's okay."

"How about I get us a bottle of vodka?"

"You know I don't drink," she said.

Everyone drank, usually starting at around ten years old, with their parents. At sixteen, you could legally buy alcohol. She had never done it, though, probably because of the way Grandmother got sometimes.

"Okay," he said. "A soda, then. And something to eat. We can have a picnic – my treat."

"That sounds good," Vik said.

So she and Kolya got some drinks, some pirozhki and

sweet pastries, went to Minny Gorodok Park, settled on the green lawn, and dug into their small feast.

She had met Kolya not long after the move to Vladivostok. He had been quite the pest at first, never seeming to get the hint that she liked to keep to herself. Eventually she'd gotten used to him, though, and even occasionally laughed at his dumb jokes.

But when he suddenly leaned over and kissed her, she was shocked to her core.

If she hadn't been so surprised, the kiss wouldn't have lasted more than a second. As it was, it took her two or three to react; then she slammed her open palm into his chest, sending him sprawling back onto the grass.

"What the hell?" she snapped.

Kolya coughed and felt his chest as if he thought something might be broken.

"Sorry!" he said. "Look, I don't know, I just thought…" He looked down, then slowly drew his gaze back up.

"I'm in love with you, Vik," he said. "You have to know that."

"No!" she shouted. "No, I don't 'have' to know that. I had no idea."

"You really don't feel anything for me?"

"You're my friend, Kolya," she said. "Or I thought you were. One of the few. I thought I could trust you."

"You can trust me," he said.

"I don't do this," she said. "The kissing and the hugging and the making out. I don't have time for it, there's no place for it."

"Yeah," he said. "No place in your life for anything that's not a Kaiju or a Jaeger, is that it? Saving yourself for your Drift partner? Well, tough. You flunked out. Maybe you should have had a Plan B."

She stared at him for a moment, then stood.

"I don't have a Plan B because I'm going to get in," she said. "I've had enough experience with backup plans. I'll take the test again, and this time I will pass. No Plan B. But I do have a Plan B as far as you're concerned," she said. "Goodbye, Kolya."

As she walked away, she realized she actually felt better. Without knowing it, Kolya had done exactly what she needed. He had called her a loser, a quitter, and she was neither. Of course she would try again. There could be no question. She had been through too much. And anyone who thought differently was just a drag at her heels.

# 33

LAMBERT AND BURKE SAT ON TOP OF GIPSY, ONE on either side of the hatch, looking out at the ship, the sea, the islands below.

"Nice view," Burke said.

"Yeah," Lambert replied.

He'd been turning it over in his head how to go about this, but he figured that when in doubt, blunt was the best approach.

"Are you going to tell me what was going on back there, Burke? If that had been a really serious fight…"

"But it wasn't, was it? Just another law enforcement action. Hell, they didn't even need us. A few helicopters and a gunship or two could have pulled them over and handled this."

"Casualties would have been a lot higher on our side," Lambert said. "Those missiles—"

"I get it, I get it," Burke replied. "Look, I'm just going

through some things right now. Personal stuff. I'll let you know when it's relevant."

"Right," Lambert said. But now the thought was in there. The ship below him was owned by a businessman tied to the Akumagami Front. Sokk and Morales clearly hadn't been working alone. Maybe they weren't even the only ones inside the Shatterdome.

What if Burke was in on it, and now that everything had gone bust was just trying to cover his butt?

But he had been in Burke's mind before. They usually drifted well together. If he was an agent of the Akumagami Front, Lambert would know by now, wouldn't he?

Mako Mori's voice was suddenly in his ear.

"You have new orders," she told him.

"We're not returning to Moyulan?"

"No. Remain deployed here until you hear from LOCCENT. I'll send you a brief on what we've learned. There is something out there, something potentially very dangerous. We don't know where it is, but given the heading of the ship, there's a good chance Gipsy is closer to it than any other Jaeger."

"Will do," he replied. "How are Vik and Jinhai?"

"Shaken, but I think they are well."

"That's good. In that case, can you do me a favor?"


Jinhai watched the gray sea below as the helicopter returned them to the Shatterdome. Mako was still questioning Vik about the bomb.

"He said so many things," Vik said. "Something about the blood of dark angels, that kind of thing."

"But he said the bomb wasn't on the boat?"

"No, it wasn't. I'm sure of that. He said they were going to meet it. They were going to be there when it exploded, the first to die in rapture."

"Then perhaps they were planning on detonating it themselves," Gottlieb said. "In which case, we may have ample time to discover its whereabouts."

"The first to die," Mako repeated Vik's words. "From what this man said – from what Morales said – they believe this bomb will bring about the end of the world, at least as we know it. Could they be attempting to open a new breach themselves? Dr. Gottlieb, I know the data she gave you wasn't real, but she might really have been investigating the deep-sea trenches."

"Yes," he said. "Of course, she may have been. That is a great deal of what Geognosis does. I just don't understand what sort of bomb would open a breach."

"He said it would make the world ready for them," Vik said. "For the Kaiju."

"The atmosphere," Gottlieb whispered. "The climate. It isn't right for them. Closer to what they would like than in times before, but not exactly right." He seemed to be getting steadily more excited.

"Newton's data. Everything Morales did – distracting us with Chronos Berserker, creating false evidence implicating the cadets – it was all so she could see his data. The answer must be there. I have to review it at once."

"Jinhai," Mori said. "Do you have anything to add? Did Morales say anything that might be useful?"

Jinhai thought about it, and about the hollow feeling in his gut.

"There was this one thing," he said. "She was comparing whatever was going to happen – the bomb exploding, I guess – to a wedding. She said, ah, that I was going to be the ringbearer, and Vik was going to be the flower girl. But she said we weren't needed for the wedding, that it could go on without us. But the way she was talking, I had a feeling about it. I don't think she thought she was necessary, either. Or anyone on the ship. I think she believed it was going to happen, no matter what."

The Secretary General pursed her lips.

"Well," she said. "Let us hope she is wrong. Now. I need both of you to pay close attention for a moment. When we return to the Shatterdome, there will be questions. But until this is all resolved, and any investigations settled, I must ask you to refrain from speaking of anything classified. Most specifically, you will not mention the Akumagami Front, or Kaiju worshippers, or the situation occurring at the moment. You needn't lie – just tell anyone who asks you've been instructed not to talk about it. The other cadets have been informed that you have been cleared of any wrongdoing. I'm certain that by now everyone in the Shatterdome is aware Gipsy Avenger has been deployed, so it's okay to acknowledge that, but no more. Is this all understood?"

Jinhai and Vik acknowledged that they did, and not much later the Shatterdome came in sight.

# 34

GOTTLIEB PARSED THROUGH NEWTON'S OLD data, wondering exactly what Morales had been looking for. Something to do with the bomb, obviously. From what little they knew of it, Kaiju blood seemed to be somehow involved, so he concentrated on the chemical analysis of the blood itself.

The problem, though, was that Kaiju blood didn't explode. It was noxious, poisonous, corrosive, ridiculously complex, but not explosive – at least not when subjected to the usual sorts of things that caused explosions: heat, electricity, violent acceleration, combustion, and so on.

Perhaps it was meant to make something else explode, then. To act as a catalyst?

He started a new search, this time on the effects of Kaiju blood. There was plenty of data on that; Kaiju blood had darkened the waters or flowed on land after the majority of battles with Jaegers. Chemical plants, oil refineries, liquefied natural gas – all had been exposed to Kaiju blood at one time or another. The blood could bring other things into contact that initiated explosions – by corroding through their containers, for instance – but no such event logged suggested direct contact between Kaiju blood and another chemical was the culprit. He was about to change tack again when he noticed something Newton had flagged, about a microchip plant in Shanghai that had exploded after the battle with Huo Da. It hadn't taken a direct hit from the Kaiju, and in fact hadn't exploded until the next day.

Newton had put a note there, too.

*Huo Da rained blood.*

That was true – Huo Da had flown, and it had been blown apart in the sky. Shanghai's financial district had been rendered so toxic as to be uninhabitable.

Was there something at the plant that reacted to Huo Da's blood?

He got up and went to one of the bins Geiszler had thrown spare junk into, rooting around until he found a board with microchips and dug one out with pliers. He placed it in a clear suppression canister, locked down the lid. Then he went to the refrigeration unit to retrieve some Kaiju blood.

Back in the lab, he got a drop of the blue liquid in a pipette and introduced it to a small opening on the lid of the containment chamber. He stepped back as it trickled down the tube, toward the microchip.

He was thinking that Newton would be proud of him for doing something so foolishly spontaneous.

The blood dripped onto the chip, and for a moment just sat there.

The next moment, everything went white. Gottlieb shook his head, trying to clear the ringing from his ears, blinking at the spots obscuring his vision.

By the time he had recovered, Security had already arrived. "Dr. Gottlieb!" one of them shouted. "Are you okay?"

His voice sounded small, far away, but Gottlieb nodded. The containment chamber was built of a synthetic polymer similar to what Kaiju plating was made of. It was rated to withstand the force of more than a hundred pounds of TNT. It was now spiderwebbed with cracks, and the titanium alloy lid had been blown completely off.

"That's rather bad," he said.

He was about to report the news to Marshal Quan when something occurred to him; for an instant, he almost dismissed it because it seemed random. Then he realized his brain must have dredged it up on purpose. He rushed to his terminal and began pulling up the imagery K-Watch had sent him, the little blue spot in the Philippine Trench.

# 35

LAMBERT LAY ON TOP OF GIPSY, EYES CLOSED, feeling the sun, teetering on the edge of a nap, thinking about Jules. He knew it didn't make any sense – a few glimpses of her at a distance, two conversations, the smell of lavender and grease and ozone. There were a lot of women in the world – hell, there were quite a few in the Moyulan Shatterdome. So what was so special about this girl?

"What's so special about her is that you're even asking the question," Burke said.

He looked over at Burke, lying on the other side of the hatch in a Hawaiian shirt and shorts, dark glasses covering his eyes.

"Huh?" he said.

"You heard me," Burke said.

"But I wasn't talking out loud," Lambert said. "I was just thinking."

"We're Drift partners, buddy," Burke said.

"But we're not drifting now."

Burke lifted his hands. "Then how did I know what you were thinking?"

Lambert just stared at him.

"Why aren't you in your battle armor?" he asked.

"Let's try something," Burke said. "Let's see if you can tell me what *I'm* thinking."

"Burke, I asked you a question. You should be in your armor. We might have to hook in at any second."

Burke sat up and sighed.

"Wrong," he said. He took off his glasses, and a blue glow spilled out. Lambert saw Burke's eye sockets were filled with cold, azure fire.

"I'm thinking it is time for you to die."

Lambert sat up, gasping. He was still on top of Gipsy. Burke lay on the other side of the hatch, in his body armor. He, too, was in the process of sitting up.

A persistent buzzing drew his attention. His comm.

"Yeah," he said.

It was Xiang.

"Gipsy," she said.

"Yep," Lambert replied. "We're here."

"I've got some coordinates for you."

He glanced over at Burke, who nodded.

"You've found the bomb?" Lambert asked her.

"I'll let you talk to Dr. Gottlieb," she said.

Gottlieb broke in almost immediately. "Hello, Ranger," he said. "Taking into account the general heading of the Akumagami ship and data from K-Watch, I believe I have located the general position of the bomb, yes. Within a range of perhaps two kilometers."

"That's not very exact," Lambert replied.

"The radiation signature is being masked," Gottlieb replied. "The bomb itself is probably not particularly large. K-Watch is working on it now. I'm sure by the time you get there we'll have a fix on it."

"Let's have it then," Lambert said. "We can at least get started."

"It's on an island, southeast of your location. Very small, not inhabited year-round. You have the coordinates now."

"Got 'em," Burke said.

"Okay," Lambert said. "We'll head that way and hope for the best."

"Watch yourself," Xiang said. "You'll be going quite near the Galathea Depth. If you fall into that, it could take you a while to climb back out."

"Not to mention the likelihood of more of these Akumagami rogues being in the neighborhood," Gottlieb added.

"We'll stay safe," Burke said.

# 36

CHERNO ALPHA WAS TOP HEAVY – IT HAD BEEN designed that way. It was built to stand its ground, to bruise toe-to-toe with Kaiju.

It was not built for speed.

And yet speed was what they were urging it to now, pushing its energy refinery and engines to the maximum.

The sea where they had first encountered Raythe had been only up to their knees, but Raythe was moving to deeper water, and soon they were almost waist deep. Off to the south, a ragged shoreline marked the northern verge of Sakhalin Island.

They were fast approaching the designated Miracle Mile.

And Raythe was gaining on them.

"Guys?" Scriabin again. "If you move off toward the shoreline, the shelf gets really shallow and then extends north. If you go that way, you might be able to cut it off."

"Got it," Sasha replied.

They churned slightly south.

Scriabin was right, of course, and soon they were barely ankle deep. They went to maximum speed and then pushed past it.

"If you burn her out, you won't get there at all," Scriabin warned.

"We won't burn out," Sasha said. "Have the oil platforms been evacuated?"

"No," the LOCCENT director replied. "There wasn't time. There's a fishing fleet standing by to get them, but we've warned them out of the water until this is over."

"One way or another, you mean," Sasha said.

Marshal Pentecost broke onto the line.

"There's only one way, Cherno. One way. You win."

"Don't worry," Sasha said. "If we don't we won't be around to get demoted, you can be sure of that."

The sun came up, a bright orange jewel emerging on the gray horizon. The frozen sea gleamed coral, yellow, orange, the ice sheets and floes becoming almost painfully bright as the Earth's star climbed into an azure vault striated by high, thin clouds touched gold on their bellies.

They could see where Raythe was now, as it broke ice in a long trail, traveling almost parallel to them. But they could see the nearest oil platform as well. It looked bizarrely like a treehouse, balanced as it was on a colossal central pylon. Aleksis's memories flashed as he recalled his visit there. Bad fish soup and good vodka, laughter and stories told after the meal. The platform was the size of a small city, with hundreds of personnel on board. He remembered cafeterias, game rooms, a bar. It wasn't Vladivostok or Hong Kong, but a lot of people would die if they failed. And more such platforms stood not far away. Plus the damage from all those deep-water wells vomiting up their oil into the ocean for who knows how long...

Although playing off of Aleksis's memories, most of these thoughts were Sasha's; Aleksis was driving them forward, one huge foot in front of the other, focused on only one thing.

Raythe.

"Deeper water coming up," Scriabin informed them. "Now or never."

No one had believed Cherno Alpha could go this fast, but she was starting to pay the price. They were drawing too much energy, and even their tremendous capacity was starting to diminish. If they had to use their incinerator turbines or Tesla Fists, they ran the risk of dropping below recommended power levels.

"So, we'll thrash it to death," Aleksis said, out loud.

They crossed Raythe's wake a few meters behind it.

Cherno Alpha dove into Raythe's trail of broken ice.

Or more accurately, fell forward and kicked against the seabed when they were at about a forty-five-degree angle.

They hit the water and went beneath it, and suddenly they couldn't see anything. They cast about blindly...

And caught something.

They both roared in triumph.

Raythe thrashed like a sturgeon on a hook, but it was messing with the wrong fisherman. Cherno was *heavy*.

Of course, they had a problem, too. Cherno was meant to be a boxer, not an acrobat. She had pendular hip joints, making her enormously strong while standing, but once down, it was difficult to get back up. If the Kaiju chose to keep pulling forward, they might be able to hold on, might even be able to climb up Raythe's back as it wore out, until they could reach something vital to punch the hell out of.

But right now, they were mostly an anchor, preventing it from reaching the oil rig.

But that was better than letting it get there.

Alarms were going off.

"The hull breach, from earlier," Sasha said. "It's not big, but water is getting in. I think I can seal off that section, but it could swamp one of our capacitors."

"Do it," Aleksis said.

The din died down. The lights dimmed and came back up.

"*Tchort!*" Sasha said.

About then, Raythe decided that it had had enough. It suddenly stopped trying to pull away and turned back, once again showing how weirdly flexible it was by bending almost double to reach them.

"Let go! Grab its chest!"

It wasn't even clear which one of them had had the thought, but they acted on it immediately. Raythe towered to its full height, thus pulling them back up to their feet.

And once planted, Cherno let loose with a haymaker, hitting just under the Kaiju's upraised arm.

It fell back into the water, but took almost no time to regain its balance and come back at them. Their back was to the rising sun, and Raythe stood completely revealed in the rays of dawn.

"*Bozhe moi,*" Sasha said. "I wish it was still dark."

In the dark, Raythe had been a menacing presence, fearful because it was largely unknown.

In the light, it was just ugly.

They caught it by an arm, put a shoulder into its bulbous belly, lifted it from the water, and then slammed it into the ice, through the roiling sea, to the continental shelf below. It twisted and surged up immediately, but they caught it with a blow to the chest. It staggered back, then rose to its full height.

"The sun," Sasha said. "I think it's having trouble seeing."

They charged and head-butted it, carried it once more

into the sea floor, pummeling as they went.

The monster twisted so their next blow hit its armored shoulder, and then came back up, grappling them, trying to pull them once more beneath the surface. They pounded its torso mercilessly, but whatever lay beneath the thick hide wasn't giving, not at all.

They struggled back to their feet, but once again the monster was climbing onto their head, seemingly obsessed with decapitating them.

"Aleksis..." Sasha began. She knew he wanted to pummel it to death, and so did she, but it was time to end this.

"Yes," he said. "Whatever."

They fired the incinerator turbines.

They looked like huge cannons, one mounted on each shoulder, and in a way, they were, but they didn't shoot shell – they fired Hell. As they switched them on, two fluids surged from hidden reservoirs, mixed, and became something like napalm, or what napalm might dream of being, a clinging gel that burned hotter than jet fuel.

Both jets hit Raythe in the face.

The Kaiju staggered back, clawing at its scalded visage, and then ducked beneath the frigid water. The fire continued burning, white-hot beneath the waves. Cherno reached down, hauled the monster up by a leg and an arm, and began trying to pull it apart.

But Raythe twisted again, slamming its burning head into Cherno. Some of the gel stuck, and now, they too were ablaze. They hurled Raythe away.

When it got back up, it shook like a dog – gobbets of flame flew everywhere, hissing into the sea.

"I don't think that hurt it," Sasha said.

Raythe charged. Cherno charged.

They came together with a crash that crews on platforms sixty miles away later said they heard.

They grappled with the upright Kaiju, neither budging or giving ground, but that couldn't last. Half of their sensors went down, and the lights dropped to emergency levels. What was worse, Sasha felt their connection in the Drift finally starting to unravel – they had joined fifteen hours ago, and that was pushing it, even for them.

Raythe's armored head lashed out, savaging their energy refinery. At the moment, the damage was mostly on the surface, but it was clear that in a few more moments the razor-sharp beak would cut through their plating.

"This is it," Sasha said. "Last stand."

Aleksis was visibly straining in his harness; his face was red, and she felt the anguish, the bloodlust, how he wanted to tear the thing apart, see its blue guts spill into the sea.

But that wasn't going to happen. Any moment, Cherno would fail, Raythe would push them into the Arctic waters and move on to ravage the oil platforms and more. Perhaps another Jaeger would stop it.

Or.

"What do we have to lose?" Sasha asked.

He reluctantly agreed. He wasn't that far gone.

"Rerouting all power to Tesla Fists," Sasha reported.

"That will leave Cherno without power," Scriabin objected. "It could take up to fifteen minutes before you have enough capacity to move."

Sasha ignored him.

"Deploying Tesla Fists," she said, calmly.

With a double cry, they yanked their arm free of Raythe's embrace.

Raythe tried to withdraw its head, but this time it was too slow. Cherno's mighty fists crashed into either side of it and held it like a vise.

Then the Tesla cells discharged, arcing 415 kW of electricity through Raythe's three-lobed skull.

The lights went out, then came back up on battery. All of their displays were down, and they fell out of the Drift with a savagery they had never felt before.

Sasha gasped and pushed the helmet from her head. From seemingly everywhere came the deep creaking of metal complaining, cables settling. The air felt stuffy and was sharp with ozone, suggesting electrical overloads somewhere inside of the Jaeger.

Aleksis was the first to totally unhook from the Pinocchio rig. He went to the manual hatch and threw it open, looking as if he was ready to carry on the fight with his bare human hands.

The stench was unbelievable, and the cold hit them like a hammer. Cherno was frozen upright, its limbs locked rigid when the power went out.

They couldn't see the Kaiju anywhere.

"Piss," Aleksis swore. He looked around, wild, on the verge of snapping. He howled into the frigid air.

Sasha took his arm. "Aleksis," she said. "We either killed it or we didn't. There's nothing to do now."

Not much later they first heard, then saw a helicopter. It wasn't a Jumphawk, but a much smaller craft with the logo of the oil company on it. When the pilot and passengers saw them standing in the opening of the Jaeger's chest, they went wild. They seemed to be happy. Then they stuck out their arms, thumbs up.

As it turned out, Raythe was still right in front of them, just below the water. Where metal and fire had failed, the lightning in Cherno's fists had succeeded. They would later be told that Raythe had three brains, and they had fried every one of them.

# 37

GIPSY AVENGER HUGGED THE COASTLINE; XIANG was right — the shelf dropped off very quickly once you went east of the coast. The Philippine Trench wasn't as deep as the Marianas Trench where the Breach had been located, but it was the third-deepest point on the planet, which was still very freaking deep. Gipsy was certainly built to survive down there — for a short time, anyway — but they didn't want to make a dive like that for no reason.

But there wasn't much in between the coast and the deeps, just a narrow strip, teeming with people.

To a Jaeger, people weren't much bigger than bugs, and although he was in theory running toward what could well be a fight for the survival of the human race, he didn't want to crush anyone on the way. Not the sunbathers, or the fishermen in shallow waters, the cast-netters on the rocks, the surfers trying to find a decent wave, the kayakers teaching their kids to paddle. Each was a person with parents, friends, desires – all of which could be literally crushed flat by a single misstep. Most people had the sense to get out of the way when a three-hundred-foot titan was wading toward them, but some of them might not have the time, or ability.

It was a relief when they drew nearer the island, where the spit of coast they were following played out, and they were moving through open if shallow sea.

"LOCCENT control," Lambert said. "I've got an island in sight. Confirm?"

"Confirmed," Xiang said.

Things had not improved with Burke; their neural handshake was tenuous, at best. Any moment he feared it would sputter out, and then they would turn into a very large offshore statue.

Probably because of the wobbly handshake, they didn't notice the missile until it was almost too late. It seemed to come from out of the sun and their radar didn't pick it up at all. They managed to grab it with the Gravity Sling when it was about fifty meters away, but before they could do anything else, it exploded. The shock rocked Gipsy Avenger back so hard, they had to take a step to keep from falling. The water rippled away from them in every direction, churning surf on the island and sending flocks of birds fleeing from their perches in the jungle.

"Where the hell did that come from?" Burke demanded.

"There's a ship about six miles offshore," Xiang said. "We didn't see it until they launched. It's got radar transparency – not that good. Technology is almost twenty years out of date."

"But effective," Lambert said. "You didn't see it."

"We weren't looking for it. But we've got it now on satellite visual," Xiang replied.

"We've seen it now, too," Burke said, zooming in on it. It sat high out of the water, several stories tall at least.

"That's a lot bigger than the other one."

"It's an old container ship," Xiang replied.

"They're out of range of our plasma cannon," Burke said. "And it's out over the trench, so we can't just run out and get it. It would be nice to have some air support."

"It's on its way," Xiang said. "Just hang in there."

"Incoming," Burke yelled.

Another missile. They caught this one a little sooner, but it also detonated, leaving them disoriented as another rocket came right behind it.

Gipsy lunged out of the way, striking with its left hand to try and deflect the third rocket.

The feedback from the blast translated as pain all along Lambert's left side. The magnetic field suspending them wavered, so when Gipsy toppled, he and Burke got a lot more shaken up than they should have.

They broke their fall with the right arm, sending miniature tsunamis scurrying through the water.

"Air support on-site," Xiang reported.

"About time," Lambert said. He saw them now, half a dozen Malay-built Osprey helicopters, moving in fast from the west-north-west. "Have them give us some cover and take out those launchers."

They were still struggling to get back up when the fourth missile arrived.

Unlike the others, when this one detonated, it was with a brilliant flash, blue tinted, like the one the Akumagami ship had tried unsuccessfully to nail them with.

This attempt went much better for the bad guys.

Lambert felt the shock of overload jolt through him, making a good start of frying his brains, just before the systems shut down to preserve their lives. Lambert and Burke fell out of the Drift and crashed to the floor. Both lay stunned for a moment. Burke managed to get up first. Lambert tasted blood in his mouth.

"Oh, crap," Burke said. "This ain't good. All systems are down. That was some kind of pulse weapon."

"Gipsy is hardened against EMP," Lambert said.

"Well, then I guess we're okay, then," Burke replied. As he spoke, battery power cut in, and communications with LOCCENT came back online. Other than that, though, Gipsy was dead in the water.

"Xiang, give me some good news," Lambert said.

"Your core isn't fried," she said. "We can start reboot immediately."

"How long is that going to take?"

"Twenty minutes."

"What about our air support?"

"The pulse got them. They're all down."

As he'd been speaking, Burke had pushed by him and opened the hatch to look out.

"We may not have twenty minutes," Burke said. "Some helicopters just lifted off from the ship."

"Well, I'm not just going to sit here," Lambert said.

"Right," Burke agreed.

In the old days, Jaeger pilots didn't usually carry small weapons – if the giant weapon you were riding around in failed, a pistol wasn't going to be much use against the Kaiju that broke it.

However, for the past ten years, Jaegers and their pilots had not been fighting Kaiju, but human opponents, and sometimes a sidearm or assault rifle absolutely came in handy.

They took the rifles out of their stays. Then Burke took another peek out.

"Look like DVs," Burke said. "Armored."

"They carry missiles too," Lambert said. "What if we stick our heads out and they lob one through the hatch? Then we're well and truly finished. As it is, I doubt anything they've got is enough to put a real dent in us."

"We don't know that," Burke said. "They had the pulse weapon, and apparently some kind of bomb made of Kaiju blood. Maybe they got an acid bomb, too."

"Maybe," Lambert allowed. "But all they really have to do is delay us until they manage to detonate their big bomb. Then we're done for anyway."

Lambert eased the hatch up and looked out. He counted four helicopters. Each pair carried what looked like cables draped between them. He didn't know what they were up to, but it couldn't be good. He aimed his rifle at one of the cockpits and squeezed off one round, then another. He couldn't tell if he had hit, much less did he see any damage. About six seconds later, however, he did notice an exhaust jet appear in the rear of the chopper's right-hand missile array.

He slammed the hatch and was locking it shut when they heard and felt the explosion. It wasn't much compared to the larger missiles that had hit them earlier, but if one slipped in and went off in the Conn-Pod, Gipsy's high-tech armor wouldn't do them a bit of good.

"They've got cables," he told Burke.

"Four DVs?" he said. "Those are no Jumphawks. It would take twenty of them to lift us."

"Maybe they plan to tie us down, like Gulliver," Lambert said.

"I'm not in favor of that," Burke said. "Not at all. LOCCENT, how long until reboot?"

"Fifteen minutes," Xiang replied.

"Is Gottlieb there?" Lambert asked.

"I'm here," they heard the scientist say.

"What else can you tell us about this bomb? Obviously these guys are Akumagami Front. They're already here – why haven't they set it off yet?"

"It's possible it isn't finished," Gottlieb replied. "Its

active component is most probably a concentrated form of Kaiju blood. I've gone through reports, and a good deal of it has been stolen in the last few months, and there seems also to have been an unusually high number of transactions on the black market. They need a certain critical mass to accomplish their aim – my suspicion is that the ship that fired on you is bringing the last of it."

"And then what?"

"Then I believe they will detonate it as soon as possible. Or, rather, inject it."

"Inject it?"

"Yes. I've just discovered that Kaiju blood seems to interact quite violently with certain rare earth minerals. These occur only in certain places—"

"Like deep water trenches," Lambert said.

"Yes. But we know from experience that merely bleeding a Kaiju out in such a trench won't create the result they desire. Water tends to not only dilute the blood but also renders its more volatile catalytic effects inert. Most likely, the island itself is rich in rare earths. If they've drilled a shaft down through it – with an oil rig or core sampler or some similar hardware – then they can forcefully inject the clarified blood directly into the magma welling up on the land side of the trench."

"Followed quickly by a big kaboom?" Burke said.

"Yes," Gottlieb replied. "A very large kaboom, I should expect. A kaboom heard round the world."

The Jaeger suddenly shifted hard enough that he and Burke were thrown off their feet.

"Okay, Gulliver," Burke said. "What now?"

"Hang on," Lambert replied. "I think this is going to get worse before it gets… even worse."

"Gipsy," Xiang said. "We have you moving. Have you recovered?"

Lambert pressed his hands against the Conn-Pod wall and studied what he could see through the optical windows – which wasn't much.

*What's happening, girl?* he asked Gipsy.

But then he understood.

"They're not trying to lift us," Lambert said. "They're dragging us. Hell, they're going to drop us into the trench."

"Calm down," Xiang said. "You're not moving that fast. You'll reboot before they get you to the trench."

"Well, there you go," Burke said. "No worries at all."

There was a little pause. Then Xiang's voice returned, sounding slightly worried.

"There's something in the water," Xiang said. "Submerged. Big. Looks like they're dragging you towards that."

"Come on, Gipsy, reboot," Burke said, kicking the bulkhead.

"You still have about seven minutes," Xiang said. "You've stopped moving."

Lambert knew that already.

"Oddly," he said, "I don't have a good feeling about this."

He heard something then, like popcorn popping about twenty yards away.

"Control?"

"I've just detected a number of minor detonations at the object," Xiang said. "I think – oh no."

"Oh no? Oh no what?"

But then Gipsy jerked, hard.

"They've pushed it over," Xiang said, her voice rising. "Gipsy is moving again, much faster—"

"They've tied us to something," Burke said. "They've tied us to something and shoved it over the cliff."

# 38

LAMBERT COULD TELL THEY WERE ACCELERATING, but suddenly gravity seemed to have been canceled, or almost so. They weren't in complete freefall – it reminded him of going down a very steep and very tall waterslide when he was a kid.

Of course, this waterslide was around six miles deep...

"Pressure's going up," Burke said, reading the minimal battery-powered instrumentation. "Very bloody quick."

Gipsy knew it, too, and her metal corpus had already begun to groan in protest. Through the thick optical windows, the light of day was fading fast, as the most ancient and enduring night on Earth enveloped them.

Xiang was still talking to them, but the signal was quickly becoming erratic. Lambert could almost feel the crushing water pressure around him, mounting exponentially with each breath he took, and the air entering his suit was quickly becoming stale and hot.

Xiang said something so scrambled he couldn't make it out.

"What was that?" he asked.

No answer. He and Burke sat in silence for a moment listening to the pinging of metal approaching its tolerance point. He heard Burke sigh.

"Listen, Nate," Burke began.

But then suddenly, beautifully, the lights came on, and Gipsy once again hummed with power.

"What?" Lambert.

"Nothing," Burke said. "Let's get the hell out of here."

Quickly, he and Burke returned to their places as the fields came back on and stabilized and the breeze in their helmets from the air scrubbers started cooling things down.

"Initiating emergency pilot-to-pilot protocol," Lambert said, moving his hands through the holo-instruments.

He looked over at Burke as the Drift began to kick in.

"A hundred percent, Burke," he said. "I need that from you, and not just for me. For everyone."

Burke nodded. "You'll get it," he said. "But you won't like it."

"Fair enough," Lambert replied.

Then they were in the Drift, and Burke's mental wall was down, and Lambert knew what he'd been hiding – and no, he didn't like it at all.

But this wasn't the time for that.

Instruments confirmed what he'd sensed earlier – they weren't *falling* into the trench so much as sliding down the now very steep slope of it. It was not, after all, a canyon with vertical sides, but as they approached the bottom it came closer and closer to that. Regardless, they were moving downhill pretty fast, and doing long, slow bounces as they went, so they weren't always in contact with the trench wall.

"We're at eighteen thousand feet already," Burke said. "Three miles. More than halfway down."

"Chain Sword," Lambert said.

The gigantic, segmented blade deployed and locked in place. In the floodlights, he could now see what they were attached to – half of a ship, a big one, probably one of many nautical casualties of the several Kaiju attacks in the area. Their end of the cable was tied around Gipsy's neck, so they were being pulled down head first.

They grabbed the cable, and with a single slash from their Chain Sword, severed it.

But, of course they were still going down. In fact, detaching the ship had the effect of bouncing them clear from the side, which here, two thirds of the way down, really did approach vertical. The wall of the trench was close, but not close enough to reach, and Gipsy was not a very good swimmer. They might impact it again before the bottom or they might not.

"Try the Gravity Sling," Burke said. "We might be able to pull a little closer."

Lambert nodded and deployed it, then sent the invisible gravitic field at the wall of the trench.

It latched on for a second, but it hadn't been built to lift something with as much mass as Gipsy; the connection broke, and somewhere deep in the Jaeger, machinery complained.

Swearing under his breath, he sent it out again, and again it caught – and this time it was enough, pulling them close enough so they could jam the Chain Sword into the rocky wall. The impact nearly jolted them out of their magnetic harnesses; the sword was half buried in the stone, but they were still sliding, cutting a long gash in the stone as they gradually slowed. They grappled for hand and foot holds and slid another half a mile before they finally stopped.

"Power core at sixty percent," Lambert said. "Oxygen supply – a couple of hours at best."

"Then let's get the hell out of here," Burke said.

# 39

SHAOLIN ROGUE'S FREE FALL CAME TO A painfully abrupt end; gravity returned, twisting Minghau cruelly in his harness. At first, he thought it was their impact in the sea, but then he realized – to both his relief and dismay – that they were once again rising.

"It has us again," Suyin said.

Indeed, Huo Da was now gripping them with all its limbs, and once again they were climbing cloudward with dizzying speed.

Shanghai was coming up fast, and once above it Huo Da went into a flat dive straight toward the towers of the business district. Shaolin Rogue writhed desperately in its grip, trying to shake loose, but it was a lost cause.

"The power core," Suyin gasped. "We can overload it."

"We can't," he said. "We'll wipe out half the city."

Everything seemed to slow down. The World Financial Center, a slender, elegant tower whose top had an aperture like the eye of a needle, loomed just ahead of them.

And Huo Da let them go.

Ming-hau and Suyin reached for one another – not physically, but in the Drift, the memories of their lives together flowing around them, leaves in a stream.

The impact against the building felt distant – the light, then the darkness in the Conn-Pod as everything came apart, whirled as if in a centrifuge – but they were together, in the Drift, growing stronger rather than weaker, giving everything to each other as the end came.


Pain returned. Ming-hau was lying on his side, blood pouring into his eyes. Through the shattered Conn-Pod, he saw rubble, smoke, a city in flames. Huo Da appeared once more, small with distance; it flew low over a building and tore the top of it off.

"Suyin," he gasped. He knew she wasn't dead; he could still feel her. But the Conn-Pod had crumpled around her, crushing her leg. Her eyes were open, but she looked like she was in shock.

"We have to get out of here," he said.

"Look," she said, dreamily. Pointing beyond him at the slash of sky visible to them.

He turned in time to see the flash of light, the bolt of energy from Crimson Typhoon's plasma cannon.

Huo Da bloomed, a blue flower in the heavens. The Kaiju had transformed again, he thought, as the toxic rain began to fall.

# 40

THE CLIMB BACK WAS A SLOW, DELIBERATE process; setting themselves, pulling out the blade, digging it in further up. At first it seemed almost impossible, but as they drew higher, the side of the trench was less and less steep, and eventually they could get all four limbs under them.

Power dropped to forty percent, and their oxygen supply was moving into the red zone. They had been climbing for nearly four miles, but they had one more to go.

But the Drift was right. For the first time since this whole business began, he felt Burke was really with him, that they were clicking like they used to. Not for long. When this was over...

"I'm sorry," Burke said.

"Not the time," Lambert replied. "Just stay with me, and let's get this done."

And so it was that finally, painfully, with almost no

oxygen to spare, Gipsy Avenger pulled herself from the edge of the abyss, rose once more above the ocean waves and went to finish the fight.

LOCCENT noticed they were back. "Gipsy!" Xiang said. "How are you?"

"Mad as hell," Lambert said. "Do we have a target, or should we just destroy everything that moves?"

They had been noticed. Helicopters were lifting off.

"K-Watch nailed it down. I've sent coordinates. South side of the island, there's a crescent-shaped lake. It's part of an old mining pit that caved in. You'll see some industrial ruins, next to it. The bomb is there."

"Thanks," Lambert said. A map of the island came up, the bomb's location marked by a blue dot.

The helicopters started firing as they approached the island. Gipsy used her Gravity Sling to snatch up a boulder from one of the little islets surrounding the bigger land mass, and flung it directly into the craft, which shattered and fell with almost unreal slowness. The others veered off, but not before he used the sling again, narrowly missing another of the helicopters.

The ship, he noticed, now stood off the east side of the island.

"Maybe we should take that out," he said. "Before they come up with any more surprises."

If the enemy had another one of those pulse bombs, for instance, they were almost certainly done for. But the bad guys had had a few minutes now to fire missiles, and hadn't. Hopefully they were empty.

Small-arms fire rattled on their armor, along with larger caliber rounds from mounted weapons. That was just noise. The helicopters circled warily behind them.

As they drew nearer to the ship, a cargo lift raised something from below decks: a long cylinder, with one brightly glowing end pointing directly at them. Instinct kicked in and they spun right as a white-hot stream of plasma crackled through the air, singing along their left flank. Howling in their Conn-Pod, they slammed the deck with one gigantic fist, sending the plasma torch flying. Then, gripping the ship along the gunnels, squeezing so hard their fingers dug into the metal, they heaved, lifted, and flipped the whole thing over. Then they hit it twice with their own plasma cannon, just for good measure. Flame ballooned out from the huge ship as they turned their back on it and slogged toward the island.

"We just got a heightened energy signature from your location," Xiang reported. "Dr. Gottlieb believes they've begun the injection process."

Gipsy set first one foot on land, then the other.

There was the lake, and next to it a bunch of equipment, set up in the ruins and camouflaged to make it invisible from the air. About fifty men and women came swarming out as they approached, firing up at them.

Ignoring the bullets spattering against them, they reached down and knocked away the covering.

"I see it," he said. "Or something."

"You're looking for a large tank of some sort," Gottlieb said.

"I don't see anything like that," Lambert reported. Gipsy cleared the rest of the wreckage, but they still didn't see anything obvious.

"It's begun," he heard Gottlieb say. "You must hurry."

"In the ground," Burke said. "It must be in the ground."

Gipsy's hand reared back, then drove down, digging into the earth. They felt something metal, cold...

They yanked it up: a sphere the size of a water tower, with blue vitriol leaking from one side.

"Got it!" Lambert yelled.

"You'd best get out of there, then," Xiang said. "K-Watch is getting some serious readings from your location."

They tilted the sphere up so it was no longer leaking, and once again, they ran as best a Jaeger could run, crushing palm trees underfoot as the earth began to shudder and slide beneath them. They splashed into the water, sprinting toward the mainland. A glance back showed black smoke billowing up from the island, fuming toward an otherwise clear blue sky.

And then the island simply exploded in their rear view; the whole thing went up in a vast ball of flame and smoke. They stumbled as the wave-front of the blast passed through them, but the power held steady, and they corrected quickly. Trees bent away from them in every direction, and the water kicked up in choppy wavelets.

"That wasn't so bad," Burke said.

Then the sea poured into the hole, a gaping wound in the Earth that ran straight down to the lake of molten magma rising up to meet it, and the two had a... disagreement, a disagreement louder than any clap of thunder Lambert had ever heard. Ahead of even the sound came a hurricane of pressurized steam, slapping them harder than any Kaiju. Gipsy toppled, went down on its knees and one hand. Warnings screamed from almost every system. The hydraulics in their left leg were reading as negative, and the cooling systems shut down.

But when it was over they still had the reservoir of Kaiju blood in the other hand intact.

Lambert looked at Burke, then at the boiling sea behind them.

"I guess we did it," Lambert said.

"Wait," Gottlieb's voice said. "Let me see – oh, thank God."

"That sounds promising," Burke said, smiling.

"Indeed," Gottlieb said. "You stopped them far short of achieving critical mass. By my calculations, they only managed to inject about fifty liters before you stopped them."

"Fifty liters?" Lambert said, incredulous. "Only eleven gallons? The whole island is gone."

"Yes," Gottlieb replied. "But it would have been worse – oh, so much worse."

"I think we're going to need a little help getting out of here," Lambert said.

"Jumphawks are on their way, Gipsy," Xiang said. "Congratulations, and thanks from everyone here. Good job."

# 41

WHEN JINHAI AND VIK ARRIVED BACK AT THE Shatterdome, Mako left them in the hands of the J-Techs and Medical. The doctors checked them out, declared them fit and sent them on their way, and suddenly they were out of it, abandoned. Whatever great events were unfolding out in the world and at LOCCENT, they were no longer in the loop.

They started toward the barracks, but halfway there, Jinhai realized something.

"I'm starving," he told Vik.

She nodded. "Of course," she said.

"Look," he said. "If you want to be alone…"

"No," she said. "Let's get something to eat."

The kitchens were between lunch and supper, and food service was cleaning up, but someone on duty managed to find two bowls of noodles with eggplant, pork, and basil. Jinhai took a bite or two of his, but

Vik just sat, looking at her food.

"What's wrong?" he asked. "We're alive, and in the clear."

"Sure," she said. "But we almost weren't. Because we were stupid. I was stupid. Lambert said he was about to start washing people out. Who do you think will be first? Us."

"Maybe," Jinhai said.

"It's a big deal to me," Vik said.

"I know," Jinhai said. "I've been in your head way too much not to know that. I'm not trying to make light of it."

"I know you're not," she said.

"Should have known we'd find them here," someone said. He didn't have to turn to recognize Suresh, but he did anyway. He saw they were all there, all of the cadets.

"What's up, guys?" Jinhai said.

"You two," Renata said. "You'll do anything to get out of training, won't you?"

For just a second, he thought she was serious. Vik was starting to get out of her seat.

Then Renata laughed a little nervously, and the rest along with her. But then the Chilean's face grew serious again.

"Look," she said. "We're here to say we're sorry. *I'm* sorry. We should have believed you, stuck by you. Sometimes I talk a better game than I play."

"It's the same for all of us," Ilya said.

"We were sort of idiots," Suresh put in.

Vik eased back into her chair. "Thanks," she said. "I really appreciate that." She sounded sincere.

"Can we join you, or are you having a private meeting?" Renata asked.

"Please, have a seat," Jinhai said. "I think we can use some company."

"Yeah," Vik said. "We were just talking about washing out."

"I know," Tahima said, as he took a seat. "That damned Ceptid simulation."

"We were thinking more about the whole sneaking-around in Mechspace and getting kidnapped," Vik said. "But yeah, the simulation, sure."

"You realize now you have to tell us all about it," Suresh said. "The whole nasty story."

"We can't say much," Jinhai said. "Gipsy Avenger –"

"– has succeeded," a new voice said.

Mako Mori had just entered the room. They all bolted up to attention.

"As you were," she said.

"So it's all over? Everything is okay?" Jinhai asked.

"All is well," she said. "You'll be filled in on details when they become generally available. For now, most of this must remain classified." She smiled. "And so we can return to training."

"Secretary General, when will Rangers Lambert and Burke return?" Meilin asked.

"Soon," Mori said. "But Ranger Lambert asked me to take charge of you this afternoon. He feels you've probably been lax in his absence. That is, if cadets Ou-Yang and Malikova feel up to it."

"Yes ma'am," Jinhai said.

"Any time, Secretary General," Vik said. "We had plenty of rest on the flight back."

"Very well," Mori said. "Meet me at the Mock-Pods in one hour."


"Here we go again," Meilin said, as the simulation came up around them.

"I should have known," Ilya said.

Ecuador, again, and Ceptid arriving from the west. They were back in the original Jaegers, just as they had been the first time – Renata and Ilya in Diablo Intercept,

Tahima and Meilin in Romeo Blue, Vik and Jinhai in
Puma Real.

"Looks like it's back to the drawing board," Jinhai
said. "Anyone have any bright ideas?"

For a moment, no one said anything. But then Vik
spoke up.

"I do," she said.

"You know what?" Renata said. "Why don't you call
this one? I haven't done such a great job so far."

Vik glanced at Jinhai. "Are you thinking what I'm
thinking?" she asked.

"Is that a rhetorical question?" Jinhai said. "Because
literally, yes. Sure. Go for it. You and I don't have much to
lose. The rest of them do. Let's put this scenario behind us."

Vik nodded and switched to the shared channel.

"Okay, Diablo Intercept, Romeo Blue, you guys get to
the shoreline and set up a crossfire. We'll stay out here and
wear him down."

"Wear him down?" Ilya objected. "If there's one thing
we've learned about this Kaiju, it does not 'wear down'."

"We'll see," Vik said. "I have tricks up my sleeve."

"Headed to shore, Puma," Renata said. "Good luck."

"Tricks?" Jinhai said.

"Well, *trick*," Vik said.

Ceptid came on.

"Let's shoot a few missiles," Vik said.

"Fine by me," Jinhai said. They let fly, with pretty much
the same lack of effect as before. Ceptid plodded forward
as if it didn't notice.

"Think they're far enough back yet?" Vik asked.

"Give them another minute or two," Jinhai replied.

They jogged a little to their left, firing more missiles,
then back to the right, shooting until they were empty.

"I think it's probably safe now," Jinhai said.

"Okay," Vik said. "Are you ready?"

"About as ready as I'm going to get," Jinhai replied.

"Then here we go."

They moved until they were directly in the Kaiju's path, and then ran straight at it.

"Puma," Renata yelped. "What are you doing?"

"Killing it," Vik said.

They put their fists up and charged into Ceptid, swinging.

The instant before they got there, it split down the middle, opened up like the ugliest butterfly on earth, and engulfed them.

And exploded. Jinhai felt mild feedback pressure, a surge of dizziness. Vik screamed, both in his mind and with her lungs. Then everything went black.

And stayed black. Unexpected terror rose up. What was happening? Was this a simulated death, or something? A punishment for deliberately destroying a Jaeger? More sabotage? Was he really dying?

But then he understood, and he began to feel a little calmer. "We're still drifting," he said.

Vik didn't answer, but he could see her, standing ahead of him, the only light in the darkness. Except now, by her glow, he could also see a door, and he knew somehow that behind the door lay the hidden place within Vik he had never seen.

She reached for the door and pulled it open.

The whole world opened.

Everything seemed calm; it was almost dark. A town lay before him, a few hundred drab little buildings tinted rose and vermillion by the rays of the setting sun.

Then Jinhai heard a sound, an awful, low-pitched groan that shivered through the earth and air. He turned away from the sunset and saw something rising.

At first, he thought it was cloud, mostly in the shadow part of the evening sky, but touched golden by the sun on its top.

But then he saw that the shadow came all the way down to the ground, and that in the ray-touched top, a face peered down at him. In the shadow, long arms and legs moved. Then the sky itself was wailing so loud it hurt his ears, and the shadow moved into the town. Fire and smoke were everywhere; the smell burned his eyes and throat. Everything was in motion, and then all was dark.

The darkness gave way to pale dawn. Jinhai was looking at the town from further away. The big thing was gone, but the town lay in utter ruin. The wailing stopped, and it was quiet enough for him to hear weeping.

Then the scene blurred and shifted. He was standing with Vik, who looked as if she was about three or four. Next to Vik stood an old man in a heavy coat and wool cap. Jinhai knew it was her grandfather. They were looking at two graves, side by side.

"Your father," Dedulya said. "My little boy. My sweet boy." He was crying. "And here, your mother, a good woman. I was proud to have her as family."

Vik stood up, and as she did, she grew older. She took Jinhai's hand, and they began to walk across the shattered landscape, to the edge of the sea, where his parents were dancing together, elegantly, despite her mother's prosthetic leg, and he felt his own longing, as deep in his heart as any oceanic trench. And he then, finally, understood.

And as his parents danced down the beach, he and Vik began to float up into the sky, and a face appeared in the clouds, a woman's face.

"*Vikushka*," the woman whispered.

Then he felt the neural handshake part, and Vik wasn't with him anymore. He was back in the Mock-

Pod, with a tech and Mako Mori standing over him.

"What happened?" he gasped.

"It's okay," Mori said. "It happens sometimes. You get lost in the Drift, especially if you have a shock of some sort. Even though you knew you wouldn't really die, some instinctive part of you probably didn't understand that."

"Okay," he said. He looked over at Vik, and saw she was actually smiling a little.

"So are we done?" Jinhai asked.

"Done?" Mori asked.

"Washed out."

"No, of course not," she said. "You won."

"We destroyed a Jaeger," he said. "We died."

"That was the only correct answer," Mori said.

"It was the original answer," Vik said. "When Diablo Intercept attacked Ceptid, it exploded. We all thought we were supposed to come up with a better solution to the fight."

"Diablo Intercept didn't know what would happen," Mori said. "They were merely trying to fight it. But sometimes the only way to beat a Kaiju is to sacrifice yourself. Sometimes there is no other answer."

"You mean like when Stacker Pentecost and Chuck Hansen used the nuclear bomb to clear the way for Gipsy Danger even though it was still strapped to them."

"Yes," Mako said. "And as when Raleigh..." she stopped, and her gaze seemed to focus past them, to something very distant.

"Ranger Lambert will be very pleased," she finally said. "With all of you. Return to your quarters and get some rest."

Rest was easy enough, but sleep proved more troublesome. There was too much to sort through, to try and come to terms with. Jinhai dozed in and out of dreams of Kaiju, distant voices, and a baby with blue eyes. A few hours before dawn, he woke and realized he wasn't going to be able to sleep anymore. The nightly curfew was already lifted, so he went to the commissary. They weren't serving breakfast yet, but a dispenser held hot tea; he got a cup and went into the Jaeger bay.

Vik was already there, sitting cross-legged, staring up at the huge machines.

"Think we'll ever really pilot one of those?" he asked her.

"Yes," Vik said.

"Me too," he said. "I didn't even used to care, but now…"

"It's different now," she said.

"Yeah. You live your whole life – or at least, your life up until now – and you think you know who you are. You tell yourself stories about why you do what you do. And then one day you find out that you were wrong. That nothing is what you thought it was, and you aren't who you thought you were."

Vik nodded.

"Yes," she said. "I got that. You worked to come here, Jinhai, because you hoped to drift with someone. You believed you wanted what your parents have. The kind of bond they have. But that's not what you want at all, is it?"

Jinhai shook his head, and realized to his shame that he was starting to cry.

"No," he said. "I just wanted – them. When I was little, they loved me so much. We did everything together. We were a family. And then – they drifted. At first it was a little, and then it was a lot. And after Huo Da – when both of them nearly died in the Drift – it was like no one else was really real to them anymore, including me. They're real to each other – they're everything to each other – but the rest of us are just kind of ghosts to them. It's not like they never try, it's just – I can tell they don't feel it."

He took a sip of his tea.

"I thought it was my fault. I thought that if I could just learn how they felt, feel that way about someone, I could somehow step into their world. Be a part of it the way I... I want to be." He sighed. "I'm sorry. I know this must sound sappy to you."

She shook her head.

"For a long time, I thought my parents were the Kaidanovskys. My grandmother told me they were. Deep down, I always knew they probably weren't. But I wanted to believe. I told myself I did. When I let my doubts come up, I felt stupid, and I beat myself up." She tapped her head. "Mentally," she said. "I'm not *that* flexible."

He actually laughed at that. It felt good.

"I didn't remember Grandpa taking me to see those graves," she said.

"You were really little. You were just a baby when Raythe came. I'm surprised you remember anything at all."

"I didn't," she said. "I mean, maybe in a nightmare now and then. I didn't know it was real. And I dreamed of my mother's face, but I didn't know it was her."

"Who were they really? Your parents?"

She held up a file folder.

"I didn't know until last night. I never tried to find out. Mako Mori gave me this after the simulation."

She opened it.

"My father was Piotr Malikova," she read. "My mother was Valentina Krupin. He was a foreman at the petrochemical plant in Tomari. She taught history and mathematics at the school there. They were both in town when Raythe came; my mother died trying to get her students to safety. My father was killed trying to shut off a chemical leak. I was with my grandmother while they were at work; when the attack started she got me to safety. My grandmother lied to me, and my grandfather went along with it."

"Do you know why?"

"To make me think I was somebody. To give me aspirations. And it did, at first, but then it just became confusing."

"Your parents may not have been famous or piloted Jaegers," Jinhai said, "but it sounds like they were heroes."

"Yes," she said. "I figured that out, at last, although I wasn't completely at peace with it. Now I think I am."

"That's good," he said.

"And what about you?" she asked.

"I'm... working on it," he said.

# 42

WHEN LAMBERT AND BURKE RETURNED TO Moyulan, they found the on-down waiting for them; Xiang, some of the junior controllers and a gaggle of J-Techs had dragged some tables outside onto the edge of the staging area, hung some paper lanterns, set up some sound, and loaded some plastic tubs with ice and beer.

The on-down was about rehashing, about going over every detail of the fight. The techs and controllers weighed in with their own remarks and questions, but Lambert and Burke were the stars, and as such were forced time and again to stand up on their chairs and make some sort of speech about the other, about the support crew – or whatever.

It should have been fun, but even after way too much beer, Lambert wasn't feeling it.

And at a certain point, and after too much beer, that wasn't enough. When they demanded he make another toast, he climbed and stood unsteadily on his chair and raised his glass.

"To all of you," he said. "To the PPDC. You give me purpose, you give me a reason to get up in the morning, to pull on my boots and go to work. I believe in what I do, which is the greatest thing a man can ask for. The second-greatest thing a man can ask for is that those standing with him believe in the same thing, have his back, will never let him down. But I guess that's too much to ask sometimes, isn't it? Loyalty. Commitment. I used to feel like I knew what those words meant. But what the hell, huh? They're just words, random syllables…"

He nearly lost his balance, as the chair wobbled dangerously beneath him. Burke reached to steady him, but Lambert swatted his hand away.

"Just…" he said.

"Hey, buddy," Burke said. "Why don't you come down? You're gonna hurt yourself."

"Now you're looking out for me?" Lambert snapped. "Screw you, 'buddy'…"

"Hey, Ranger," someone said. "Come on. Let's go get some air."

He looked down and saw Jules, holding her hand up to him. Then he looked around at all the faces, which a moment before had been laughing, smiling, but which now looked shocked and confused.

"Yeah, okay," he said.

He took the offered hand, and she led him away from the light.

"I like a man who can hold his drink," she said, as behind them the sounds of revelry began again.

"That's too bad," he said.

"I'll tell you the truth," she said. "I'm a little drunk myself."

Once beyond the harsh floods, they could see the stars above the mountains. A warm breeze came through, and Lambert was acutely aware that they were still holding hands.

"You were right, by the way," he told her.

"Yes? Right about what?"

"They did switch Chronos Berserker's Conn-Pod. It was the spare I took the kids into. I didn't think of that. I should have."

She smiled. "The spare wasn't fully functional," she said, "so I didn't think of it at first, either. But then I realized it didn't have to be. So I did a little checking. For my Ranger pal. And I found out that not only did someone switch them, they tried to be sneaky about it."

"Yeah," he said. "Thanks for checking on that."

He looked out at the night. Somewhere an owl called – a distant, lonely sound.

"What was all that?" Jules asked. "Back at the on-down?"

"Burke," he said. "My buddy, my chum – my Drift partner. He's leaving."

"Leaving Moyulan?"

"Leaving the PPDC. Going into the private sector. He didn't want to tell me. Almost got us killed."

"I wouldn't want to tell you either, if I was him," she said.

"What's that mean?"

"You're a true believer," she said. "Burke isn't. He's a good guy, but he's not you."

"It's just – it's not the first time my Drift partner has left," he said. "I can't seem to… Is there something wrong with me?"

She turned to face him. In the starlight, her eyes were – impossible.

"Ranger," she said. "Nathan Lambert. There is not a thing wrong with you."

Later, he honestly couldn't remember who made the first move, which would become a bit of a problem. But now it didn't matter, and he became lost in her lips, her eyes, the warmth of her against him.

\* \* \*

Mako smiled at Lambert as he joined Quan and Gottlieb at the conference table.

"Are you feeling well, Ranger?" she asked.

He was not. His head hurt, his stomach was queasy, and he had a head full of half-memories which he was pretty sure would be embarrassing when – if – he got them sorted out.

"Tip top," he lied.

"I'm sorry I didn't make it to your – debriefing," she said. "I hope everything went well."

"The on-down?" he said. "Not my idea…"

Quan surprised him by stepping in.

"Everyone worked very hard," he said. "The Ranger most of all. Order is important, but everyone needs to blow off a little steam, now and then. I approved the on-down."

"You'll get no argument from me," Mori said. "But I think we can do with a more formal discussion of what happened."

"I agree," Lambert said, although he really wanted to be back in his bed, with a pillow over his head.

"We'll get to the breakdown of the action in a moment," Mori said. "But I've been in communication with Sydney, and I've made my recommendations. With some caveats, my suggestions have been accepted.

"The events leading up to the sabotage of Chronos Berserker, the murders of Braga and Sokk, the abduction of cadets Ou-Yang and Malikova, the battles in the Philippine Sea and the destruction of the island are all now considered to be part of an ongoing investigation into the Akumagami Front and any other individuals or organizations which may pertain. As such, all of these events are considered classified, and as such are not to be discussed by members of the PPDC. This includes cadets."

"Are you giving out a story about what happened in the Philippines?" Lambert asked. "After all, the island did sort of explode."

"A number of press outlets have already reported it as a natural eruption, similar to any number of volcanic eruptions that have occurred in that part of the world. We have encouraged this theory without actually endorsing it."

"Understood," Lambert said. "I'll have a talk with the cadets. But it's hard to keep news like this down."

Quan shrugged. "We can't stop what is already out there," he said. "But we can seek to contain it, at least for a while, until we can determine whether this was a one off, or part of a much more serious, widespread threat."

"The threat is very real," Gottlieb said. "We must be more vigilant than ever. From what I can tell, Morales believed that her 'K-Bomb' would trigger a catastrophe so large it would re-form the world to Precursor specifications. If she was right, and their plan had gone ahead, the world would at this moment be beset by tectonic action the like of which no human being in any era has ever experienced. We could expect extinction of animal and plant life on an unprecedented scale. It might, indeed, be greater than the mass extinction at the end of the Permian period, which up until now had the dubious distinction of being the greatest in Earth's history. Also, I might add, probably caused by volcanism."

"But she did not succeed in detonating the entire bomb," Quan said.

"No," Gottlieb said. "She did not, thanks to the Ranger here and the efforts of many others. Nor am I certain her calculations were correct. I think her bomb might have done a great deal of damage, but perhaps not wreaked the global havoc she aimed to inflict. Still, this 'bomb' is a quite simple device. Anyone with a sufficient quantity of

Kaiju blood and an oil rig could create one."

"Your recommendations, Dr. Gottlieb?"

"From a scientific point of view? We must expand the mission of K-Watch to cover all of the deep-sea trenches, not just the deepest and most active. I myself will immediately begin research on the range of interactions between Kaiju blood and the various rare earths. But we absolutely must limit access to the blood itself. The supply should be finite, with no Kaiju coming into our world. We must try to obtain what remains for the PPDC."

"I have already proposed preliminary measures to the council along those lines," Mori said. "Let me have any further recommendations in writing, so I can pass them along."

By the time the meeting was finally over, the worst of Lambert's hangover had passed. He just wished he had a clearer memory of the night before. He kept meeting people in the halls who seemed to be suppressing smiles, as if they knew something he didn't.

He stopped to have a look at Gipsy. It hurt to see her banged up, but he knew that was a temporary condition; she would be ready to go again in a few weeks, probably even sooner. But even after she was fixed – once again, he no longer had a Drift partner. Where was he going to find another – one of the cadets? The thought was more than a little depressing.

He was just about to leave when he saw Jules approaching. She – like so many others he had met today – had an odd look on her face.

"Ranger," she said. "How are you?"

"A little shaky," he said. "Too much beer, I guess."

"Great on-down," she said.

"Yeah," he said. "Just great." He kept trying to rearrange the blurry events of the night before. He remembered yelling at Burke, and Jules pulling him away. And – something else? Had they…?

Jules cleared her throat. "So," she began, "did we – do you remember… um…"

"What?" he said.

"Nothing," she said. "Just – never mind. I better go, I've got this – work to do."

"Yeah," he replied. "Me too."

Then they hurried away in opposite directions.


Mako Mori stepped once again into the Kwoon. This time she selected no weapon at all. She took six long, centering breaths, and began to move, feeling her breath, the blood in her veins, her bare feet sliding on the floor.

She contemplated Jinhai and Vik's Drift; she had seen their recording and was still absorbing what she had learned. She had been wrong about Jinhai, projected her own feelings for her adopted father onto him. Vik's tangled history with her own identity was not entirely resolved, but what she'd seen was promising.

She had believed she could help them, and that in doing so she might find her own answers. Now she doubted that she had helped them at all, but they had helped her.

She had always been propelled by ghosts, she understood now. The ghosts of her parents, of the Tokyo that was, had pushed her along until she finally got revenge for them. Then she had lost her adoptive father and Raleigh, for whom no vengeance could ever be had, not really. So instead, she had carried them as a burden, seeking them in the Drift. Usually she found Raleigh, sometimes her father.

But somewhere along the line, she had become terrified of being alone, of just having herself in her head. She had become attached to memories, which in the Drift was a fatal mistake. So she punched and blocked, kicked, dodged, turned her way through the kata, the imaginary battle.

And then, as he often was, Raleigh was there, behind her closed eyes, sparring with her. It was wonderful, and it was sad, and it was as real as any Pons-generated Drift. Real, but... less.

Raleigh stopped sparring and stood back.

*Mako. All you have to do is fall,* he said. *Anyone can fall.*

"I know," she said. "I understand, now... Goodbye, Raleigh."

He smiled, and then she was once more fighting alone.

She could still find Raleigh and her father in the Drift if she needed them – but she no longer needed them.

She would never truly be at peace; life was not peace, it was struggle, and ideally it was growth.

She still had much to do. What she had learned from the wreck of the Akumagami Front plot was that there were more questions than there were answers – about who was behind them, where their funds came from, what other plots they might be fermenting. And there were several other disturbing strands that she thought might bear pulling on, strands that might not lead her to the Kaiju worshippers at all, but in other directions. She felt, somehow, that something big was coming, perhaps something without precedent, unanticipated – not merely another Breach, but something even worse. The Precursors learned. They adapted. They wouldn't make the same mistake twice. She didn't know what was coming, but she feared they might not be ready for it when it came.

And there was another thing; something that she had pushed aside for far too long.

It was time to find her brother. Time to find Jake.

## ACKNOWLEDGMENTS

Thanks to my editor, Cat Camacho. Also at Titan, I am grateful to Natasha MacKenzie for design and Hayley Shepherd for copy editing. To the folks at Legendary, thanks for letting me explore a corner of a fascinating imagined universe, and specific credit goes to Lisa Lilly, Jamie Kampel, Barnaby Legg, and George Tew. George was invaluable in helping nail down particulars about the world of Pacific Rim. Much appreciation to Evgeniya Mukharyamova for helping with a fine point of colloquial Russian, and David Dunlap for lending me a small bit of his expertise in Japanese.

## ABOUT THE AUTHOR

GREGORY KEYES was born in 1963, in Meridian, Mississippi. When he was seven, his family spent a year living in Many Farms, Arizona, on the Navajo Reservation, where many of the ideas and interests which led Greg to become a writer and informed his work were formed. His first published novel was *The Waterborn*, which was followed by a string of licensed and original books. He has a BA and Masters in Anthropology and lives in Savannah, Georgia with his wife, Nell, and two children, Archer and Nellah. He enjoys writing, cooking, fencing, and raising his children.